GOLDEN ROSE PART 2

KENYA STEMMONS

KANSAS STREET PUBLISHING

CONTENTS

Chapter One

FALLEN ANGEL (JANUARY 2025)

Golden loves all her classes and teachers at a fashion design school in Atlanta called the Southern Art and Design Institute. She can't imagine learning how to be a successful fashion designer anywhere else. She loves how challenging her assignments are and how her instructors reaffirm her talent. Golden is even making friends on her small campus, despite the betrayal she suffered at the hands of her best friend who, a few months ago, tried to lure her into becoming an escort. Between the previous year's reveals of her deceased father's business partner LeBaron, revealing himself after hiding his true identity for months to find out her best friend was in on the deception; tech school was a welcome change of scenery.

She is getting used to the faster pace of living in Atlanta in comparison to that of her midwestern hometown. Her classmates are smart and ambitious as well, so she fits right in, especially after her work experience designing the sex-themed rooms in a million-dollar Las Vegas mansion the year before. Her only regret was abandoning the project after the mansion's opening night, but the news of her grandmother's passing was all Golden could think about.

Last year, Golden learned about LeBaron's identity, and the truth caused her so much confusion and anxiety. However, he was the only one offering a way out of the chaos of her life and a way for her to pursue her career in fashion design. Golden's thoughts of her grandmother helped the opportunity of her future shine through all her grief. So, she settled on figuring out LeBaron's motivation for reentering her life later. She didn't care if LeBaron was the one who'd got her into tech school; she needed an immediate escape from her grief and could not refuse his offer.

There were so many changes to Golden's life that fashion design school couldn't have come at a better time. Plus, LeBaron finalized the school's application and financing for her. All she had to do was show up. She was grateful for him removing the burden and stress of applying to school, even if she still had unanswered questions about who he is and why he waited so long to tell her about his relationship with her father. Golden found out that LeBaron and her father Diamond were more than business partners. They were like brothers. So, this made his unexpected presence in her life even more confusing.

Golden didn't really talk to her mother Althea after her grandmother's death or in the days leading up to her departure for tech school. She was still processing the fact that Althea knew LeBaron. She was questioning why he hadn't disclosed anything about himself, especially since he was always in the background of her and her mother's lives by secretly sending them money. Golden recounts LeBaron's last visit when he admitted that he regularly sent her grandmother money to take care of the household bills. But Golden remains resentful toward LeBaron because of his absence and his dishonesty. Golden felt that his presence could've shielded her from her mother's drunken outbursts and the constant barrage of men that darkened their doorstep, taking advantage of Althea's grief-stricken state.

Althea also had unanswered questions about LeBaron's motives for disappearing after his so-called best friend's murder showing up in her daughter's life. She wondered why LeBaron never reached out to help her or Golden after Diamond's murder. She questioned how LeBaron could spend every day with Diamond since they were teenagers only to abandon his best friend's family in their gravest hour of need. Althea was so deep in the grief of losing her lover, best friend, co-parent, and provider, that LeBaron's absence was a hazy fog at the time. But seeing his face as he stood in her living room a few months before Golden left for fashion design school brought the past barreling back in disjointed waves. She didn't question LeBaron's absence at the time of Diamond's death, because she was trying to put together the fragments of her shattered life.

Now the past had a new clarity that Althea was prepared to dissect. She had to figure out why LeBaron was back and trying to burrow himself into her daughter's life after ignoring them for over twenty years. When Diamond was murdered, Althea was in survival mode and grief and suffocated her entire being like a weighted blanket. Over the years she used drugs and alcohol to keep her grief at bay. Back then all Althea knew was that she had a toddler to care for while her own mother was in prison. The only remnants of Diamond were about $60,000 in cash that he had stashed and the house that she, Golden, and Diamond's grandmother shared.

In the weeks after LeBaron's visit to their house, Golden and Althea were left to their own thoughts. Neither of them dared to express their concerns to one another. Although, judging from her mother's quiet demeanor after LeBaron's unexpected visit, Golden was positive that she and her mother had the same thoughts about his presence, potentially changing the trajectory of their lives, in the past and in the present.

Seeing her mother drunk and experiencing verbal abuse from her traumatized Golden to such a degree that she had to detach from a part of herself to survive. It didn't help that Althea was a young parent who suffered from her own traumatic upbringing that stemmed from Mother Rose's verbal onslaughts, which never ceased for Althea or her daughter.

Golden always heard people describe her father as a man who "didn't play." As much as she wished she could corroborate those sentiments, the truth was, Golden couldn't remember much of her father. The only memory of Diamond was him holding her above his head as he spun in a dizzying circle while they laughed themselves silly. However, after meeting LeBaron and observing his character, she knew her father was more than a pleasant memory; he was a drug lord, feared throughout the Midwest. She only wished she had her own memories of him that spanned longer than the four short years before he was gunned down by his enemies.

Marquez was the only bright spot in the days after Golden learned about LeBaron's identity. Marquez's love for Golden rivaled that of no other man she'd been involved with. But Golden doesn't feel the same and is incapable of reciprocating his unwavering love. Marquez knows Golden's tumultuous relationship with her mother better than anyone. He holds out hope that she'll get help, deal with the ghosts of her past, and be the companion of his dreams, full of love and affection.

He also knows that Golden's grandmother provided the only stability Golden ever had and was who she inherited her gentle nature from. Her grandmother gave Golden all the love her heart could muster for as many years as her body allowed. Golden took the passing of her grandmother the hardest of anyone because she was more like a mother than Althea, Mother Rose, or any other woman in Golden's life could ever be.

Marquez loved Golden from the time his family moved across the street when they were both in middle school. His love never wavered, even now in their mid-twenties. Marquez quietly works on being a better man for Golden while building his economic portfolio in hopes that she will see him as more than a lover, but also a life partner. He wants to take care of Golden and be the best man for her. That wasn't going to be cheap, so Marquez worked as a mechanic by day and studied the stock market by night, making trades before work every morning.

Marquez knew Golden was too fragile to consider a relationship with anyone, especially after LeBaron showed up. He was excited that Golden had the opportunity to go after her dream of becoming a fashion designer. When Golden asked his opinion about going away to fashion design school, Marquez knew the best thing was to let her go. He put aside his selfish desires to be with her in favor of Golden's happiness and the possibility of her dreams being fulfilled.

Marquez now calls Golden every few days to check in since she started her second semester. During her first semester, she would make nightly calls to Marquez. He encouraged her to stay the course and finish. Golden frequently asked him if she was good enough and if she could even hang with the other students and their talent?

Marquez would always answer these questions with a resounding "yes" and reaffirm Golden's talent and desires to be a fashion designer. He even had her recall her most iconic looks throughout the years. He never admitted to Golden that every day in high school he would wait by the front window of his house waiting for her to walk out the front door so he could be the first one to see her that day without hearing the critiques of the envious high school girls and horny teenage boys.

He encouraged her not to focus on *how* she got there but *why*. Golden felt unworthy of the right to attend such a prestigious fashion design school in Atlanta because the opportunity was given to her by LeBaron rather than her earning it. However, as the days went on and the more she eased into her school routine, the *why* became more evident. Throughout the months, their conversations started to modulate between "why am I here" to "I belong here." Marquez couldn't be more satisfied with Golden's progress, despite her still grieving her grandmother.

Top designers frequently visited her school looking for fresh ideas, assistants, seamstresses, and content creators. Golden was showing real potential to her professors, and her impostor syndrome slowly subsided. Marquez reminded her of how proud grandmother would be if she was still alive, knowing that Golden was chasing her passion and using her God-given talents.

She remembered grandmother saying, "You got ta' use yo' gift, baby. God thought you so special, that he blessed you with this gift. Don't slap God in the face by not using it."

Grandmother always had a way of making Golden understand life's complicated lessons with a simple phrase. *Damn, I miss her so much,* Golden thought.

Golden's thoughts are interrupted by her cell ringing. She picks up immediately, knowing who it is. Golden had a presentation earlier that day and was expecting Marquez's call.

"Hey, beautiful." Marquez's baritone voice soothes Golden.

He feels her smiling through the phone, although she always acts like she's unimpressed with his compliments.

"Hey, how are you?" she asks brightly.

"Okay. Let's get to it. How'd your presentation go?" Marquez presses. They'd known each other for so long that pleasantries were no longer needed.

"It went well. Thank you again for sitting up with me last night while I finished my presentation slides. I think I got a good grade. Everybody seemed to be nodding during my presentation, so I guess that was a good sign that I was making sense." Golden lets out a nervous laugh.

"I know you did great, babe."

Marquez lets the *babe* word slip. He usually only calls Golden *babe* in his head.

Silence ensues. Golden hates it when Marquez calls her pet names or shows her too much affection, because she doesn't feel the same way. She doesn't want to hurt him though, because he'd been there when she needed him the most. In fact, he was always there, now that she thought about it. Marquez has been a soft place to land for years, always giving encouraging words and a listening ear. When she really is being honest with herself, he is the only man who shows her what true love looks and feels like. Oh! And the sex is the bomb!

She wouldn't have made it through the loss of her grandmother had it not been for Marquez. Heck, when she thought about it, she may not have made it through her childhood without him. He is in her life when everyone else has flaked or betrayed her.

"I know, I know. Too much, wasn't it?" Marquez asks nervously.

He can't help his love and adoration spilling over into his conversations with Golden. She was the love of his life, and she didn't really know to what depths his love went. He fears she may never know.

Golden lets out an uncomfortable chuckle, then more silence.

"Well, thanks for checking on me to see how my presentation went. I'm gonna get on in here and study for this other test I have coming up on Friday," Golden lies to avoid talking about her feelings.

"Okay, do yo' thang, chicken wang!" Marquez attempts to sound uninjured and hangs up.

Golden stands still in her tiny, single dorm room. An immense feeling of guilt sweeps over her. *I'm gonna have to tell him soon. It's gonna break his heart.*

The last thing Golden wants to do is share how she really feels about Marquez. She loves being loved but knows she can't reciprocate his feelings. She falls backward onto her bed with her arms flailing at her side as she contemplates how she will tell Marquez that all she wants is friendship—with benefits of course.

But is it even fair to still wanna fuck?

"Ugh!" Golden lets out an angry sigh.

But how can I go on hurting the only person who's consistently there for me? she wonders. *Am I that selfish?*

Golden shakes her thoughts of their complicated history and refocuses her energy on studying. Although she doesn't have a test coming up, Golden likes to review her class notes every afternoon to solidify the information in her mind. This way, studying for a test is a breeze when the time comes. She opens her laptop and checks her school email to make sure there are no new threads for her pattern design group project. Golden loathes group projects but is excited about learning new ways to cut patterns for different body types.

There are no new emails from her group, but there is an email entitled *Look at this!* So, being curious, Golden clicks on the email and a video begins playing.

Golden watches the familiar lights of Pinky's Kitten dance around the room so fast that her eyes grow wide with anticipation. She knows the club from anywhere since she'd worked there for months before going to Vegas with Tatiana. She listens while horrified at the distorted bass of the music threatening to blow the speakers of her laptop. The music drowns out the catcalls from in the background. Topless dancers bounce their asses to the music. She knows all the dancers in the video by name. Then, without warning, the video pans to her on her hands and knees, licking her lips and staring seductively at the crowd while money is raining on her naked body.

Golden's jaw drops in horror! She scrambles to close out of the video, but it keeps playing. Then she hears an unfamiliar man's voice say, "Come over here, shawty."

Golden watches herself bewitchingly crawl over to the man, sucking her bottom lip, pausing to pinch her nipples and knead her breasts. The video stops, Golden's face frozen, then it starts to play again.

Golden sits with her eyes wide still in shock as she watches the video replay. Hot tears begin streaming down her face. Golden shakes her head in disbelief as her eyes dart to the "to" line of the email and she realizes that the video was sent to the entire student body's email addresses, including faculty and staff. Golden stares at the email.

Who the hell sent this email? Golden thinks, blinking away her unrelenting tears. *Why would someone send this?*

She grows furious, because she needs answers. Her mind is ablaze with questions leading with who, what, when, where, and why—but she doesn't have any answers. She knows some people she crossed paths with at school may not have liked her, but nothing would warrant such a wanton and vicious attack. She needs to find out who sent the video, but more importantly, why. What do they want? She also wants to know why the video was sent to all the student body, staff, and teachers. And how the hell did whoever it was make the connection between her, her school, and Pinky's Kitten. No one knows she's going to fashion design school except for three people other than herself: Marquez, her mother, and LeBaron.

As her mind races, her cell begins to buzz with a call coming from one of her classmates. They had met in the first semester and had evolved into close friends.

"Golden, you, okay?" Ashley hesitantly asks.

Golden's thoughts are flying so fast she doesn't process Ashley's question. After a moment of silence from Golden, Ashley repeats her question.

"I asked if you are okay."

"Huh?" Golden asks distractedly.

"I just got this email...and I...umm...think it's you. And it's only because you shared with me a little about your past and you know I would never bring that up." Ashley's voice trails off because she can sense Golden's anxiety.

"What are you talking about?" Golden asks.

"I, um, saw this email that was sent to me, so I clicked on it." Ashley's voice begins to shake. "I thought it was for one of my classes and then this video of you dancing at a strip club pops up."

Before Golden can answer, she sees another incoming call from a number that isn't saved in her phone.

"Hold on, girl," Golden says irritably. "Hello, who is this?"

"Damn, girl. I didn't know yo' ass was that fine," the unknown male voice answers back.

"Who the fuck is this?" Golden shouts. The call ends and her cell automatically switches back over to Ashley.

"Hey, girl," she says. "Let me call you back. I gotta handle some shit."

"Oh, okay. And Golden, if you need anything, I gotchu." Ashley affirms and hangs up.

Golden hurries back to her laptop to look at the source of the email. Her computer skills aren't the best, but she knows someone who can get to the bottom of it: LeBaron. Golden hadn't spoken to LeBaron until that night at her grandmother's house when he stood before her and her mother, admitting he'd been lying to Golden about his identity since he met her.

Golden shakes off the worrying feeling growing in the pit of her stomach. Although she hadn't spoken to LeBaron in months, he would pick up her call and help in any way possible if and when she ever needed him. So, she swallows her pride and silences all her questions about the past and scrolls to LeBaron's name in her contacts list. Then, taking a deep inhale, she presses the call button.

The phone rings once on Golden's end before she hears the deep baritone voice of LeBaron answer. "What's wrong, Golden?"

Golden can't hold back her tears any longer. She starts relentlessly sobbing. Through gasps of struggling to get breath into her lungs, she tells LeBaron about the email she received and the video of her dancing at Pinky's Kitten. She fights to keep the panic from her voice, but she knows that the possibility of her being expelled may be hanging in the balance. The school may think she sent pornography to the students and staff.

"I can forward the email to you." Golden's body trembles as the tears pour from deep embarrassment and shame.

"No, don't do that. Whoever sent the email may have encrypted it as a virus. I need to see what you see. I'm gonna remote in," LeBaron coolly replies.

Golden had forgotten she was still using the laptop that LeBaron gave her. *Of course, he can remote into my laptop,* Golden thinks. A small part of her is relieved at LeBaron's access to her laptop.

She watches as her laptop commences to type coding script without her doing anything. She notices her mouse move on its own and the video starts to play from where Golden paused the video. Then she sees the mouse quickly pause the video.

"I need to have one of my tech people come over there to check things out and see if we can find out where this video came from. In the meantime, I need you to remain calm. Do you need anything?" LeBaron asks in an even tone and waits for her to reply.

When Golden is still silent and doesn't respond, LeBaron adds, "Okay, my tech person should be there within the hour. You'll know it's them. Don't open the door for anyone else. Not even anyone from your school." LeBaron declares his final orders.

Golden doesn't protest or ask any questions. She hears the strain in LeBaron's voice; a tone Golden had never heard before. His voice contains an uncertainty he tries to disguise. That's when she gets scared for the first time.

As Golden ends the call with LeBaron she sees another incoming call and ignores it, then places her phone on "do not disturb." Simultaneously, her laptop chimes with email notifications. Golden hurries to her laptop and snaps it shut. Then she paces the room, her thoughts swirling.

Who could've taken that video and why the fuck send it to my school email? And why the fuck now? Now, when I'm doing so good.

All Golden can think about were the tough weeks that she had after her grandmother passed away and how she had to pick up the pieces that remained of her soul.

Golden can't think of any enemies that would want to hurt her that badly. Most of her enemies are girls from strip clubs she used to dance at, and she doesn't think any of them have the guts, let alone the intellect, to send an email to her entire school. Plus, none of those girls know Golden is enrolled in a fashion design school in Atlanta. She sits on the edge of her bed and starts rocking back and forth, trying to calm the dread growing inside. *Who could've done this shit?*

Golden's thoughts lead to her old mentor and friend, Tatiana. Tatiana had already betrayed Golden once by purposely seeking her out, knowing who she was, but that was under the guise of LeBaron to get close to Golden and observe her. Then, for a millisecond, she wonders if LeBaron is behind this sick and twisted act of sending her stripping videos to her entire fashion school's email roster. But Golden quickly puts that thought out of her head because LeBaron had only tried to help Golden since he met her. She recalls that he sent her grandmother money for her over the years to make sure Golden and Althea weren't living on the street. A warmth fills her chest at the thought of LeBaron sending money to Grandmother to make sure she was okay.

Oh no! I wonder if my teachers saw that shit already?

She holds her head in her hands and presses against her temples as a stress-headache starts to form in the front of her forehead.

Just then, there's a sturdy knock at the door and Golden freezes on her bed. She remembers LeBaron's warning not to trust or talk to anyone until his tech person gets there. The knock comes again, more urgent this time.

"Hey, Golden. It's me, Ashley. I know you're in there. I was just checking on you. Golden...hey...Golden, are you in there?" Ashley asks.

Ashley continues to knock fervently and Golden covers her mouth and dares not breathe.

"Okay, well, I'm leaving now. But you hit me if you need me." Ashley pauses. "I'm sorry, Golden," she half-whispers, and Golden hears her soft footsteps retreat down the hallway.

Golden listens for the all-too-familiar ding of the elevator arriving at her floor accompanied by the closing of the elevator doors. Ashley is gone and Golden releases her breath—she didn't realize she was holding it. Golden walks over to her closet. She pushes aside all her outfits to reach the very last hanger that contains her grandmother's knitted gray shawl she used to wear while she watched her stories in the afternoon. Golden wraps herself in the shawl and imagines what type of comforting advice her grandmother would give. All she could come up with is, "*It's gonna be alright, baby.*"

Golden snaps out of her comforting thoughts about her grandmother when there's an urgent knock on the door. A woman's voice echoes in the hallway.

"Hello. Golden. My name is Ace and LB sent me over here to check on your problem and get some answers."

Then things go quiet. The silence is comforting to Golden because she knows this is the person LeBaron sent to analyze the video and find its source. But she wasn't expecting a woman.

Golden hesitantly cracks the door open and a brown-skinned woman in her mid-forties, her locs neatly tied back in a bun, meets Golden's emerald eyes.

"Hey, Golden."

They continue to lock eyes for a moment while Golden hesitates. She needs to be sure this person isn't going to harm her. She remembers her mother telling her that if you look a person in the eyes long enough, you will see all you need. Ace's eye contact doesn't waver from Golden's, weary gaze with smudged eyeliner around the rims from crying. The two continue to stare at one another for an uncomfortable amount of time—under normal circumstances, but this is far from normal. Golden decides to step aside, seeing no threat or intent of malice in Ace's eyes or demeanor.

Ace quickly scans the room. She finds Golden's laptop and opens her own large briefcase containing her laptop with cords and external hard drives, which she quickly places onto Golden's desk. Golden suddenly feels safe and sits back on her bed to watch Ace work. The tapping of Ace's fingertips on her keyboard unexpectedly lulls Golden to sleep until she feels a gentle nudge on her thigh. Golden opens her eyes to Ace looking at her. She sits up with a start, slightly frightened because she didn't plan on falling asleep. For a moment, she thought she dreamt the whole stripper video debacle. But Ace's kind brown eyes remind Golden of her somber reality.

"So, did you find anything out, like who did this shit to me?" Golden asks with furrowed brows as she hugs her long, ebony legs to her chest.

"Yeah, I think we got a lead. LB is catching a flight to take care of it. I spoke to him while you were resting," Ace says in an even tone, then pauses. "Look, Golden, I ain't gonna lie to you because I get paid not to. But that damn video went to all the students and staff here at the school. I also hacked into the administrator's emails and they're discussing how appalled they are and how they must uphold their reputations and the reputation of the school." Ace hesitates. "They're thinking of expelling you."

Golden gasps. "What the fuck? I mean, how can they do that?" Golden gets out of her bed and pushes past Ace in one swift movement, using her five-foot-ten frame to easily stand from the bed to the middle of the small dorm room. Ace is just as quick and nimble and stands to face Golden. Ace holds up her hands in defense to let Golden know she is only the messenger.

"Look, I told LB what was going down and he already has your legal team working on a statement for you to buy a little time before they try to meet and put your expulsion to a vote."

"My legal team?" Golden asks worriedly.

Ace cocks her head to one side and says in a softer tone, "Yes, Golden, your legal team." She nods reassuringly. "Look, LB is gonna take care of you. Trust that."

The pair once again stand in the middle of the room in silence, eyes locked, studying each other's faces. Ace breaks the silence.

"Oh, and I also sent an email to your instructors letting them know that you are going to take a few days away from classes to take care of some personal business. If you need anything else, I programmed my number into your phone. So, call or shoot a text if you need me. It was nice to finally meet you, Golden." Ace turns to leave.

"Finally?" Golden questions and rushes forward to try and spin Ace around, but she is stronger than Golden anticipates. Her shoulders stay square, and she turns her head to reply.

"I ran with yo' pops back in the day. When all this blows over, hit me up and we can chop it up." Ace touches the dorm's door handle and pauses. Then, in one swift move, Ace is out the door, closing it quickly behind her.

Golden stands stunned and alone in the middle of her room, too shook to speak. *You knew my dad? This day is getting weirder by the second.*

She waits for the familiar sounds of the elevator to chime, but it doesn't come, so Golden opens her door to see if she can catch one last glance of Ace. But she's gone.

CHAPTER TWO

THE MEETING

LeBaron steps off the private jet, the bitter Chicago cold stinging his cheeks and numbing his face. The wind cuts through his designer wool peacoat as he descends the jet's steps and the crunch of salt shatters under his dress shoes. His jaw tightens as the cold whips through his bare head, nose, and neck like a pit-bull off its leash. He'd long forgotten how the brutal cold from Lake Michigan sweeps through the city streets. Chicago holds a type of cold that is only mildly bearable to its inhabitants. The city had turned his heart to ice so long ago, but it quickly demanded respect.

He quickens his pace as he scrambles to the SUV in anticipation of the heated seats awaiting him. As he slides into the softened leather, all the memories he buried long ago rush to the forefront of his mind with that first gust of the city's biting wind—letting him know it was still alive. Chicago is one of those cities with a palpable pulse. As LeBaron piles into the SUV, a shiver tingles down his spine, not only from the cold but from the past crashing into his present.

It had been years since LeBaron fled the Windy City with Diamond in search of new territory to establish their drug empire. His throat tightens from the memory of making that initial decision to leave everything and everyone they knew to strike out on their own. As his SUV exits the tarmac, his mind drifts back to the early days when he and Diamond first learned to hustle. His tense muscles slowly relax as the heat from the seats gently warms him. With the airport in his rearview, he can hear Diamond's voice replay like it was yesterday, laying out their plans to take over the Midwest corner by corner. Diamond had always been the mastermind and LeBaron was the brute force it took to create and maintain their enterprise. As he looks out the tinted windows, his clenched teeth grind in anticipation. Knowing who he has to confront about Golden's cyberattack has him on edge. As LeBaron gets near the heart of the city, his memories become more vivid.

He recalls how, in the beginning, he and Diamond had a strong supply connection in Chicago but wanted their own piece of the pie and didn't want to work for anyone else anymore. They wanted to deal in weight. They didn't want to be two-bit hustlers anymore and share their profits with a boss who wasn't as smart or as business savvy as them. So, they found a new drug connect and headed a few hours south of Chicago to set up shop. It wouldn't be easy to start on their own, but they were optimistic because the drug dealers in their new target area were loosely connected, disorganized, and non-territorial. LeBaron and Diamond could easily take over the drug scene there.

Within eight months, they established themselves as the new players in town and business was booming! The old heads who were running the two largest gangs in the area started noticing their pockets were light and they put a target on LeBaron and Diamond's backs. Another chill runs down LeBaron's spine, bringing him to the present. He's starting to remember the true cold of Chicago.

Damn, I can't believe it's been over twenty-five years.

LeBaron's eyes are glued to the city streets as he travels from the airport to his hotel. The city has subtle changes, but it's still "the Chi." He goes to his hotel first to change out of his traveling suit and make a quick shopping trip. He needs appropriate clothes if he is going to survive the brutal January windchill.

Being back in the city has LeBaron on edge and rightfully so. He'd gotten soft being a lawyer away from the drug game. Nowadays he prefers white-collar crimes instead of those that can land him conspiracy charges, costing him the remainder of his natural life.

He makes a mental note of all the things he needs to do and the people he needs to see in the next few days to resurrect the man he had long ago buried. Chicago reminds him of Diamond because Chicago always meant him, Diamond, and...he stops himself before his mind utters the third name. He clinches his right fist and covers it with his leather-gloved left hand as his driver takes him to his downtown hotel.

Every corner he turns brings back bittersweet memories. He hadn't anticipated the emotional charge the city would hold for him. He needs a moment to regroup at the hotel—to strategize his next move. He knows his opponent well. They will already be expecting him, because they have knowledge of everything going on in the city. LeBaron takes his time and will only make contact when everything is in place. He has a back-up plan for his back-up plan.

LeBaron arrives at the hotel, checks into his room, and calls to check on the calf-length wool coat with a heavy silk lining he's ordered from one of his favorite coat makers in the city. He had requested specialized inside pockets to inconspicuously hold his favorite automatic hand-held gun, a Sig Sauer P322. He loves its reliability and the feel of the trigger. He was able to bring it on his private jet.

The coat manufacturer confirms that his coat is ready—he paid an extra $5,000 to rush the job. He was pleasantly surprised to learn that the coat manufacturer/retailer is still open after all these years. Their quality and discretion are unmatched in the city. Buying a coat from them had been a rite of passage among the elite entrepreneurs, politicians, and anyone looking to make a name for themselves in the city. One could look at the cut and quality of the coat and surmise that it was a Marks Brother's coat.

LeBaron calls the front desk and asks the concierge to order some business casual outfits consisting of jeans, sweaters, and boots from nearby designer stores and boutiques to supplement the clothes he brought with him from his favorite black designers. LeBaron stays fashionable because it's a part of his DNA. Coming up in the 90's, everyone had to be dressed to impress. He never lost the importance of fashion, even after becoming a lawyer. He remembers one of his first bosses in the drug game telling him that your clothes make a statement about you before your words ever do. LeBaron lets his clothes communicate "don't fuck with me," before he ever opens his mouth.

He is keenly aware that he needs serious firepower, because where he is going, no one should venture without protection. He was going into the belly of the beast and needed to buy some guns that he couldn't bring on his private airplane. He arranged a deal with another connect from his past who had passed down his gun business to his two sons. Chicago was like that; businesses were handed down from generation to generation. That's how things were done in crime families, and the people expected it.

LeBaron connects with the gun dealers and arranges to have a compartment built within the car he bought prior to coming to Chicago. He made his moves within days of each other because his visit to Chicago was unexpected, but he promised Diamond long ago that he would protect Golden. Even though he wasn't involved in her daily life, he kept watch from afar so that she wouldn't stray too far off course. When Golden called him for help, he had no other choice but to fly to Chicago and face the past. As soon as he knew he was traveling to Chicago, he had started to formulate his plan.

He had known the places he needed to go and the people he needed to talk to, and he didn't need any witnesses. He kept his driver on duty but had his car delivered to the hotel. He spent the morning and afternoon studying maps of the city, entrances and exits of buildings he would be visiting. He heard Diamond's voice in his head: "*Always know where the window is in case you gotta jump outta one.*"

After ordering room service, receiving his new clothes and coat, LeBaron is ready to hit the city. He uses the service elevator to access the hotel's garage and get to the car he bought before arriving in Chicago. The car was just as it appeared in the photos: a matte black Audi RS 5 Coupe. It's fast as hell and can maneuver in tight spaces—the perfect getaway car.

LeBaron reaches under the driver's side wheel-well to access a magnetic key holder containing the car's key fob, where he had instructed the seller to conceal it. He unlocks the car, pops the trunk to lift the baseboard, and reveals a hidden compartment with a keypad. He enters his code into the keypad. Inside is a .22 caliber handgun, a 9mm with two extra 12-round magazines, and an AR-15 with three additional loaded clips, as also instructed. Satisfied, he closes the secret panel and positions the trunk covering back in its place. He's impressed with the work done by the gun dealer.

LeBaron slides into the soft black leather of the luxury vehicle. He had the car's GPS disconnected before taking possession of the car. He was assured by the seller that the GPS was an important feature in the car and it couldn't be done. LeBaron didn't argue with the seller but had Ace send one of her team members to take care of the GPS system before he landed. LeBaron, taking another page out of Diamond's kingpin book, made sure to always have a team in place in whatever city he moved through. You never knew if a price was on your head and you might need help to flee. Although this trip was short notice, LeBaron always kept his eyes and ears locked on Chicago, his hometown, having crossed so many up-and-coming dealers, especially after Diamond was gunned down.

LeBaron presses the start button, igniting the engine. He loves the way the engine revs to life and lets him know it's ready for whatever may come their way. LeBaron slowly pulls out of the hotel's garage, the anticipation of the city pulsing through his veins. It's been years since he drove on the city's streets. He decides to cruise through his old stomping grounds on the west side where he and Diamond first learned to hustle.

Summertime Chi and wintertime Chi are two totally different places. Summertime Chi is full of greenery. People are out laughing, cruising their boats on Lake Michigan, exploring the Navy Pier. Families walk in their neighborhoods, oblivious of the danger surrounding them. Wintertime Chi is dark and dreary. Winter reflects the true nature of the city that is harsh, cold, and doesn't give a fuck about you or the people you love. The entire city looks like a black-and-white film, complete with a gray washed-out hue. Salt on the roads melts the snow and ice, turning the city streets into multi-levels of depressing grays. No greenery can be seen for miles. All the leaves on the trees are gone and all that remain are twigs reaching to the heavens, begging for spring to return. The city appears dead and lifeless, but LeBaron knows the city burns hot with life under the surface.

A smile plays in the corner of LeBaron's mouth as he reminisces about how ambitious he and Diamond had been to take over the streets of Chicago, block by block. They wanted it all! LeBaron recalls the masterplan Diamond concocted to replace their plug, Fat Ron.

Cutting out Fat Ron would be a death sentence, but they could get their dope at a cheaper price from a plug who was new to Chicago, straight from Florida by way of Puerto Rico. The new plug guaranteed dope that was uncut and a better price, which meant more money coming to Diamond and LeBaron's pockets. That decision changed everything. Forever.

This lasting thought brings LeBaron to park in the back of a warehouse-turned-night club. He doesn't remember taking the turns to get to the club, because his body has been on autopilot, his mind lost in deep thought. He sits in the comfortable leather seats of his car as his body stiffens in anticipation of his next moves. He knows a confrontation is possible. He deliberately opens his car door slowly and steps down on his left foot—donned in Italian leather ankle-boots—onto the pavement to get a feel for the sole of his foot on the frozen Chicago concrete. He then puts all his weight on this left foot and glides his tall frame out of the low-seated car. The only part of his deep chestnut skin that is exposed is his face. He adjusts his gray, slim-cut slacks and buttons his double-breasted, matching suit jacket under his open custom wool coat. He takes his time adjusting his clothing, making a show to whoever is watching that he is confident, and he knows exactly where he is. He wants to show he's there for a purpose and isn't afraid of whoever may be watching. Finally, he adjusts his long wool coat, breathes his hot breath into his black, leather-gloved hands, closes the car door, and strides toward the back door of the night club.

A security guard stands at the back entrance wearing a heavy leather trench coat and a black knit cap with leather gloves while taking in LeBaron's theatrical display of exiting his car with a frown of disapproval on his thickly bearded face. LeBaron spies the security guard's eyes shift toward him and then slightly to the right of him where he assumes another armed security guard lies in wait for a signal to attack. LeBaron had anticipated being watched the moment he turned onto the block of the warehouse. LeBaron calculates his every move and slowly walks up to the security guard with measured steps while holding the security guard's attention with an intense gaze, signaling that neither of them will be the first to look away.

Before the security guard utters a word, LeBaron's voice booms, "Tell her LB is here."

He cocks his head and twists his smirk thinking, *Who does this nigga think he is?*

The guard's smirk slowly leaves his face, turning into a scowl directed at LeBaron. He holds his earpiece, apparently listening to the communication device in his ear, he's being given and undoubtedly disagrees with, but he isn't the boss and only a worker bee. The security guard doesn't respond to the voice on the other side but continues to scowl at LeBaron and run his tongue over his teeth in an apparent dick-measuring contest that he doesn't know he's about to lose.

Another command must've come over the communication device; the security guard jerks his body ever so slightly and he begrudgingly waves LeBaron closer and opens the back door. LeBaron doesn't become smug. He knows his name still carries weight in the city and opens doors—particularly these doors. It isn't his fault the security guard doesn't know who he is, but by the looks of the guy's demeanor, he quickly learned that LeBaron is no one to fuck with.

Another security guard is waiting for him on the other side of the door. He nods, a signal to LeBaron to lift his arms to be patted down for weapons. LeBaron complies with the unsaid request. The security guard completes his search and motions for LeBaron to walk down a narrow hallway with a single door at the end. His strides confidently in the direction of the door, his footsteps echoing down the long, concrete hallway and accented by each step of his Ferragamo Oxford lace-ups.

When he gets closer to the door, another security guard comes into view, peering through the small sliver of a window in the steel door, watching him walk toward him. The security guard opens the next door, closing it tightly and locking it behind LeBaron. The armed guard steps in front of LeBaron, leading him through a winding path of hallways. LeBaron inconspicuously looks in the corners of the hallway and in the rafters of the warehouse, clocking the cameras without lifting his head. Some are motion-activated with red blinking lights, indicating they've been recording since he and security came within a fifty-foot radius. Some cameras move with the pair and follow them down the hallway. LeBaron hears soft music in the distance. They must be getting close to the section of the warehouse that is being used as a club. The two walk through two plush, black-velvet-tufted double doors that lead to an area behind the DJ booth.

LeBaron quickly scans his surroundings. He counts nine security guards in total: one is posted in each corner of the main floor, two guards are on the second-floor balcony, two guards are on either side of a booth in the VIP section, and one security guard leads LeBaron.

"That's far enough." He hears a familiar, Puerto Rican-accented female voice purr from the inside the VIP booth. "Why are you here, LB?"

LeBaron stops at the sound of her voice. His ears pound as his heart hammers in his chest and his words stick in his throat. He hadn't expected his body to involuntarily betray him at this moment. Despite his stoic act of indifference, this woman still holds prominence over his emotions; this much is undeniable, even after all this time.

"Rica, hello. It's been a long time." LeBaron takes a deliberate pause that impregnates the air of the nightclub floor with anticipation, lust, resentment, and lastly control. His voice holds a slight hoarseness due to the sudden dryness of his throat. The two let silence permeate the air for what feels like an unnatural amount of time, making the surrounding guards who are witnessing the exchange feel uncomfortable.

"Leave us," Rica orders the room in a booming, authoritative voice.

The head of her security, standing to the right of the VIP booth, breaks protocol, whipping his head around to face his boss with concerned eyes. He would never advise leaving her unprotected, but he also understands his boss is keenly aware of how to take care of herself and had survived long before he came to her employ. His jaw tightens in disagreement, but then he settles his anger on the face of LeBaron as if to say, *Make one wrong move, and you're dead.*

LeBaron offers a twitch of his eyebrow in understanding toward the head of Rica's security's unspoken threat. With that, the security-head motions for his men to clear the room swiftly. The room is so quiet, all that can be heard is the HVAC unit blowing warm air throughout the vents. LeBaron hears rustling from inside the VIP booth, a spark of a lighter, then a deep inhale, followed by the familiar smell of Rica's clove cigarettes. The smell transports him through decades and he envisions sixteen-year-old Rica holding a clove cigarette, trying to act older than her age so her brothers would let her hang out with them and their friends. He remembers trying to focus on his purpose for his visit as he stares at the red lipstick ring around the filter of Rica's cigarette. He is a fruit fly caught in her web. He is mesmerized.

LeBaron listens to Rica take three deep inhales and exhales of her cigarette before putting it out.

"Why the fuck are you here, LB, after all these fucking years?" Rica demands.

LeBaron is keenly aware that he has to play his cards right, so he weighs his next words very carefully.

"I came here seeking a truce." LeBaron lies.

In one swift move, Rica slides out of the VIP booth, taking two quick steps to come face-to-face with LeBaron.

"What the fuck right do you have to ask me any-fucking-thing, you fucking piece of shit coward?" Rica clicks her tongue against her front teeth.

LeBaron fights Rica's intoxicating smell of clove cigarettes and Channel N°5 parfum lingering in his nostrils in an attempt to fight her allure and the closeness of her body heat.

"Hey, what the fuck is going on in here? Where's Marco? Where's security?" A voice calls out from behind the DJ booth.

Rica takes a half-step back from LeBaron's face and softens her expression a bit as Camilla demands her question be answered.

"Ma! What the fuck is going on?" Camilla asks.

She approaches the pair as they stand silent as if Camilla hadn't loudly asked a question of them both.

Rica breaks the awkward silence. " A ghost from the past, coming back to haunt me, but he was just leaving." Rica shoots LeBaron a deadly look. LeBaron looks at the floor, daring not to make eye contact with either Rica or Camilla.

"Perhaps we can talk tomorrow. Dinner maybe? Talk about why I'm here and when I'm leaving," LeBaron offers.

Rica raises an eyebrow and smirks, aggressively closing the distance between them.

"I tell you when to leave, LB. You're in my city and I run shit! Understand?"

"I understand. I mean no disrespect," says LeBaron with a sincere nod. "I should've reached out first but I thought you were expecting me."

"Who the fuck is this nigga? He gotta lotta balls talking to you, and where the fuck is Marco?" Camilla asks with greater urgency while reaching for her hip holster. Rica raises her hand to calm her daughter's urge to shoot and ask questions later.

"This gentleman was just leaving. I'll see you tomorrow at seven, LB. My car will pick you up." Rica gives LeBaron a knowing smile. "Remember this is my city now and nothing gets done without me knowing about it."

LeBaron gives a curt, understanding nod.

"Our place?" he asks before he can catch the words escaping his mouth. Rica's nostrils flare in anger.

"Seven," Rica commands and then gives a hand-signal, making Marco reappear with his security detail to escort LeBaron to his car.

"So, you just ain't gonna explain nothin,' Ma? Who the fuck was that nigga, and why he got you all shook? I ain't never seen you at a loss for words. Is he the new competition or something? Do I gotta send the Circle Boyz after him? I mean, say the word and it's done, Ma." Camilla begs Rica to allow her to unleash her crew on LeBaron.

Rica tiredly holds up her hand to quell her daughter's questions.

"He's a part of my past and I didn't ever think he would have the balls to show up again," Rica says with a snort. "But I should've known better. I should've known he would come."

Camilla looks at her mother's twisting expression, questioning what is happening. She can't understand why this stranger has her mother—one of the strongest and most ruthless women she's ever had the displeasure of knowing—so upset she would send away her security detail to be alone with him. She knows there's more to this story, but she isn't going to press the issue. She can feel her mother's vulnerability window closing with frightening speed. So, she decides to change the subject.

"Me and the Circle Boyz gonna do our rounds tonight. Collecting on the new Oxy pills we got. Gonna be a lot more money to wash through the club and I want us to be ready. You talk to Rico yet about the changes needed with the drops?"

Camilla's questions about the family's business drone on. All Rica can focus on is how LeBaron looks after all these years and how incredibly attracted to him she still is. He still sports a low-cut with subtle waves that are now accented with a little gray around his temples and in his goatee. His skin is still a smooth, deep chocolate that glistens with the tiniest bit of sweat on his forehead whenever he's nervous. While Camilla talks, Rica keeps thinking about his full lips when he asked, "Our place?"

"Ma! Hey...Ma!" Camilla shouts. "You hearing me? Damn, you spaced out! Anyway, I'm about to head out. I got a couple things to do before I meet up with the Circle Boyz tonight, and I got a meeting with that new restaurant owner tomorrow morning. We need a new place to wash our money. You need me to ride with you to meet up with ol' boy tomorrow night?" Camilla skeptically inquires.

"Naw, I'm good. I got it." Rica looks at Camillia, raising her right eyebrow as if to say *leave things alone and don't ask any more questions.* Camilla, understanding, leaves without another word.

Chapter Three

CAMILLA ROSE

C amilla's head is still spinning from last night when the mysterious stranger from her mother's past popped up. She plans to take care of all her pickups so she can spy on her mother's dinner with LeBaron. Her curiosity throws her off her game a bit, because she's in her head, trying to stay ten steps ahead of her mother. That will never happen. Rica has always been secretive. Half the things that Camilla knows about her family business she's learned from secondhand accounts. But the interaction between her mother and LeBaron seemed strange. In fact, their dynamic seemed more intimate, and Camilla found herself feeling like a third wheel at the club last night.

Camilla needs to put on her game-face if she wants to intimidate her newest money-washing business, so she shakes her uncertainty. Camilla makes her rounds, collecting from one of her many pickup points throughout the city. The family drug business can't run smoothly and discretely without using several legit businesses to cover their illegal activity. Camilla doesn't mind doing the pickups any other time but winter.

The cold has become less brutal in December, but by January, winter unmistakably takes up residence in Chicago and a deathly stillness permeates the bitter cold air. Chicago winter isn't letting up anytime soon, especially because this is only the first part of winter—the holiday season. Second winter comes after the New Year when the Chicago cold is at its most unforgiving. Camilla loves this time of year though, because most of her customers are either lonely, wanting to fill voids created in childhood, or they want to party harder than usual. Either way, she's ready and willing to provide her customers with their drug of choice. She's as ruthless a businesswoman as she is a drug dealer, and everyone on the west side of Chicago knows it. Her family name carries weight in the city, and Camilla isn't afraid to flex.

When Camilla was five years old, Rica met Ramon Sr. at a nightclub a year after Diamond was killed. Ramon Sr. was born in Puerto Rico and moved to Chicago to handle the Central American side of business. This was when he met Rica and the two fell in lust at first sight. He was impressed by her beauty and ambition, which made Rica an attractive wife. Rica, on the other hand, was attracted to Ramon Sr.'s wealth and status. However, before they married, Rica made it clear that she and Camilla were a packaged deal. Although Ramon Sr. never wanted to be a stepparent, he reluctantly accepted Camilla and Rica to agree to be his wife.

Eleven months after their wedding, Rica and Ramon Sr. welcomed her first son, Ramon Jr. and Rico a year later. Ramon Sr. was ecstatic and felt lucky to have handsome sons with a beautiful wife. Although Camilla was Rica's daughter, she was oftentimes left out of family photos and group trips. Ramon Sr. felt on top of the world with his empire growing and two heirs to his empire. However, Ramon Sr.'s reign in Chicago lasted for only three years when he was killed while gambling. Tragedy struck the family again when Rica and Ramon Sr.'s eldest son Ramon Jr. was killed in a drive-by shooting when he was fifteen.

After Ramon Sr. and Ramon Jr. died, Rica made an agreement with the Martinez family to train Rico in the drug business and equip him to take over when he turned twenty-five. The Martinez family agreed to Rica's terms that she would run their Chicago business until their son came of age because she'd proven that she was an asset after Ramon Sr.'s passing. However, the Martinez family made it clear that Camilla had no rights to Ramon Sr. 's empire and made Rica agree that Camilla can have no direct dealings in Martinez's main business of cocaine and gun running.

It was unheard of for a woman to run drug empires, but Rica had proven her loyalty and knowledge of Chicago to secure more territory for the family. Since Rica struck a deal with the Martinez family to exclude Camilla from the business, Rica groomed Camilla to be a keen business woman with instincts for sniffing out distrust. Unfortunately, Rica never treated Camilla like a daughter, only a business partner. This left Camilla feeling undeserving and in a constant state of proving her worth to Rica. She also felt expendable under the authoritative supervision of her mother.

At twenty-seven years old, Camilla is eager to please her mother with the assistance of her crew, the Circle Boyz. But her time helping her mother run their empire is coming to an end as her brother approaches twenty-five. She can tell her mother is having a difficult time with the idea of relinquishing the business to Rico. Camilla has known her time in the family business would be short-lived, especially since she wasn't Ramon Sr.'s daughter. The crime family in Puerto Rico only recognized legitimate children born within a marriage.

So, Camilla ensured her own success by earning a real estate license and building a formidable real estate empire that belongs to only her. While building her real estate business, she still picked up some drops from local family-owned businesses in the downtown area that were repaying small loans. These mom-and-pop businesses took out loans from her family when the government-issued PPP loans didn't cover their expenses during COVID, a time when a lot of small business owners were failing. Camilla's family charged minimal interest for these loans, but the bigger win was the access given to them to launder more cash from the sale of Oxy, cocaine, heroin, Percocet, Xanax, Ritalin, and Ambien. Camilla convinced Rica to start moving Fentanyl during the pandemic, as well as pushing more prescription drugs that had become more desirable to their customer base once their doctors started refusing to refill.

Camilla is on her way to one of the drops when her phone rings. "Aye, I'm gonna hit you back, Meech. I'm at the spot."

She doesn't wait for a response from her right-hand and hangs up. Meechie knows not to give too much conversation over the phone because there is always the prospect of someone listening in. The last thing they're going to do is incriminate themselves over an open line.

Camilla is visiting a new restaurant that can't secure the financial backing it needs to open because a key investor has decided to drop out at the last moment. Camilla always keeps her ears to the street and has learned about the new restaurant struggling to open. It could be the perfect place to launder money through. She knows the owner's desire to succeed was greater than their morals. The owner had reluctantly agreed to Camilla's terms, and they'd seen lucrative success together in the first month of the restaurant's opening. Today is the first pickup of the restaurant's loan installment. Camilla hates the first meeting, because it always goes one of two ways; either the owner doesn't have the first installment and makes excuses, or the owner has the first payment but wants to renegotiate terms because now their business is successful, and they've grown a moral compass overnight. In both cases, Camilla would have to flex and let the owner know that non-compliance would be paid with their life and the lives of their families.

Camilla double-checks her Glock before exiting her vehicle. She cocks the gun to load the chamber in case she needs the kind of backup that everyone understands—a cold barrel to the temple.

Camilla drives to the back of the building through the small alley where the restaurant receives their deliveries and parks her SUV outside the metal door. She quickly enters her pin on the keypad outside the door. As she turns into the hallway, looking to her left then right, she sees a silhouette of a woman in what appears to be a short trench and heels. Camilla curses under her breath at the restaurant owner, because she told him to get the hallway light fixed last week when they met.

She walks toward the silhouette and the woman shifts her weight from left to right. The woman starts to advance toward Camilla with her hips swaying, causing the bottom of her jacket to swing like a bell in rhythmic time with her steps. As she gets closer, the woman's features become clearer as the lighting improves. The pale-yellow light from the hallway bulb reveals the woman's glowing white teeth that she's showcasing a bright smile that stretches across her smooth, deep, caramel skin. The woman stops in front of Camilla, tilting her head to the side with her dangling earrings still swaying from the movement of her hips.

Camilla's breath hitches in her throat, and she seductively licks her lips because the woman standing before her is absolutely stunning. Her short-cropped hair beautifully frames her onyx, almond-shaped eyes. Camilla reaches for the woman out of habit, her eyes hooded with desire.

"Hello there, beautiful. Why you come back here in this filthy hallway? I was supposed to meet you in the office, remember?"

"I know, babe. But you were taking too long, and I wanted to surprise you," Elyse purrs in her raspy, sexy voice. "Plus, I can't do this in the office."

Elyse's voice trails off as she steps into Camilla, wrapping her arms around her neck and kissing her lips softly. The kisses start as pecks, then deepen as their breaths become rapid with excitement. Camilla pins Elyse against the wall while passionately kissing her and running her hands down the sleekness of her pixie cut.

"Spread your legs," Camilla demands.

Elyse's smile spreads across her lips in response while Camilla continues to kiss her deeply. Camilla smiles inwardly because her plan to seduce her lover at work is playing out even more beautifully than she planned.

"Yeah baby, just like that," Camilla whispers into Elyse's ear while undoing her belted trench coat.

Camilla then trails her fingers inside of Elyse's trench and lands on the outside of Elyse's lace panties. Camilla is pleased for her fingers to find Elyse in a lace bodysuit teddy. She slaps Elyse's ass, squeezing it while making her moan from pleasure. Camilla slowly traces the edge of Elyse's teddy while kissing her deeply and finding her soft center. She circles her two first fingers around Elyse's bundles of nerves as Elyse lets out a breath of pleasure. Then Camilla dips one finger between Elyse's folds while holding up her leg with the other arm.

"Mmmm...I see you already wet for me, huh, baby?"

Camilla's fingers eagerly rub over Elyse's engorged mound, seeking to give her partner a release.

"Let me see how wet you gettin' for me, baby. Oh shit!" Camilla's moans fill the slightly dark hallway as she slips one finger in and out of Elyse's warmth. Her own breaths shorten as she is aroused by her woman's pleasure. Camilla quickens her motion and increases the pressure of her fingers to bring Elyse to her pinnacle.

Elyse's wet, soft center openly responds to her lover's expert touch as Camilla lifts one of Elyse's legs to waist level.

"Yeah, baby, that's it, open up for me." Camilla coaxes Elyse while thrusting two fingers inside of her, massaging her engorged G-spot.

"Damn, I love this sweet, fat pussy!" Camilla opens Elyse's mouth even more as she drives her tongue into partner's mouth.

"Mmmm...that pussy smells so sweet. Is it my pussy, baby?" Camilla asks, quickening her pace and pressure on Elyse's clit.

"Mmmm...yeah," Elyse moans.

"You gonna make that pretty pussy come all over my hand, baby?"

"Yeah...Mmmm...fuck yeah, baby." Elyse pants between shortened breaths as Camilla strokes her G-spot with more force, causing the leg she's standing on to shake. "Oh shit, baby...I'm coming."

"Well, c'mon then, with that pretty fucking pussy, baby. Come for me." Camilla moans in a throaty tone that makes Elyse's pussy pulse in anticipation of her lover's request.

Panting, Elyse feels her release building from the bottom of her spine and through her core as she shudders in ecstasy.

"That's my good girl," Camilla coos, kissing Elyse on the chin and softly biting it.

Camilla releases her leg so Elyse can shakily stand on her two feet. She begins smoothing out her trench coat, looking deeply into her lover's eyes.

"Thanks, babe, I needed that. Had a stressful morning."

"You know I got you. Go clean up and I'll meet you in the office," Camilla commands, giving Elyse another deep kiss, then sticking her fingers in Elyse's hot mouth while she licks her essence off her lover's fingers.

"Nasty ass!" Camilla teases, kissing Elyse again.

"You love it." Elyse giggles.

"Touché, my nigga. Touché. Now go get cleaned up! We gotta check these books and get this business done."

Camilla smacks Elyse on the ass to get her going while Elyse giggles, skipping away to the bathroom.

Camilla adjusts her necklace over her plush, beige sweatshirt. She concentrates on her own body pulses as she thinks about getting Elyse into their bed when she gets home. After adjusting herself, she continues down the dark hallway thinking maybe the darkness wasn't so bad as she makes her way to the back office to meet the restaurant's owner, Rich. Camilla softly knocks on the office door. An irritated voice beckons from behind the door for her to come in. She knows from the forced irritation in Rich's voice that violence was going to take place; Rich was going to attempt to grow a conscience and renegotiate terms. Before entering the office, Camilla takes her gun out of her back holster and turns the safety off, gently placing the gun back in its holster and tugging her jogging suit shirt over it.

"Hey, Rich, what's good? You got my money and the books for this week?" Camilla doesn't feel like fucking around with Rich.

She has to let him know that she's in charge and that he's still dealing with a gangster who just so happens to be a woman.

"Umm...hey...I've been doing some thinking about this loan thing and the conditions." Rich nervously runs his fingers through his short hair. His face turns red from his heart pumping blood throughout his body.

"I mean, I can pay back the loan, but this other stuff with running money through here. I'm just not comfortable with it." Rich pauses to check Camilla's reaction to his words but her stony face doesn't give him any pause.

"But business is good and I can repay the loan in a few months. How's that sound?" Rich rambles off his question.

Camilla lets a smile slowly creep across her face. She hates when men, particularly white men, think they can sweet-talk their way out of anything—that the rules don't apply to them.

"You know what, Rich? I'm gonna spare you all the Samuel L. Jackson *Pulp Fiction* theatrics of a lengthy monologue and just get to the fucking point." Camilla moves closer to Rich, standing next to him and taking a seat on the edge of his desk, making him visibly uncomfortable.

While still smiling, Camilla leans in close to Rich's face and whispers, "Listen to me, you fucking piece of shit. You *will* honor our agreement or this pretty, little wife of yours and your fucking picture-perfect family will all be a memory. Or did you forget that little tidbit of the deal?" Camilla awaits an answer.

Stuttering, Rich answers, "Naw, see it ain't even like that. I was just having a rough day, ya know? I wasn't thinking."

"Don't make me blow your fucking head off right now, Rich. It's fucking Monday and my patience is thin. I will blow your brains all over this office and will sleep like a baby tonight. The choice is yours."

Just then, the door opens and Elyse appears, nonchalantly taking the seat across from Rich's desk. She pulls out a .22 from her purse and rests the weapon on her lap, pointing at Rich's desk approximately where his dick would be. Elyse cocks her head with a forced smile that doesn't reach her eyes, matching Camilla's.

"Now wait just a minute," Rich stammers. "What's going on here? We're just talking, right?"

"There is no talking. The time for talking was when we were negotiating. That time has passed. Now we are conducting the business arrangements we both agreed to. I've kept my end of the bargain, now it's time to keep yours." Camilla pauses for the weight of her words to penetrate Rich's tiny brain.

Rich's eyes dart from Camilla to Elyse.

"Now Rich, if I pull my pistol out, I'm not like my fine ass companion here."

Camilla nods toward the direction of Elyse.

"I will shoot your dumb ass. Now get me my money and your laptop so we can review your books."

"Ummm...okay, sure. It's just...ummm...I got the money right here in the drawer." Rich's hands shake as he opens his desk drawer to retrieve the bank bag containing his weekly loan payment.

"And your laptop?"

"Yeah, it's right here." Rich points to the closed laptop on his desk.

Elyse, still holding her .22, gracefully crosses the room with her long, athletic legs. Placing her .22 back into her purse and swapping it for a flash drive, she balances the laptop on her knees and begins downloading software onto Rich's laptop.

Rich's attention is snatched by Camilla's authoritative voice.

"Now, Rich, my accountant is gonna install some software to help you keep track of your expenses and revenue. You'll also get emails with suggestions on how to better your business. Well, let me take that back." Camilla chuckles. "These won't be suggestions. We will tell you what to do to improve your business."

Rich gives a bewildered look.

"Okay, I understand," he replies, defeated.

"Good, I'm glad we have an understanding, Rich, because I would sure hate to visit Gwen and the kids."

Elyse removes the flash drive and places the laptop back onto Rich's desk and gets up to leave while Camilla grabs the money bag, hands it to Elyse, and opens the door for her.

"See ya next week, Rich."

Camilla has had days when she hated her life of crime but today is not one of those days. She loves the way people fear her and her crew. She loves the power she feels, knowing that she holds people's lives and futures in her hands. Like her mother Rica, she also has a ruthless streak. But she doesn't like showing that side of herself, because she's scared she may be pushed to a point of darkness she knew lay deep inside of her that she may never recover. She's never accessed that side of herself, but she knows what she's capable of and always keeps the raging beast inside on a tight leash. She's always had a primal need for revenge and violence against her enemies, but she wonders if it came from her mother or her father. She sometimes even wonders if she's a psychopath. She'd learned that it could be hereditary, but she doesn't know much about her father, so she's always kept a tight lid on her temper in fear of what may be unleashed.

With thoughts of her family tree swimming in her head, she heads to her crew's warehouse to receive a new shipment of Oxy. She's excited because more products mean more money. Making money is one thing that Camilla excels at and the skill that her mother and Rico both rely heavily on her for. She drives in silence the rest of the way to the warehouse with the smell of her woman at her fingertips. A smile plays on her lips with thoughts of following her mother and LeBaron tonight.

CHAPTER FOUR

POISONED APPLE

LeBaron made reservations for The Village before landing in Chicago. It was the place he, Diamond, and Rica—the trio—used to go when they were young adults, plotting their Chicago takeover. Many dinners were spent at the corner booth in the back of the restaurant. The trio liked the privacy of the booth because it stopped wandering eyes and questions about what three young, urban kids were doing in a nice Italian restaurant they surely couldn't afford.

Rica is the first to arrive. She knew LeBaron would be early, too, despite her sending a car to his hotel. So, she planned to arrive before him and was seated in their booth an hour before LeBaron arrived. She can't believe how nervous she is to see LeBaron again. She gets angry at herself for checking her lipstick in her camera phone and slams it facedown.

"Hello, Rica." That low baritone voice is unmistakable. Rica lifts her head and forces her face to be emotionless.

"I see you beat me here as always." LeBaron tries to force a smile, but he knows the two of them share too much history to fake pleasantries. "May I?" LeBaron motions with his hand to the available seat across from Rica.

She nods and LeBaron slides into the booth, unbuttoning his suit jacket simultaneously. "Let's cut the shit, LB. Why are you here?" Rica asks LeBaron in a tone as the chilliest Windy City winter night.

LeBaron leans onto the table to get as close to Rica's face as possible. "You know why the fuck I'm here, Rica. Stop playing with me." LeBaron notices two diners in the booth next to theirs shift in their seats as they hear the disrespectful tone in LeBaron's voice. LeBaron nods in the direction of the diners. "Some of yours?" he asks. "Damn, you think so little of me, Rica? You think I'm here to hurt yo' ass, after everything...after..."

"Look, LB, I don't know what the fuck you thought, but I ain't the same little helpless girl you and Diamond up and abandoned over twenty years ago. I run shit now," Rica says with finality. LeBaron starts to protest, but Rica holds up her hand to silence him. She calms her voice. "I run shit now and everyone answers to me. All those pipe dreams you, me, and Diamond had as a crew...well, I made that shit happen, even after yo' coward ass left."

"Is that really what the fuck you think of me, Rica? That I'm a fucking coward? After Diamond..." LeBaron stops and starts speaking again. "Before he passed, we came up with a game plan for me to execute if anything ever happened to him. That's why I'm here."

"Here you two are, a French 75 for the lady and an Old Fashioned for the gentlemen," says the server while placing their drinks on the table. "So, do we want to start with some appetizers?" Their server asks.

An awkward silence lingers between Rica and LeBaron, neither of them acknowledging the presence of the server. "Okay, I'll just come back then. Take your time." Releasing a curt smile, the server eagerly leaves the table.

Rica reaches for her glass with perfectly manicured, blood-red stiletto nails and delicately fingers the stem, taking a much-needed sip of her cocktail. LeBaron follows suit, not realizing how much he needs his drink as well. His throat immediately burns and loosens with the peppery taste of the rye whiskey now coating the back of his throat. The two sit for a moment longer, enjoying one another's presence in the bustling restaurant. Memories begin to flood both of their minds—thoughts of the two of them with Diamond, plotting and planning the city's takeover; Rica scheming on how to get her uncle to front them some dope so they could stop being corner boys for Fat Ron.

"Aye, remember when you and D bought those matching chains from Chika and them? Damn things turned you and D's necks green?" LeBaron can't help bursting out laughing from the memory, which is out of character for him because he's usually very stoic. Rica tries to stifle her laugh but can't when she thinks of Diamond's and her matching green necks and how they furiously looked for Chika for revenge.

"Whew, I was fightin' mad at that bitch! I remember me and D swearing we was too fly with that fake shit on." Rica chuckled. "Swearing we was gonna stunt on the whole hood with them chains. You know I still got the club pictures from the night we first got them? Fucking memories." Rica's voice trails off.

The two sit in a more comfortable silence that comes with knowing a person for a lifetime; sitting in their presence is comfort enough. "So, you finally gonna tell me why you're here, LB?"

"I'm here about D's little girl, Golden. She had some shit go down and I wanted to know if you were behind it," LeBaron blurts, because he's unsure about Rica's reaction at the mention of Golden's name.

Rica lets out a snort, shaking her head. "So, wait, LB. Let me get this straight. You wait over twenty years to come here and ask me about a child that D had on me and then left me for? Nigga, you must be fucking crazy!"

Commotion stirs at the booth across from them and Rica raises her hand letting her crew know she's okay. She lowers her voice. "Look, LB, I don't know shit about shit, let alone some little girl. What the fuck I look like, fucking with some little girl of my dead baby daddy?" Rica asks. She arches her eyebrow and her eyes pierce into LeBaron's as she awaits his answer.

"Let me show you something, Rica." LeBaron reaches into his suit pocket for his phone and pulls up the video of Golden at the strip club. Rica watches the video intently and can't stop the smile from spreading across her face in satisfaction. LeBaron grows murderous watching her enjoy the video.

Meanwhile, outside of the restaurant, neither Rica nor LeBaron know they are being watched by Camilla. She's had a weird feeling from the moment she met LeBaron, and she knows that only a man with power could sway her mother to abandon all reason and recklessly dismiss her security. She followed LeBaron to his hotel and waited for him to leave, then followed him to the restaurant where he currently sat across the table from her mother. If Camilla didn't know her mother's murderous tendencies, it might appear that Rica and LeBaron are on a date. While watching the pair, Camilla decides to call her brother Rico.

"Yo,' bro, I don't know who the fuck dude is, but he got Ma trippin' and actin' all weird and shit. Like a love-sick high school chick. This shit is weird, bro. But I'm gonna get to the bottom of it," Camilla tells her brother through the car phone.

"What you mean, she acting like a high schooler?" Rico laughs, because he can't imagine his mother being anything but cold and calculating.

"And she doin' that thing where she blinks her eyes and plays with her glass like when she tryin' to be sexy and shit. Yo, this shit got me heated, bro! Who the fuck is this nigga? I ain't never seen him before today and now she meetin' with dude all out in public. I can't remember the last time Ma was out in public like this. I'm gonna figure this shit out, bro. And why you all calm?" Camilla is dissatisfied with her brother's response. *Yo,' why the fuck this nigga so calm*? She's thinking.

Camilla always feels like an outsider when it comes to important aspects of the family business. Her mother trusts her to run the Oxy side of the business and manage some of the real estate they own around the city, but her mother relies heavily on Rico to run the dope business and all the other dirt. Rico is the muscle of the operation. Camilla is three years older than her brother and more experienced in the drug game, because Rica had kept her precious heir to the throne out of the dirty side of the business, hoping to keep his record clean.

Camilla loves being a big sister to Rico, but she doesn't love being treated like an afterthought by her mother. Rico will inherit the family business when he turns twenty-five. He has a great family lineage reaching back to Puerto Rico. In contrast, all Camilla knows about her father is that he was black and gunned down in a drug deal. As far as she knows, her father didn't belong to any major crime family. She honestly doesn't even know if she was a mistake. All she knows is that Rica and her father met in high school and started running drugs back in the mid-nineties. She's never known her father Diamond, and the only father-figure she has known is Ramon Sr.—he merely tolerated Camilla for Rica's sake.

As an outsider in her own family, Camilla has formed her own family. The Circle Boyz are loyal to her. But Camilla can't hide the jealousy she feels about the secrets Rico and her mother share. Camilla thinks to herself, *She even named his ass after herself.* But she loves her brother and trusts him with her life, as he does her. Rica is Rico's only confidant. He can't share the ins and outs of his business with his girlfriend—he needs to make sure she has plausible deniability if anything ever goes south. Camilla confides in Rico about her dreams of having her own real estate empire. Plans she never fully shares with her mother, because she doesn't want to hear her criticisms.

I bet Rico knows something about this nigga, Camilla briefly thinks and tucks the thought away into the corners of her mind for later.

She chalks up Rico's secrecy about the stranger as part of a business deal her mother and brother cooked up without her, yet again. Camilla has known Rico would be coming into power and that she would have to make her own moves soon or be pushed out of the family business—further reducing her role in the family business to a flunky, running simple errands for her brother. Camilla isn't going out like that. She plans to carve out a piece of territory with her Circle Boyz—with her brother's permission—and focus on selling Oxy and real estate. She initially resented her mother insisting she get her real estate and brokerage licenses, but now she understands that her mother knew she may no longer have a seat at her brother's table and would need a table of her own.

"Yo, I'mma hit you back, bruh," Camilla tells her brother and hangs up.

She knows something isn't right about the stranger. She's going to find out what scheme her brother and mother have concocted and how the newcomer is involved. Camilla uses the zoom feature on her phone to spy on Rica and LeBaron. Rica's demeanor is relaxed, but her face is still tense. Camilla can't decipher this new posture of her mother's at first, but then she recognizes her mother's actions as nervousness. She likes this man. Rica's words play in Camilla's mind while she watches her mother squirm under this man's gaze: "Niggas ain't shit and only good for two thangs, money and dick. And you can live without the dick but not the money." Camilla shakes her head at her mother's words, mumbling to herself, *Should've took your own advice, Ma.*

***

"And…so what? Another young slut shaking her ass in the club. What's new about that?" Rica spits her words at LeBaron. "I mean, she got skills though. I'll give her that."

"Look here, you crazy, jealous ass…" LeBaron allows his words to trail off as he gathers his composure. Rica raises an eyebrow, ready for the disrespect to pop off so she can have a reason to air LB out. She's wanted to for years anyway. LeBaron slides back in the booth and presses his back to the overstuffed leather booth.

"Okay, are we ready to order yet? I see you finished those drinks."

The server arrives at the table at the most inopportune time. Both Rica and LeBaron shoot her a dirty look.

"Okay then, how about another round? And may I suggest the calamari and antipasto platter to start? How about a large Caesar salad with grilled chicken to share?"

Rica waves her hand in agreement and the server dashes off to put in the order.

"Oh, and put a rush on those drinks," Rica adds before they leave to place the order to the point-of-sale station. "They sure know how to spend your money here," Rica says absentmindedly.

She regrets not taking a few pulls from her one-hitter before getting out of the car. She had wanted to be clear-headed for the meeting, because LeBaron is cunning and always out-maneuvers his adversaries. Now, she wishes she had something to calm the swirling thoughts and memories of her partner in crime and former lover, Diamond.

"You ever think about me over the years?" Rica asks before she even realizes the question has passed her lips. She keeps her head hung, focusing on an imaginary spot in the white, starched tablecloth.

Their eyes dart to each other's, searching for the answer neither of them will give—not in this lifetime. LeBaron pulls his eyes away from the deep sea of Rica's.

Focus, man...damn. But he can't help it. *Those eyes, those fucking eyes*, he frantically thinks, taking a bated breath and thoughtfully looking into Rica's eyes.

"You know, can't a woman alive hold a candle to you, Rica, never have and never will." LeBaron looks at the pulse of Rica's blood pump through her jugular vein. He sees her pulse quicken ever so slightly. "Intelligent, ambitious, clever, and ruthless as fuck."

Rica allows a smile to crawl across her faintly painted red lips.

"You know you always had a way with words, LB. So again, tell me why we're here? Huh? You come back after twenty years—uninvited I might add. You show up to my club unannounced—again, uninvited. Then you invite me to our place and show me a video of some stripper and get mad when I don't play your little guessing game." Rica grows annoyed because she almost fell into LeBaron's seductive trap of compliments.

"Lastly, and most importantly, you disrespect me to my face. So, for the last time, why the fuck are you here, LB, but more importantly, when are you leaving?" Rica leans in with her last question, folding her hands in front of her on the tablecloth.

"I always liked that you got straight to the point, Rica, so let me do the same. The girl in the video is Diamond's daughter like I said." He pauses and checks her jugular vein; it's pulsating quickly. He knows he's past the point of no return and he needs to ask what he came to Chicago to ask. "This video surfaced at her school in every single student's school email address. Even the faculty got the email and now they're calling for her expulsion."

"So, what the fuck does that have to do with me, LB?"

"You did it, Rica. Well, not you personally, but your son did it. But what I can't figure out is the why."

"Wait, wait, wait. Hold up, LB. You mean to tell me, not only did you come here unannounced, but you came here to accuse my son of what? Sending a fucking email? Be fucking for real! You done lost it now!" Rica said.

LeBaron knows Rica's lying about her son's involvement. She hadn't mastered the art of lying to him, even after all these years. He knows that if he accuses Rico directly, she'll overact, proving she's guilty and has something to do with sending the email.

"You see right there, the guy sitting by the stage handing her fistfuls of cash? You see that tattoo on his arm?" LeBaron asks, pointing to the video on his phone.

Rica can't say anything, because the still shot of the video clearly shows her son with a family tattoo that all members got when they turned fifteen to initiate them into the family business.

Rica sucks her teeth. "Okay, so what? My son loves stripper bitches and what?"

"You mean he likes watching his sister's half-sister dance in the nude? You know his half-sister, Golden?" LeBaron lets his sentence hang in the air, because he knows Rica is now calculating her next move and trying to anticipate LeBaron's. If she admits she sent Rico to record Golden, Rica would have to reveal her ulterior motive, but LeBaron already knows what it was. Rica also knows that if Rico ever finds out that his mother had him purposely drive to a strip club, film, and upload the footage to hundreds of people's emails, he would be at risk. His face could now be identified in a lineup for any number of crimes he has committed and always blamed on a fall guy.

"You know revenge porn is a punishable offense now, right?" LeBaron asks sarcastically as a small smile plays across his lips. His sentence penetrates the silence while Rica quickly works out LeBaron's powerful threat.

LeBaron and Rica know that Rico had been clean up until this point, but if Rico's face could be identified and an allegation of revenge porn charged against him, then the allegation alone would bring attention to his family's drug business. The FBI has been looking into them for decades but has never had concrete evidence to prosecute a top player.

But what LeBaron doesn't know is that Rico had robbed a gas station the same weekend, even though he had a pocket full of cash; he only did it for the adrenaline rush. Knowing that he has the backing of one of the largest Puerto Rican crime families spanning from Wisconsin down to the Mississippi, he let his wanting for reckless behavior win over his responsibility to his family.

Rica knows that if Camilla ever finds out she has a half-sister her mother never bothered to mention that her only daughter would possibly hate her. However, Rica doesn't want Camilla or Rico to ever find out about Golden until she is ready to tell them, and she has never thought she would be ready to reopen those deep-rooted wounds of the past. So, Rica weighs her next words very carefully.

She lets out a small chuckle. "Okay, LB. Yeah, that's my son in the video. And yes, that was me who had him record that little girl and send it to her school. But I guess you wanna know why, huh? Well, LB, we ain't got that type of time and this conversation is over." Rica abruptly slides out of the booth and storms off in the direction of the front exit with the two fake diners in tow. One of the diners turns around and stares menacingly at LeBaron, as a warning and turns away just as quickly, catching up to the other diner and Rica.

Camilla sits in the car watching Rica stepping away from the table with her long white, cashmere trench coat floating behind her.

Now what the fuck he say to her to make her stomp off like that? Rica wonders. She's never seen her mother stomp away from a meeting like a spoiled child who was told *no* after asking for their favorite snack. Camilla zooms in on the stranger's face with her cell's camera. She watches LeBaron sitting in the booth with a smug grin on his face, taking a sip of his watered-down drink. He sits back while amusement plays across his face as the server brings him his meal. Camilla needs to clear her head; she has so many racing thoughts and questions swirling.

CHAPTER FIVE

SOFT PETALS

Camilla pulls up to her condo that she shares with her girlfriend Elyse. The lights are still on upstairs. Camilla uses the garage door opener and drives her Jeep inside, hoping Elyse is getting in the shower so she can join her. Before she left the restaurant, she texted Elyse, letting her know that she was on her way home and to be ready.

Camilla stays in her car waiting for the garage door to close while keeping her hand on her piece that lies in her lap. Her mother always told her that most gangstas get robbed at home because their guards are down. Camilla vowed it would never be her.

She gets out of the car and is welcomed by the sweet aromas of her favorite vanilla candle and Elyse 's cooking commingling in the air. Camilla walks to the microwave to retrieve her plate of glazed lamb chops, butter-whipped potatoes, and garlic green beans—one of her favorite meals. She sits at the white and grey marbled counter to enjoy her food and sends some texts to the Circle Boyz to check on the business. She wants to see how the pickups went this evening and make sure no one came up short. She also wants to check up on Meechie to see what he found out about LeBaron. While she was at the restaurant, she sent the short video and pictures of him to Meechie to run through their connection at the local police station. She didn't want any surprises.

> *You talk to ol' boy yet?*

Camilla texts Meechie while taking another bite of her potatoes, savoring the butter and garlic.

> *Naw not yet*

Meechie texts back.

Camilla puts her phone down, satisfied she would have answers in the morning. After finishing her plate and rinsing it off, she heads up the spiral staircase, down the hallway, and enters the master suite. Elyse is singing one of her original songs. Camilla stands still for a moment and closes her eyes, listening to Elyse's alto bravado sing the sweetest love song ever written about a lover's passion. She smiles to herself because she knows Elyse wrote the song about Camilla after they first met at the club and were drawn to one another like magnets. Their attraction was electric and volatile at times, completely consumed by passion.

Camilla opens her eyes, now calm and centered. She reminds herself she's home and safe. She doesn't have to pretend here or be tough to get respect, because she's home, and home is love.

She undresses and joins Elyse in their steamer shower. Camilla bites her lip as water runs down Elyse's perfectly round ass. She admires her woman's physic. She follows the water running over Elyse's short, tapered natural haircut, down her neck, to her toned back where the water pools for a moment in the small of her back, then spreads out over Elyse's beautifully rounded hips, down her thighs and calves. Elyse feels the hungry stares of Camilla devouring her body and coyly turns her head. "So you just gonna stand there watching or you gonna come get this pussy?"

Camilla bites her bottom lip, undresses, and steps into the water, hugging Elyse tightly and pressing her breasts into Elyse's back. Elyse turns her head and passionately kisses Camilla's lips.

"Mmmm...you taste good." Elyse purrs.

"Alexa, play, 'I Wanna Freak You' by Jodeci," Camilla calls out. The song and seduction begin in tandem. Camilla grabs the body wash and lathers Elyse while hungrily tonguing her. Elsye grabs the body wash and lathers Camilla, mixing saliva, water, and the lubrication their bodies are making. Camilla slides her fingers over Elyse's clit while pinching her nipples with her other hand, making Elyse moan while she presses her body further into Camilla. Their breathing quickens as Elyse covers Camilla's mouth with hers, thrusting her tongue deep inside while they exchange air. The lovers moan in pleasure as Camilla moves her mouth from Elyse's tongue to her breast, eagerly awaiting her mouth with erect nipples. A spasm of sensation runs through Elyse's body, tingling into her now softened, swollen lips, her clit engorged with pleasure. Elyse massages Camilla's clit and grabs a handful of her soft, supple ass.

"I fucking love you." Elyse moans between gasps of pleasure, rocking her body into a tense rhythm until they both climax and their bodies slowed from getting their fill of each other.

"Rinse off and get that pretty ass on the bed. I wanna fuck you," Camilla orders Elyse while she breathes into her mouth and tongue kisses her deeply again. Elyse follows orders and gets out of the shower, dripping wet onto the heated, dark stone tiles and tiptoeing to the bedroom. Camilla is right behind her, admiring the sway of Elyse's ass on the way to their king-sized bed with a tufted, royal blue velvet headboard. Elyse lies on her back in anticipation of her lover while

Camilla slides her face between Elyse's thighs and begins to slurp and suck Elyse's clit while twisting her nipples with one hand and gripping Elyse's ass in place with the other. Camilla's mouth is locked in place, and she isn't going to let up until she feels Elyse's body tremble to each massage of her expert tongue. The two make love until their bodies clench and relax in ecstasy into a softened heap of sweet and sticky flesh.

Camilla reaches over to grab a pre-roll from the mirror-encased nightstand. She looks at her reflection and smoothes her curly bob back into place. She sparks her pre-roll, takes a deep inhale, then exhales while letting the events of the day float into the recesses of her memory. She relaxes against Elyse's breast while both of their breathing calms and slows. They lie in silence while taking turns getting lifted.

"So how was your day?" Elyse asks between holding in her smoke.

Camilla takes a deep drag, holds her breath while the weed smoke fills her lungs, and then lets it out. "It was really fucking weird. Ma is up to something." She exhales.

Elyse reaches over Camilla's naked body to grab another pre-roll and sparks it. She knows that whenever Camilla starts talking about her mother, the conversation could get deep. She isn't high enough to listen to another bitchfest about Camilla and her mom's fucked up relationship, especially since Camilla is constantly trying to prove her worth to her mother—that she is capable of running the family business. But Elyse knows as well as Camilla that Rica is never going to hand the business over to her. Rico is going to inherit the family business, because the business belongs to *his* family. Camilla is her mother's first-born, but she wasn't born into a worldwide drug empire. She will always be second to her brother. This doesn't stop Camilla from trying to prove her loyalty and usefulness to Rica though.

"So, what happened, babe?" Elyse asks, uninterested.

"This fucking nigga just pops up outta nowhere and my moms was acting all different, going out to dinner with this nigga. Not having her security around, just moving all different. Matter fact, she actually looked like she was flirtin' with dude when they was out at dinner."

"Oh, so, you went with them to dinner?" Elyse asks while taking another drag and absentmindedly drops ashes onto their silver, silk sheets.

"Naw, I followed her sneaky ass," Camilla replies, placing her roach in the ashtray. "Something is going on yo', and I'm gonna figure that shit out."

"Why the fuck you care, shit? It ain't like it's gonna change nothing! Your brother still about to get the throne and you gonna be out on yo' ass with the Circle Boyz, looking stupid." Elyse had grown tired of biting her tongue when it came to Rica. It's no secret Elyse doesn't like Rica and the feeling is mutual.

"Bitch, what the fuck you say?" Camilla asks in a calm tone.

Elyse shifts her weight and sits up, "I..."

"Naw, bitch. What the fuck you say? Don't stutter now. Say that tough shit with yo' chest!"

"Naw, I was just sayin' you care so much about what she thinks, and I mean, she just focuses on your brother." Elyse says weakly.

Camilla abruptly gets out of bed. She isn't gonna argue with Elyse right after making love to her. She can't decide whether she's madder at her mom for treating her as less than equal to her brother or more mad at Elyse for pointing it out.

"I'm going out." Camilla takes a quick shower to wash off the sex and dresses in a tan sweat suit paired with a cream pair of Yeezys. She grabs a tan overcoat with matching skully. She remote-starts her truck to warm it up while she checks her text messages. One thing about the drug business is that there is always something or someone to do.

She gets a text from Meechie saying,

> *I got a hit. At the spot.*

Camilla knows that Meechie has information from the police officer they have on payroll. Most drug dealers pay narcotics officers or beat cops for information or to keep them out of jail, but Camilla keeps an evidence room clerk in her pocket. He usually knows when all the busts are happening, and he can make evidence disappear and reappear. He's the best person to have on your team when you need information or to build a case against your competition. Camilla knows that Meechie would want to deliver whatever news he gets from their snitch in person. So, Camilla gets in her truck and heads to one of the Circle Boyz's spots where they count the cash at the end of the night. They never meet in the same place and don't have to, because Camilla keeps at least a dozen houses available to them throughout the city using her brokerage and real estate business as a cover.

Camilla drives up to one of the fronted homes in Calumet City and pulls all the way to the side of the house to enter through the back door. She gets out, locks her truck, and runs up to the house before the cold can set in. She does the Circle Boyz's secret knock on the iron-laced security door. Every person in the Circle Boyz has their own unique knock and they even have a special knock to give if someone is with them trying to use them as a decoy to rob the spot. She knows someone is at the door listening and waiting. The person on the other side of the door decides it is Camilla, pops about three locks and a steel-bar security lock to open the door. "What up, Black?" Camilla daps up Black, her head of security, as she squeezes past his six-five, two-sixty frame.

"Shit!" Black gives his coined response.

Camilla makes her rounds through the kitchen and into the living room, speaking to all the Circle Boyz. Her crew consists of twelve—eight men and four women. The Circle Boyz are more than a crew; they are each other's chosen family. They are all on the same level and no one person is over another, not even Camilla. Everyone plays their role according to their strengths, but every member has an equal say in the business dealings. If one member isn't as knowledgeable about real estate, then another member educates them, so they're always teaching one another and leveling up. This also means if one person gets popped by the police, the whole organization can keep going. It also cuts down on the jealousy factor, and anyone wanting to "snitch or be a bitch," as Meechie so cleverly says.

The founding members of the Circle Boyz are Meechie and Camilla. They met in middle school and instantly fell in sync, because they were the flyest kids in school. Camilla found out that Meechie's dad was serving life in prison for drug dealing and his mother was a small-time, local drug dealer who slang for Rica here and there. They both came up with the name Circle Boyz because they saw how other organizations crumbled because one member wanted more power or money. But Meechie and Camilla thought by treating their organization like a true circle, with no beginning or end, it cut down on someone having to strong-arm others to get their way to the top of the organization. The more money they all made together, the more money everyone got. Simple math.

Camilla locates Meechie in his favorite spot at the small, circular kitchen table with the money counter, rubber-banding bundles into thousand-dollar stacks. Meechie briefly looks up to see Camilla walk in and gives a quick nod, so as not to miss any bills that stop the machine. "What up, Milla?"

"Chillin'. Glad to get out the house, my fuckin' woman trippin'."

They both laugh, because Camilla is always arguing with Elyse over one thing or another.

"I been told yo' ass, fucking with a black girl named Elyse is a bad idea." Meechie lets out a small laugh, shaking his shoulder-length locs under his black skully.

"Anyways, nigga. Enough about her ass. What you find out from Pops?"

Meechie stops the money counter, which he never did while they spoke about the information they got from Pops while at "the spot," because everyone in the house was an equal member. There were no secrets among them, theoretically. Camilla knows that the information Meechie receives from their resident Chicago Police Department snitch is no run-of-the-mill gossip, and it's for her ears only. Camilla, turning on her heels, heads for the back door.

"Hey, Black. Me and Meechie out back about to blow one."

Black nods in agreement as he opens the door for the two of them and they head to the garage. The Circle Boyz have a rule to never keep drugs, guns, or even alcohol in the same vicinity where they count money. They either smoke in the garages of the homes they use, or they wait until they're in a trusted surrounding. They still never keep large amounts of money on them the same time they carry drugs or guns.

The two make it into the detached garage—thankfully none of the crew are there—and the smell of gas lingers in the air even with the high-level air filtration system. The Circle Boyz don't want to bring any undue attention to their activities, so there can be no more than three of them at a house at a time because numerous cars in the driveway draw attention. Also, they never play loud music, gamble, or smoke where nosey neighbors could see, smell, or report suspicious activity.

Meechie shows Camilla the text Pops sent. It was an old *Chicago Sun* article, dated 1992, with LeBaron in handcuffs on the front page with the caption, *Young phenom basketball star, LeBaron Tate, loses scholarship due to drugs*. Camilla scans the article, looking for clues as to why Rica seems so enamored with LeBaron's presence. Camilla moves her lips while reading the article. "Hold up, he went to Marshall. That's the same high school my momma went to. I remember her tellin' me once about it on a drunk night. You know Rica don't say shit personal about herself." Camilla looks at Meechie as they nod in agreement.

"Keep reading, my G," Meechie urges as he preps a cigarillo to roll.

Camilla keeps scanning the article and her eyes grow large when she reads the name *Diamond Rose* in a picture caption. Camilla reads aloud, "LeBaron pictured with friend Diamond Rose." The two of them were in their school basketball uniforms.

Camilla lifts her head with her mouth agape, befuddled by the article's revelation. "So, my dad and LeBaron played ball together back in the day?" Camilla asks Meechie.

"Yeah, that ain't all. Pops said that's how yo' moms got started in the drug game. When LeBaron was kicked off the team because they caught him with a gun, yo' daddy and momma teamed up with him to really just say fuck it and start they own drug gang." Meechie finishes rolling the cigarillo.

"Pops said the three of them was always together. The hood called 'em the Musketeers and shit. They was all planning to get out the hood on the back of that LeBaron dude going to the league, but since that didn't happen, they all got into the game instead. Got linked up with a local connect and started slangin'." Meechie shrugs his shoulders, sealing and twisting his cigarillo in his mouth.

"So, what you gonna do, Milla?" Meechie asks, snatching Camilla out of her racing thoughts with the flick of his lighter.

"I'm gonna find out why this nigga is here. Clearly, Rica ain't gonna tell the fucking truth! Maybe that nigga came back to frame her, try and finesse some money outta her since she's the connect now. But naw, that nigga don't look like he hurtin' for money." Camilla grows silent, mulling over the possibilities for LeBaron's return after over twenty years.

"Well, whatever you gonna do, you know I gotchu." Meechie says as he daps up Camilla and takes a pull off his blunt.

"Preciate you," Camilla replies.

"Since you took an interest in the nigga, I had two of the homies follow dude, so we know his motion." Meechie says between puffs of weed smoke. "He staying at one of the hotels downtown. I got one homie watching the back entrance and the other watching his car. I'll tell you what though." Meechie stops.

"What?"

"Dude ain't no joke. He move like he ain't new to this shit. Dude move like how I was taught to move, so I told the homies to hang back cuz dude is likely to know we or somebody is watching him."

"Hmm...interesting." Camilla reaches out to take the blunt from Meechie and inhales. "Yeah, keep the homies on him. I'm gonna talk to my brother and see what he knows. I got a funny feeling about dude. Something is in the air and I gotta make sure bruh ain't holding out on me. A'ight, I'm gonna holla at you in the am. Let me get back home to this crazy girl." Camilla laughs, takes another deep pull of the blunt before passing it back to Meechie.

"Holla. Hit me up," Meechie adds as he daps up Camilla one last time.

Camilla uses her drive home to try and put together the pieces of LeBaron's return and his connection to her mother's past and, most importantly, her father's past.

Chapter Six

LOVE ALLIANCES

Camilla stretches a kink from her neck as she rises from the white, leather couch she spent the night on, rather than in her plush, king-sized bed with Elyse after their argument. She hates fighting with Elyse. She'll need her partner's level-headedness and ingenuity if she's to pull off the plan she'd thought of last night. There are a few missing pieces she needs to place before she can put her plan into action.

Camilla stands up to stretch and feels a twinge in the left side of her neck—an old basketball injury from her high school days. She yawns, heading up the large, spiral staircase to her and Elyse's bedroom. A high-powered jet massage from her shower could release the tension in her neck and entire body. As she reaches the top of the steps, she hesitates, thinking of an apology before opening the door. She softly twists the bedroom doorknob and is shocked to see Elyse awake sitting in the middle of their king-sized bed in an upright fetal position with her arms wrapped around her knees. Elyse is just as alarmed to see Camilla and wipes the early morning tears from her red eyes.

Camilla creeps closer to the bed, hanging her head in shame. She hates that she's the cause of Elyse's fragile state. "Hey, bae. Look, I'm sorry," Camilla says.

Elyse springs from the covers and storms past Camilla.

"Hold on. Wait, bae, let me finish," Camilla pleads as she follows Elyse to their large bathroom. "Hold on, Elyse. For real, you were right about my mom."

Elyse stops mid-step and whips her head around in disbelief. Camilla never admits Elyse is right when it comes to Rica. Camilla always defends Rica's actions blindly, always hoping for Rica's love and attention, but instead receives harsh tones, disrespect, and feelings of inadequacy.

"Wait, what did you say?" Elyse asks. She needs Camilla to repeat herself to make sure she isn't still asleep.

"You right, bae. All this time I knew you were right about my mom, but I thought that if I didn't admit how shitty she's treated me then it wouldn't be true, but it is and always has been. I just didn't know why she treats me like a fucking plague! I never did anything to her but exist, and my presence irritates her."

Camilla pauses, allowing her words to penetrate Elyse's ears, and her own as well. Camilla had these thoughts over the years but never voiced them out loud. She always held out hope that her mother would change one day and embrace her, that she would tell her how proud she is of her. But that day had never come. Camilla is now coming to grips with the fact that she will never hear her mother say that she is proud of her.

"I'm sorry, bae, for all the times I came at you when you were only trying to be there for me and support me." Camilla hangs her head in shame.

"I guess I was just fucking frustrated with myself that I would rather hurt you than deal with my own fucking issues. Can you please forgive me? Please, I'm begging you. I swear I'm done with that shit of trying to prove myself to my mom. I spent a lot of time thinking last night. And…and…I'm ready to get out the game." Camilla's breath hitches in her throat, because she doesn't know that her stream of consciousness is taking her to the conclusion of walking away from everything: her mother, the Circle Boyz, the business, and her brother.

Elyse stands frozen in silence at Camilla's revelation. All the things that she talked about with Camilla now seem to be coming full circle. Elyse had always advocated for Camilla to leave the drug game and take her real estate career seriously. She had pushed Camilla to not only be a licensed agent as well as a broker so she could keep all the money from her deals to herself, but to also create her own real estate company. Elyse realizes she isn't breathing and inhales. She wobbles a bit from lightheadedness. She can't believe everything Camilla is saying, and she isn't going to be easily swayed by Camilla's overnight revelation. She knows how manipulating Camilla can be.

"Naw, bae. It's not like that this time," Camilla answers Elyse's unspoken question. "I've done a lot of thinking over the past year about getting out and how I would do it. I just never had the courage to do it. But seeing how I left you last night tore me up."

Elyse tilts her head. She knows Camilla is embellishing her feelings.

"Okay, let me stop. It ain't all about you. I'm tired of living in my brother's shadow too." Camilla says as she firmly plants her feet, squares her shoulders, and claps her hands in front of her. Her posture mirrors her words and Elyse takes notice.

"I'm tired of feeling like I'm second to him and my mom always keeping their little secrets. I'm tired of all that shit. And I just really want to start over. But I can't do this shit unless I know you with me." Camilla's eyes plead with Elyse to give her another chance.

"First thing's first," Elyse says, walking closer to Camilla and grasping her two hands in hers. "Let's brush your teeth."

The two–burst into laughter and hugs. They know they need each other, but Camilla also knows that Elyse is ready to walk away if she doesn't change. Camilla squeezes Elyse a little tighter at the thought of almost losing her.

Camilla crosses the bathroom, looking in the mirror at her reddened eyes and curly hair; it's matted from sleeping on the couch without her satin pillowcase. She's startled by her own appearance. Her decisions weigh heavily on her heart as she squeezes toothpaste onto her electric toothbrush and Elyse joins her at their double sinks. Both are caught in their own thoughts, processing Camilla's revelation as they take extra time brushing their teeth.

Elyse spits out her toothpaste and gargles mouthwash, spitting it out and quickly turning to Camilla. "So, how you plan on pulling this off? You know she ain't just gonna let you walk away, right?"

"I know, but I got a plan. I just need to work out a few things first. Can we talk about it over breakfast?" Camilla's half-crooked smile draws Elyse in.

"I can be persuaded with breakfast." Elyse smiles in return.

"Okay, get dressed." Camilla pats Elyse on the butt. "We can still beat traffic this early."

Elyse nods in agreement and slips her silver, silk nightgown over her head, nipples erect in anticipation. "But first, I'm gonna need you to get down on your knees and make it up to me, Camilla Rose." Elyse smiles with her eyes and heads to their steamer shower with Camilla close behind.

Chapter Seven

COUNTER PUNCHES

Meechie is heated.

"Aye, Milla, I got the drop on dude. He up here at Harold's on seventy-fifth. This nigga got the nerve to be all out in the open! Nigga just casually eating chicken like he not out here causing ruckus and left the Chi after his homeboy, I mean yo' daddy, got shot."

"Ok," says Camilla. "I'm on my way. I'm right around the corner anyway. Later."

I can't believe this nigga just out here like it's sweet, Camilla thinks.

She drives a few blocks to the location of the chicken shack where LeBaron is. Sitting in the truck a few cars away from the store window, she watches LeBaron. He looks like he's having a casual meal, but everything about him makes him seem out of place, from his low-cut fade to his outfit—snug, black turtleneck topped with a black, cashmere sweater that's perfectly fitted and wraps around his torso, and the tailored, black slacks. Camilla surveys her surroundings, making sure she hasn't missed an invisible security detail.

Once she's satisfied that LeBaron is alone, she climbs out of her truck and steps onto the pavement. She lightly fingers the trigger of her .22 in her puffer jacket pocket; it's easy to conceal and doesn't have a safety lock. She and LeBaron lock eyes through the window as soon as she crosses the street and walks in the door while the warm, humid air of fried chicken smacks her in the face. They do not release their distrustful stares as she slowly approaches his table.

"Hey, welcome to Harold's." A young woman from behind the counter half-heartedly greets Camilla, not looking up from her duties at the cash register.

Camilla doesn't respond. She stands at LeBaron's table. "Mind if I sit down?" Camilla asks.

LeBaron stops eating his food and wipes his mouth, tossing his greasy napkin onto a pile of bones. He motions with his hand for Camilla to sit in the free seat opposite him. "Sure, Camilla. Have a seat."

Camilla doesn't let her surprise at LeBaron knowing her name show. If she were in his position, she, too, would've taken the time out to know her enemy. LeBaron rests his hands on the table on either side of his empty food basket to show Camilla that he has no intention of reaching for a weapon. She follows suit and takes her hands off the trigger of her .22. Camilla sits in the metal chair and places her hands gently on the table, interlacing her fingers, while never taking her eyes off LeBaron.

"So, to what do I owe this pleasure, Camilla? I haven't seen you in such a long time. Not since you were little. Of course, before your..." LeBaron trails off. "Not since your father was killed."

Camilla sits staring at LeBaron, measuring her next words carefully. She isn't here for a family reunion or to reminisce about a father she can't remember. But LeBaron may be the only one to give her the answers about her father she yearns to hear. She wants to know about his personality. If he was a jokester or the serious type. She wants to know what he was like as a business partner. Was he ruthless or fair with his workers and clientele? How did he meet her mother and how did they work together? Why was he murdered? And most importantly, did he love her?

Before Camilla can ask anything, LeBaron starts talking.

"So, me, your dad, and your mom met in high school. Did you know that? Your mom had stolen some weed from her older brother and convinced us that we could sell it for a slightly higher price, make the money back, and re-up before your uncle ever realized the weed was gone." LeBaron leans back in his chair, lifts his eyes to the ceiling with a smile on his face while he momentarily gets lost in the memory. "Your mom was made for this shit, even back then."

He tells her that once they sold the little bit of weed to students they knew wouldn't snitch, Rica quickly realized she had enough money to re-up and cop some more. They bought more product from a local connect, Fat Ron, and never looked back.

"She taught me and Diamond the game she learned from your uncle, RIP." LeBaron balls up his fist, kissing his thumb, looking to the heavens as a form of respect.

"She got us hooked on the fast money, quick. Not sure what's worse: the addict addicted to the product, or the pusher addicted to the money."

Camilla listens in awe to her mother's origin story and admires how she got it out the mud and had two niggas following and believing in her from the start. She doesn't want to interrupt LeBaron by asking any questions because this is the most she's ever heard about her mother growing up and how she got in the game.

LeBaron fondly reflects. "Had us following her around like little schoolboys while she called the shots. She been a fuckin' boss, no doubt about that." LeBaron confirms Camilla's thoughts aloud. "We were just happy to be in her world, ya' know? Then her and D fell in love and had you."

"That's a good story, nigga," Camilla spits out. "But you forgot to add the part about how my dad had me, abandoned me, and then got himself killed. Don't try and paint that shit out to be a fucking Hallmark movie." Camilla's ears were getting hot with anger.

Her stare is broken by the waitress walking over from the counter. "Okay, baby, I got a three-piece wing, mild with fries. Imma get yo' drank in a minute, a Dr Pepper, right?" Camilla, bewildered, nods in agreement.

Camilla sits stunned, looking at the steam wafting off her freshly fried chicken with the mild sauce perfectly covering each wing. Her mouth starts watering. She swallows her spit just in time for the waitress to bring her soda with the top half of the wrapper still on the straw. Camilla reluctantly removes the wrapper and takes a large gulp. She looks up at LeBaron.

"I thought you might be hungry. Did I get your order right?"

Camilla nods yes. She digs in with more questions swirling in her brain now than when she initially sat down.

"How'd you know? Camilla asks.

"I make it a point to stay in the know about people of interest to me."

"Is that so?" Camilla asks between bites of her chicken wings. "So, tell me this. Since you know so much about me, why don't you tell me why my mother never talks about you or my father? If the days were so good, then why doesn't she fondly reminisce?"

"Well, I can't speak to her reasons, Camilla, but I can tell you this..."

"Cut the smooth shit, motherfucker, cuz I don't like yo' ass and I fo' damn sho' don't trust you either. Thanks for the trip down memory lane. But why in the fuck are you here?" Camilla stares down LeBaron to emphasize the seriousness of her tone.

She hates when men try to placate and satisfy her with stories or compliments on how much of a boss Rica is and was. She knows her mother is a boss more than anyone else. She watched her mother single-handedly build a drug empire from the ashes after her stepfather died. Not only did she do it without being born into the family, but she did it while securing a spot in the family while her second-born son came of age and was able to take his father's place. She even watched Rica push through her eldest brother's death without so much as one tear. Camilla sat ringside, watching Rica rule her drug empire with as much ruthlessness as any drug dealer she's ever come in contact with, so she doesn't need a bedtime story about a woman she knows all too well.

Camilla repeats herself, "Why the fuck you here, my G?" Camilla wipes her mouth and takes a sip of her soda.

LeBaron doesn't react to Camilla's abrupt question. He smugly sits back and answers, "Ask Rica why I'm here."

"Naw, nigga, I'm asking yo' ass. Why the fuck are you here? You supposedly came here after not seeing my mom for twenty-five years, then you show up here on our doorstep. You don't seem like you hurtin' for money and you for damn sure don't have people here. Rica don't fuck with you. So, again, why the fuck are you here?"

"It's none of your business."

Camilla realizes she's wasting her time and decides to leave. She learned a long time ago not to let another person manipulate her emotions to persuade her of the truth. Camilla had had many experiences with people who had narcissistic tendencies, namely her mother.

LeBaron's actions set off her narcissist alarm. Narcissists attempt to gaslight you into thinking your intuition about them is off, so you question your own mind. Camilla is smart enough to end the conversation, and she rises from her seat. "I don't know what your play is, but I intend to find out. Stay safe out there."

Camilla turns to walk away, feeling LeBaron's smug smile following her exit. As she crosses the street and climbs into her SUV, Camilla calls Meechie's number from her call log. "That nigga hiding something." She says when Meechie answers then she quickly hangs up and sits for a moment while her thoughts run wild. She tries to calm her mind. Rica's thoughts are in the back of her mind saying, "If it don't make sense, then it don't make sense."

Camilla originally thought LeBaron was back in the Chi to make a play for the family business or stake an original claim in what he, Rica, and her father started over twenty years ago. *No*, she thinks, *that can't be it*. LeBaron was clearly successful without Rica and her father, so he couldn't be there to stake a claim on the family business. She quickly pushes that plan out of her head, because in trying to take over their operation, LeBaron would be going head-to-head with one of the oldest drug families in the States that still had blood ties to Puerto Rico. Going against the family is pure suicide, and *no one is that stupid*, Camilla thinks.

More money must be his play. *He can't be here to make money with my mom*, she thinks. *So, he has to be here to protect his money*. She starts up her SUV. Camilla knows just where to get the rest of her answers—or at least a starting point.

Chapter Eight

TRUTH SEEKER

Camilla pulls up to her brother's girlfriend's house thinking, *He's probably still asleep since he worked the club last night.* She and her brother Rico usually trade off nights so one of them is always at the club, letting the other handle business for their crew or Rica.

Sitting in her car, she scans her surroundings. When she's sure she's safe, she reaches inside of her center consol' for the garage door opener labeled *Tricee*. She opens the garage door and drives in. She hates coming to her brother's girlfriend's house. His girlfriend had lived there for about six months with her school-aged kids and was getting tired of relocating them just so their house wouldn't get hit by thieves. Tricee figured that if anyone came inside her crib, she was gonna give them what they came for.

Camilla likes Tricee more than any of her brother's girlfriends. She's the only one who doesn't take crap, nor does she tolerate cheating. Rico tried to cheat and failed miserably, because Tricee is one of those girls everyone likes. She's one of the prettiest girls in the hood with a good heart, so no one wants to see her hurt. It also helps that her father, Blue, is the leader of one of the most respected motorcycle clubs in the city. When you hear that distant growl of forty Harley Davidsons pulling up, you know you're in deep shit. Tricee's dad took a liking to Rico after his father died. Blue was one of the first people Rico's father linked up with when his family sent him from Puerto Rico to Chicago. Blue and Rico both dealt with the death of his father by working on motorcycles. One day while working in Blue's garage, Rico saw Tricee at Blue's shop fixing her own motorcycle one day while doing an exchange with her dad. He couldn't take his eyes off her honey-colored legs crouched down, fixing her bike. After he handled his business he struck up a casual conversation with Tricee and was turned on by her wit and beauty; and the rest is history. Blue was okay with the relationship because he knew Rico at his core, not the persona he showed out in the streets.

Camilla pulls into the four-car garage and sees Tricee's BMW truck and her brother's AMG. She gets out of her SUV and goes to the keypad on the wall, enters a four-digit code, and waits for the keypad to flash green. After that, she rings the doorbell next to the keypad. The doorbell rings like a regular doorbell, but it also activates green lights that are posted in every room that run on a separate generator. Camilla patiently waits for the light in the garage to turn green. She chuckles to herself about a time when Black didn't wait for the green light and just headed inside Tricee's crib; he was met with the sound of a twelve-gauge being racked at his back.

The light in the garage turns green and Camilla proceeds to the backdoor. Rico is waiting behind the latticed-steel storm door for Camilla in one of Tricee's fluffy pink robes. She shakes her head and laughs while climbing the steps.

"What's so damn funny? It's early as a mu'fucka'!" Rico snorts.

"Aye, remember the time Tricee pulled that gauge on Black because he didn't wait for the green light, and she wasn't takin' no chances to figure out who it was either?"

"Aye, that nigga ain't come over here for like two months after that happened, even after my girl apologized. That shit was funny though. You want some coffee?"

"Yeah, I'll take some. Ya'll got all the good shit over here. Make me a mocha-choco-latte." Camilla says sarcastically.

"Yeah, okay." Rico laughs and gets to work making one of his famous lattes because Camilla doesn't know the difference between the different types of espressos. Rica made Rico work at the neighborhood coffee shop for a week because he pistol-whipped one of the drug runners for being five minutes late picking up. Rica wanted to send a message to Rico to learn when it was suitable to be ruthless and when a simple conversation would suffice. Rica was surprised to find out that Rico enjoyed working at the coffee shop. She passed by the shop on the fourth day, expecting to see Rico begrudgingly serving customers, when in fact, she saw her son serving coffee with a smile. His entire being radiated happiness. Rica parked her champagne-colored Range Rover in front of the coffee shop, left the SUV running, opened the glass door, and bellowed, "Let's go." Rico looked up in fear, bent his head, took off his apron, and folded it on the counter. He followed Rica out of the store. They both settled into Rica's SUV and the coffee shop was never spoken of again.

Camilla feels a pang of hurt for her brother. If they had grown up in a different family and under different circumstances, Rico may have been content with owning his own coffee shop. She thinks about herself as well while she watches him focus on the task of making one of his infamous lattes. *Where would I be if not selling drugs?* Her mind drifts to thoughts of running a mortgage brokerage with Elyse. She even lets her thoughts wander to her and Elyse getting married.

"Here you go, sis." Rico hands Camilla a glass coffee mug that has the perfect color of caramel coffee topped with foam in the shape of a leaf and a light dusting of cinnamon, brown sugar, and spice mixture. Camilla takes a sip as the full-bodied espresso floats over her tongue, finished by the creaminess of the foam and sweet spice blend.

"Got-damn, bro! This shit is good!" Camilla exclaims and takes another sip and almost forgets why she's come. Rico leans against his black, marbled countertop and admires his sister enjoying his concoction.

"Yeah, I added a little bit of brown sugar syrup cuz I know you like yo' shit sweet like hot chocolate." Rico lets out a laugh.

"Yeah, this the one, bro. Damn!" Camilla takes another sip and the two sit in the kitchen enjoying each other's silence. Rico knows that if Camilla is at his house, then whatever she wants to talk to him about must be important, so he waits patiently. He knows halfway through her latte, Camilla will feel relaxed and ready to divulge her purpose for the visit.

"Thanks, bro. I really needed this. You got anything to go with this?"

"I thought you'd never ask. My girl made some cinnamon rolls for the kids this morning. Let me heat you up one."

Camilla slows down sipping her latte in anticipation of her cinnamon roll. It smells heavenly in the kitchen now, because not only does Rico have a commercial-grade espresso machine, but he also has restaurant-grade kitchen appliances as well. She can smell the cinnamon roll from the convection oven and her mouth begins to water in anticipation. Rico serves Camilla the warm, homemade cinnamon roll on an all-white porcelain saucer with a gold fork. Rico watches with a small smile playing on his lips, fully knowing what Camilla's reaction will be after tasting Tricee's cinnamon rolls.

"Mmmm…" Camilla moans in culinary ecstasy. Coming to her brother's house reminds her of how neither of them grew up in a picturesque family with two working parents, a house with a white picket fence, and a dog. Instead, they grew up around guns, dope, weed, pushers, murder, and chaos.

"Damn, bro! Tricee know she can throw down, bruh! This shit too good!"

"So, what's up, sis?" Rico asks with his crooked, half smile. "To what do I owe the pleasure of your company?"

"Yeah, about that." Camilla has almost forgotten why she was so upset only an hour earlier after her meeting with LeBaron.

"So, remember I was telling you about dude who showed up the other day at the club, actin' all cozy with Ma?"

"Yeah, what about him?" Rico asks while easing onto the kitchen barstool next to Camilla.

"Well, Meechie followed that nigga up to Harold's and I popped up on the nigga." Camilla pauses, waiting for Rico's reaction.

As anticipated, Rico aggressively turns to face Camilla. "What the fuck you mean, you met up with this fool?" Rico's eyes burn into Camilla's, and she leans in toward Rico to gain a position of power.

"Look, I went there alone and made sure he was alone. You do know I can take care of myself, bro? Right?" Camilla pauses. "Right?"

Rico shakes his head and rolls his eyes in disgust. *She always tryna prove she so hard and don't need nobody*, Rico thinks.

"Look, the nigga had my food in his hand as soon as I pulled up. It's like he knew I was coming or something."

"Wait, what the fuck you mean, Milla?" Rico asks as he bites his lip and clenches his fists.

"Damn, G, I wouldn't have to go on missions myself if you and Ma wouldn't keep me iced the fuck out!" Camilla spits out.

Rico shakes his head. "That ain't fair, Milla, and you know it."

"Oh, ain't it?" Camilla strains her voice while cocking her head.

"I called you the first night I followed the nigga when he met up with Ma at that restaurant. After watching them, I knew there was more to the story that you wasn't givin' up, so I decided to get the shit straight from the source."

Rico clenches his jaw tightly but remains silent. He knows the exact night Camilla is talking about. He was holding back, on their mother's orders from a few months prior that were still fuzzy around the edges. Rico is more of a foot soldier and does Rica's bidding with no questions asked. Camilla has always been the more strategic of the siblings and they both know it. Rico needs Camilla to know what is going on because LeBaron only means trouble for the family business, especially since Rica has been keeping this man's identity a secret from them. *I knew Ma was up to some foul shit when she sent me to that club,* Rico thinks.

"Damn, Milla. I'm sick of being in between you and Ma's shit!"

The siblings stew in their feelings in silence. They know through experience not to speak out of anger, because things may be said that can't be unsaid.

"Look, Milla," Rico says in a calm, slow voice. "All I know is that a few months ago Ma asked me to go to this city a few hours away. She texted me a pic of this broad and told me that I need to find ol' girl, follow her, and get video of her doing dirty shit at the strip club. I mean, I thought the shit was weird, but what got weirder was when she said, and I quote, *whatever you do, don't fuck her cuz I know yo' ass and yo' type.*"

"So, what did you do?"

"Just like Ma asked me to do. Me and the homie drove to this city. I had B—you know B, right?" Camilla nods in agreement. Rico asks to make sure Camilla is following his story, because she's staring off to the side and not paying attention to him. She often does this when she's trying to figure out a solution to arising problems.

"Yeah man, I know B. So, what happened? Camilla is irritated, waiting for her brother to finish his story. He always likes dragging out stories when he knows more about their mother's plots.

"Okay, so anyway. B ran some face recognition shit and found out the strip club the broad was supposed to be featured at that weekend, and we pulled up on her." Rico pauses for dramatic effect to make sure Camilla is still listening to him spin his tale.

"C'mon, man. Stop stallin' before I tell Tricee that you went to a strip club outta town." Camilla raises a threatening eyebrow.

"Damn, why you always gotta take it there?" Rico pouts because he can't draw out his story any longer. "Okay, anyways, we went to this hole-in-the-wall strip club. But when ol' girl came out, I swear it's like she had them mu'fuckas in there mesmerized."

Camilla sits back in her chair, arms folded, and sucks on her teeth. She knows her brother has an affinity for strippers—and any woman with a pretty face and fat ass for that matter.

"Naw, sis. This woman was something special. The girl was super cold. Hair, makeup, outfit, music, the whole package. And mu'fuckas must've knew it too because they was at the stage like some hungry hyenas just throwing all they damn money in the air." Rico stops to see if his sister believes his story, but she doesn't look convinced.

"I mean, I hear you, bro, but you know how you get over them hoes." Camilla leans in with a whisper in case Tricee is near.

Rico shakes his head, disappointed that Camilla doesn't believe his story.

"Okay, look. I saved some of the video because you know, well, anyway...you know me. Hold on, let me get my other phone."

Rico leaves the kitchen and quickly returns with another phone.

"Okay, look," he demands.

The video starts off with a completely dark screen and Camilla thinks that he made a mistake. Then music starts and a dim spotlight in the center of the stage shines on a silhouetted figure. The sparkles of the mysterious woman's bra and panties brilliantly reflect and dance in the spotlight with the slightest shift of her body. Camilla notes the woman's skin tone glows with a blue tone from the stage lights. The stripper takes her time and basks in the spotlight. She listens to the catcalls of her admiring audience with her hand powerfully placed in the dip of her waist while her right arm creates a right angle that shows her beautifully sculpted muscles. Then, the lights begin to pulse to the beat of the music. "Under the Influence" by Chris Brown blares over the club's speakers, but the woman doesn't start dancing yet. She just lets the dollars reign down on her while she flexes the muscles of her long legs and the anticipation of her audience grows to a loud roar. She doesn't move until more money is thrown. The music pauses at just the right moment and the club goes dark. Then the beat drops and the stripper goes berserk on the pol', her body twisting and rolling while she grinds her hips to the beat and the crowd salivates for her clothes to hit the stage. She removes her bra as the men shout obscenities to show their appreciation of her body.

Camilla notices the lights catching a glint of something shiny to the left of the stripper. She must've seen it too, because the stripper whips her head around as her ass-length ponytail drifts in the air behind her. The sparkle of light is reflecting off the flawless diamonds of Camilla's brother's favorite Cuban link platinum bracelet encrusted in diamonds. The stripper locks eyes with Rico and seductively walks over.

The camera angle was taken from the side, so the stripper couldn't see she was being recorded, because all phones were confiscated at the club's door.

The stripper steps off the stage. Security magically appears to gently guide this beautiful gazelle toward Rico, as she saunters on her tiptoes. Rico greets her with a large smile and a wad of cash. He slowly makes it rain all over the stripper. Camilla can tell the money excited the stripper just as much as it excited Rico to drop it, one by one, over her erect nipples. The video zooms in on the stripper's face as she turns away from Rico and begins twisting her nipples and grinding his lap. Rico keeps his stack of cash flowing while he grabs another stack and generously gives his tithe for the night. Then the music changes, and security comes to escort the stripper back on stage.

Camilla had been to many strip clubs in the past, but she had only been mesmerized a handful of times by the strippers. This woman was exceptional. She had beauty, stage presence, and physique. She knew not to give the audience anything until they paid their dues in cash. Camilla can't help but notice the familiarity of the woman's face but can't place where she may know the stripper from, which makes Camilla even more curious as she sits in silence well after the video has ended.

"Yeah, I know, right?" Rico says as he watches his sister's eyes widen at the sight of the video. "And just imagine being there. Ol' girl is the truth! That's when I understood Ma's warning to not get involved with her. Just to make sure I had someone film her dancing on me and to make sure her face was clear in the video."

Now that Rico replays the interaction back in his head, he begins to see that his mother, once again, was playing on his unwavering loyalty to her. He never asks questions of Rica, not ever. He never wonders why this small town, why this particular stripper, and why it had to be him in the video. Rica's instructions were very clear.

"So, what happened after that?" Camilla asks while sitting down and finishing the rest of her latte.

"Nothing. I did what Ma asked me to do."

"And?" Camilla presses.

"Ma told me to me to send her the video to one of the burner phones. She said it had to be a burner phone and the video had to be under one minute. She kept pressing the issue about the phone being a burner phone and untraceable. And she kept telling me to make sure the bitch's face was in the video." Rico huffs and leans back on the barstool.

"So, wait. Ma told you to drive to another city, find some stripper chick, record her dancing, and then come home?" Camilla is trying to put the pieces together in her head.

"Yeah, that's it. Then..." Rico trails off.

"What, man?" Camilla insists "Spit it out!".

"Damn, chill." Rico puts his finger up to his mouth as if to quiet Camilla's voice, because Tricee may be listening. Camilla composes herself. She understands Rico's desire to keep Tricee out of as much family business as possible so she can have plausible deniability.

"Then, like two days after B and I came back, that nigga you talkn' about showed up. But I didn't think nothin' about it then. But now, it don't seem right." Rico leans back and rubs his chin while deep in thought.

"Gimme the name and address of the strip club you went to, and whatever else you got," Camilla says. "I'm gonna send myself this video and see if I can get a location on this bitch. I'm about to get to the bottom of this shit." Camilla pours the rest of her latte out in the sink and quickly washes the glass mug.

"Wait, hold on, sis. What you thinkin' about doing?"

"I'm gonna get some answers and ask questions that you should've asked Ma the first time. Look, Rico, if this was just some other dude in town sniffing around to get a few dollas or a connect, then I wouldn't even trip. But this dude LeBaron started with Ma when she first started slangin' back in the day. He may have a whole other angle we don't even know about."

"Who told you that about him and Ma?" Rico asks inquisitively.

"You already know my connect down at the precinct stay with tha' info. He ran down what he knows, but that's not enough. I wanna know who dude is and if he's connected to this mission Ma had you running to find this stripper." Camilla confirms. "Plus, he knew my Harold's order and everything. He sat there talking to me like we were old friends. I'm telling you, bro, this man is bad news, and if Ma out here going to dinner with the man and allowing him to walk around the city untouched, then you already know he got something on her. Think about it, bro."

The two sit in silence for a moment. Rico has never been one who was able to figure out conspiracies or double-crosses, but Camilla is especially equipped to sniff out her mother's bullshit, especially since Rica is the one who taught Camilla the art of deception.

"Aye, go ahead and send that info to my burner," Camilla barks.

"A'ight." Rico knows not to question Camilla when she gets in detective mode. Once his sister has a conspiracy theory in her head, she doesn't stop until she has proof that her theory is solid. He has to admit he admires her tenacity—she never quits and her hunches are rarely wrong. She is also usually 100 percent right in identifying situations where their mother had her hands in some dirty shit that she didn't want them to know about.

Camilla's burner vibrates in her small, leather cross-body wallet. She retrieves the phone and buries her head while Rico starts making them a snack, because Camilla let her cinnamon roll get cold. He knows Camilla is about to get jittery from the espresso and adrenaline pumping through her veins. Rico whips up a quick snack of fresh fruit, crackers, and cheese as he would for his step-kids.

Camilla does a Google search for one of the still pictures of the stripper's face and comes up with a few hits at other strip clubs and the stripper's social media. The social media site only contains one picture of the stripper's face; the rest of the pictures and videos are of other dancers. Camilla begins to grow an appreciation for the stripper's lack of online presence.

Camilla goes through the other stripper's pictures and looks for tags of other people to try identify and locate the mysterious stripper. Camilla finds a post from the stripper that contains an advertisement for a party at one of the strip clubs, and a comment reads, "Sorry about your grandma, I know you gonna miss her. I loved her cooking every Sunday at Mount Calvary."

Camilla is elated when she sees that Mount Calvary was tagged in the post. So, Camilla clicks on the tag and goes down a rabbit hole to find the social media page of the church. She then views the postings around the date that Mount Calvary was tagged on the other post and hopes her search will lead to the grandmother's funeral. She knows that more than anyone, black church folks love to post full obituaries online. An obituary is a special tool that every con-artist uses as a way to get into the family, steal inheritances, and generally cause all kinds of hell on the unsuspecting family members.

"Jackpot!" Camilla yells out.

"What? What'd you find?" Rico comes from behind the stove where he had started on dinner. He enjoys being at home waiting on the kids, cooking for Tricee and spending time with his sister. He would normally be out making rounds and collecting money. He hates being in traffic and dealing with the day-to-day business of a criminal.

"I found the name of the stripper's grandmother who passed a few months ago. After that, this search will be easy. I found the church she went to and her obituary. Hold on," Camilla trails off.

"What?" Rico asks.

"It says she was survived by her granddaughter Golden Rose and her mother Althea. Then it says she will join her grandson, Diamond Rose." Camilla goes silent.

"Wait. Ain't that? Hold up, Milla, let me see that phone." Rico snatches the phone from his sister's frozen hand. He moves his lips while reading the obituary. Then he re-reads the obituary to himself.

The pair sit in silence, processing what the obituary means.

Camilla breaks the quiet. "So that bitch knew I might have a sister out there and kept it from me?" Camilla stands up in a rage.

"Hold up, Milla. You don't know that! Ma wouldn't do no shit like that Milla." Rico pleads.

"Oh, she wouldn't?" Camilla feels the heat inside of her body start to radiate at the center of her chest, then quickly move up to her neck and face.

Rico sees the rage brewing inside Camilla as her cheeks flush with anger.

"That fucking bitch! That fucking bitch!" Camilla kept repeating. She sits in Rico's kitchen barstool with a thud.

"I can't believe it."

Rico knows to give Camilla some time and lets the silence between them permeate the air as he walks back over to the stove to stir his spaghetti sauce he'd started last night. The deafening silence is broken by the laughter of kids approaching the front door—Rico's twin stepchildren arriving home from school. They are a welcome distraction. Camilla's demeanor softens as she welcomes the kids home and asks about their day. She rarely, if ever, gets to be there when they come home, which is a great excuse for the kids to postpone their homework.

Rico attends to his fatherly duties as Tricee leaves for work at the hospital and the babysitter is just making her way into the house. Rico signals to the babysitter that he is leaving and gives the kids hugs and reminders to get to bed on time and brush their teeth. Camilla gives the kids an extra-long hug, because today she is in need of more affection.

Camilla gathers her things and heads down the back steps toward the garage with Rico behind her as he sets the alarm and waits to hear the babysitter set the locks to the back door. In the garage, Rico goes into his secret stash and starts rolling up. He knows they both need to relieve some stress and talk about the information they found out just before the kids arrived.

The two sit in the garage for the next two hours smoking, planning, and plotting how to find out more information on LeBaron and her possible half-sister Golden.

"I can't believe we got the same last name, bro! That shit's wild!" Camilla says between puffs.

Rico shakes his head in disbelief, because Camilla is the only sibling he still has after his older brother was killed. He doesn't wanna share Camilla with this new stranger.

"So, you tryna' get to know her or somethin'?" Rico asks sarcastically.

Camilla looks at the hurt in her brother's eyes and the longing in his question. "Naw, bruh. Just trying to figure all this shit out. But I do wanna know why Ma didn't tell me about her."

"Yeah…true."

"And why the fuck keep it a secret? That's the part that's fucking me up. And was she ever gonna tell me?"

The two sit quietly reflecting with more questions than answers.

"I'm gonna drive to that town tomorrow and get some answers. There's so much shit on the line, bro. I gotta move wisely."

Camilla is determined to put the pieces together before Rica finds out that they have discovered her half-sister. Camilla leaves Rico's house feeling a sense of closeness with her brother. It's one of the first times he sided with Camilla over their mother. They realized they needed one another more than ever if they were going to stay a step ahead of Rica and learn what she already knew.

PAST MEETS PRESENT

C amilla barely slept last night. She kept going over her plan, as well as a contingency for every potential issue that may arise when she meets her half-sister. Before getting on the road, Camilla pumps her brother for more information about the conversations he had with their mother. She's trying to understand her mother's motives for sending Rico to take that video and keeping Golden a secret. Camilla is looking forward to the drive to sort things out in her head and craft a solid game plan before arriving at the strip club where the video was taken.

"So, you all ready to go?" Rico asks as Camilla packs her travel car, a beige Buick Envoy. The police never pull her over when she drives this vehicle, no matter the time of night or neighborhood. It helps that the car has retired law enforcement license plates, courtesy of a retired police officer she keeps on her payroll.

"Yup, got all my shit packed last night. Couldn't sleep, thinking I might have a sister and Ma kept her from me all these years. Then to

make it worse, had you go and spy on her. Shit's just wild. Still tryin'
ta wrap my head around it." Camilla sighs, thinking about why her
mother kept this secret for so many years.

"I know, right? Shit's crazy, but you know I gotchu" Rico affirms.

"Yeah, I know, bruh," Camilla replies.

"Make sure you stay strapped."

"Oh, you already know. I stay ready!" Camilla replies confidently.

"You taking Meechie wit chu'?"

"Naw, I'm going solo on this one. Too much personal shit on the
line. Plus, I might need a minute to slide down the wall." Camilla
nervously chuckles and Rico joins in with her, just as nervous. They're
always able to find humor in the midst of their chaotic lives.

"Well...lemme know when you touch down. And lemme know
anything else you find out." Rico gently urges. He wants to say more
but leaves his next breath hanging in the air.

He wants to let Camilla know that his love is sufficient for her, and
she doesn't need to seek the love of their mother, much less the love
of a stranger. He wants to tell her how much he admires her ability to
see business opportunities and how smart she is. He wants to let her
know that she is the best big sister anyone could ever have, and he isn't
willing to share her with anyone. But he holds onto his thoughts.

"A'ight." Camilla hangs up.

She feels a warmth of closeness with her brother that she hasn't felt
since they were kids. She feels like she has her little brother back and
that brings a smile to her face.

She packs a week's worth of clothes, even though she only plans
on being gone for a few days. She doesn't want to draw attention
to herself as a new face in a small town, so she knows she has about
three days tops until the locals start trying to place her. Camilla kisses
Elyse softly on the forehead before leaving. She stands over her sleeping

body, admiring her beauty. Camilla feels lucky to have her. Elyse stirs under the weight of Camilla's focused gaze. Not wanting to awaken her, Camilla tiptoes out of their bedroom and downstairs.

Camilla puts the address of the strip club into her GPS on her cell. *Three hours and fifteen minutes,* Camilla thinks. *Okay.*

She doesn't mind road trips, because it gives her time to work out all the thoughts swirling in her head. She has to figure out who LeBaron really is and why he's resurfaced after all these years. She also needs to figure out how and where this stripper fits in all this mess between her mother and LeBaron. Camilla is convinced the stripper is the missing piece, and she isn't going to stop until she finds the link.

Camilla pulls up her road trip R&B playlist, complete with Mary J., The Isley's, Joe, Maxwell, Marvin Gaye, Faith, Mario, and a few hip-hop artists to get her through the three-hour trip. She loves old school music, when the lyrics had meaning and men wanted to prove their love to their women instead of calling them bitches and hoes.

Camilla makes it to the small city in no time—faster than she expected. The strip club is nowhere near opening time, so she decides to check in to her hotel early. She drives around the town, trying to imagine the life the stripper led. Camilla is glad she brought her laptop with her, because she wants to do multiple page searches at a time and needs a wider screen than her cell offers. After checking into her hotel room, she gets to work on her laptop using the tiny desk. She quickly crosses the room to retrieve her hotspot from her bag—she doesn't want any of her internet activity to be tracked in any way. She always travels with a hotspot that's attached to a reloadable credit card so she can minimize her digital footprint. *It's getting harder and harder to be a criminal,* Camilla thinks as she turns on her VPN as an added layer of security.

Camilla is somewhat grateful for the criminal lifestyle she grew up in, because it gave her the resources and knowledge to find things people wanted hidden. She also doesn't have any false notions that people are good. Growing up in the game and being exposed to its dangers made Camilla acutely aware that things are never as they seem, and people are always out for themselves.

Continuing her internet research, Camilla would now search Facebook for Golden's grandmother's church. *Bingo!* Camilla thinks as she easily finds Mount Calvary Church's page. Camilla scrolls through the public page of the church and scans the pictures for any shots taken at Golden's grandmother's funeral.

Camilla's finger pauses on her keyboard; knowing the name of her potential sister feels surreal. She has to pause for a moment for a reality check and to center herself. She hears Elyse's voice from their conversation from the night before. Elyse had told her to think through her choice to find Golden, because the truth may destroy life as she knows it. She keeps Elyse's warning in mind.

To Camillia's dismay, there are no pictures of Golden in the photos, only pictures of the grandmother lying in her casket. Naturally, Camilla stares at the dead woman's photos, trying to find facial similarities between herself and the deceased.

Camilla switches gears and searches for Golden directly. Any questions she needs answered will have to come directly from Golden and not from internet searches of her late grandmother. So, Camilla searches the name of the strip club and is taken to the page. She searches the strip club's page and pictures added by customers when leaving reviews of the club. She can't believe that she doesn't find any pictures of Golden. She has to keep referencing the picture Rico had taken the night he saw her with the images on Google and Yelp.

Something ain't right, Camilla thinks. *How does a beautiful woman who clearly knows how to stun an audience not have a digital footprint in 2025?*

Camilla decides to search for Golden's criminal record. She knows from running a nightclub that there are always fights breaking out and innocent bystanders sometimes go to jail, simply for being at the wrong place, at the wrong time.

Before he died, her stepfather would give Camilla special projects to work on that he said no one else could do because they weren't smart enough. Realistically, he gave her research tasks that no one else wanted to do and honestly didn't have the patience to complete. Camilla learned how to navigate the public information sites and the internet. Her specialty was researching potential business partners' legal records to reveal their past convictions, court orders, and court rulings. One thing a criminal can't hide is their record unless it's expunged.

Camilla searches the county clerk's database for court records for any of Golden's criminal activity. And there it is. Golden received an eviction notice about six months prior. Camilla loves eviction notices because they show the address of the property the person was evicted from and possible addresses where the person may currently have their mail forwarded. Camilla puts both addresses into her phone, starting with the forwarding address. Camilla leans back in the hotel's small desk chair, satisfied with herself for finding Golden so easily. However, she still feels apprehensive, and there are questions in the back of her mind about why internet images had been scrubbed of Golden's face. There was no way a woman—and stripper—that beautiful didn't have an online presence. Camilla keeps that thought tucked into the back of her mind as she grabs her coat and keys, heading to the location of what could possibly be her sister's house.

***

Camilla easily finds Golden's house. It's only fifteen minutes from the hotel. She parks down the street, surveilling the house for signs of movement. It's about five p.m. now, and Camilla's stomach lets out a loud growl. She's forgotten to eat. Just then her cell buzzes.

"Hey, babe." Camilla answers her cell with a sigh.

It's Elyse's comforting voice on the other line. "Hey, babe. Hadn't heard from you and you promised to call when you got there."

"I'm sorry babe," Camilla replies. "Got caught up."

"Well...did you find her?" Elyse asks eagerly.

"I'm sitting down the street now. Ain't seen no movement yet though."

"Well, you be careful. You don't know what the fuck you walking into. And if it has anything to do with Rica, you know you really gotta watch yo' back," Elyse warns.

"Yeah, I know," Camilla replies solemnly.

Elyse takes the hint and can hear by the tone of Camilla's voice that she doesn't need any chastising.

"Well, did you at least eat yet?" Elyse asks, deciding to change gears.

Camilla's stomach tells on her and lets out a loud grumble while Camilla laughs. "I think my stomach heard you. Naw, I ain't eat yet."

"Well, you found the house. Get something to eat, then come back. You know how you get when you get hangry." Elyse lets out a small, weighted laugh. She has been so worried about Camilla's mental state. Her partner is in the midst of a life-changing experience, and she isn't there to support Camilla. "I wish I was there with you, bae."

"I know, but you know I had to do this alone. I'm gonna let you go and find something to eat." Camilla rushes off the phone. "I love you and will call you soon."

"Okay," Elyse replies softly. She doesn't want to fight or add any more stress to an already stressful situation. "Love you."

"Love you too, bye."

"Bye."

Camilla sits in silence for a moment, weighing the gravity of her choice to find Golden. *Elyse is right*, she thinks. She does need to get something to eat. Plus, she hasn't completely thought out her plan or what she is going to say when meeting Golden for the first time. She starts her SUV and heads to a restaurant she had searched for before she got on the road. She decides to order her food and pick it up curbside—the fewer people who see her, the better.

Camilla finishes her meal at her hotel and is running through what she will say to Golden when her phone buzzes; it's her mother. In all her haste, Camilla forgot to tell her mom that she wouldn't be at the club tonight.

"Hey, Ma."

"Where you at?" Rica demands.

"Had to take care of some business right quick, not gonna be at the club tonight, but Meechie..." Camilla starts her lie.

"Fuck Meechie. I'm askin' about you. Where the fuck are you and why ain't you here, Milla?" Rica barks out her questions as usual.

Rica has never really shown Camilla her nurturing side. Their relationship has always been transactional, as far as Camilla recalls. But that's how Rica is with everyone besides her son. If you can't do anything for her, then she doesn't have a need for you.

"Ma! Like I said, I had to take care of something and Meechie is gonna be at the club tonight instead of me. It just popped up last-minute. Some shit with the Circle."

Camilla knows that Rica doesn't like to involve herself with anything the Circle Boyz have going on so she would be able to deny any of their activities if she ever gets picked up. Rica made it known around Chicago that her wealth was gained from the death of her husband who left her some money. Then, she started the night club with her newfound wealth. Of course, no one in law enforcement believes this lie, but no one has ever mounted enough evidence against her, not even so much as a parking ticket. Rica has been smart enough to distance herself as far as possible from the illegal side of her business, although she runs drugs and prostitutes through the club. But she could easily deny knowing any of those activities take place.

"You know I don't like knowing shit, Milla. You make a move, you let me know. Got it?" Rica always demands respect and the last word. Just as Camilla starts to answer, Rica hangs up.

Camilla sends a quick text to Meechie.

> Sorry, forgot to tell Ma I was gone. Told her you got it.

Meechie replies with a black heart emoji.

Three dots appear on Camilla's phone as Meechie types another text, then nothing. Camilla puts down her phone and makes a mental note to tell Meechie what's going on. She feels a pang of guilt, because she's never kept anything this important from him, but she's a little embarrassed that she was still seeking her mother's favor. She's also embarrassed that she thinks LeBaron could be a key to her mother's past and explains why Rica acts like she's never loved Camilla but only tolerates her. Camilla wants to know more about her mother's past, and possibly her dad. She figures that she will have to get the information on her own, because Rica is a closed book.

Camilla decides to watch a movie on her laptop instead of going back to spy on Golden's house that evening. Even if she got up the courage to knock on the door, she still doesn't know what to say. Her tattered mind needs some rest, and she'll have clarity in the morning.

***

Camilla wakes up refreshed and ready to confront Golden. She wants to see her face-to-face. She wants to know how Golden speaks and what her voice sounds like. She wants to know if they have the same features. She wants to know if Golden knew their dad and what were her memories of him. She wants, most of all, to know if Golden knew that she existed.

She checks her messages and replies to the few she can. The rest will have to wait until she gets back to Chicago. Camilla makes a call to check in with Elyse. Camilla lets her know that she hasn't seen Golden yet, and they discuss the possible ways Golden could respond to her showing up on her doorstep unannounced.

"You know I appreciate you, right? Camilla asks Elyse.

"Yeah, bae, I know," Elyse replies affectionately. "So, are you ready?"

"Yeah, I think so. If not, I betta get ready, huh?" Camilla asks, unsure of herself.

"You know you don't have to do this. You don't have to go chasing some...ghost."

"What you mean *ghost*?" Camilla asks as her head snaps back in defense.

"I'm just sayin', what you think you gonna find by talking to this girl? Your dad is gone. What else is there to...never mind." Elyse stops mid-sentence.

She knows that discussing Camilla's parents is always a sensitive subject and grounds for an argument, especially when it comes to Rica. Elyse doesn't want to add undue stress to Camilla and thinks it best to end their conversation.

"Listen, bae, I gotta get ready for work. Call me afterward, I wanna hear all about your...ummm...sister," Elyse concedes.

"Okay, talk to you later." Camilla taps the *end call* button on her cell twice and tosses it onto her bed.

She hates it when she and Elyse argue. Maybe Elyse is right. What is Camilla really chasing? The ghost of a murdered father that her own mother didn't even talk about? She often wonders what type of man her father was. All she really knows about him is that he and her mother grew up together, they started their drug empire with LeBaron in their teens, and that Rica had been the boss. But what she can't understand is why her father left Chicago and, ultimately, her. She always wonders if she was a planned or accidental pregnancy. Did her dad even know she existed? There are so many unanswered questions, and Camilla holds a glint of hope that Golden will be able to fill in the missing links of her past.

Chapter Ten

FRACTURED MEMORIES

Camilla pulls into the spot on the street where she had parked her car yesterday, watching Golden's house for any signs of life while building up the courage to knock on the door. She sits for so long that her warm breath fogs up the windows of her SUV, but she isn't ready to get out just yet. So, she turns on the car and gets the heat rolling to defog the windows against the brutal midwestern cold. As she sits waiting for the front windshield to defrost, her phone vibrates. She runs through possible scenarios and what she will say to whoever opens the door.

Will I say hello? she wonders. *Who will open the door? Will it be my potential half sister or someone else? Will I be prepared to answer their questions? What if they don't answer the door? Will I come back tomorrow?*

So many questions swirl in her mind. Camilla's throat tightens and her mouth waters as she feels the familiar signs of nervous vomit brewing at the pit of her stomach. She remembers her phone buzzed before her inner monologue and decides to check the message.

> You got this bae. I'm so proud of you.

A text from Elyse gives Camilla the little push of strength she needs to put her SUV in drive. She pulls in front of Golden's house, stopping at the dilapidated chain-linked fence with its gate drooping off the hinges. This gate is the only obstacle standing between her and the answers she desperately needs. She isn't going to let the fear of the unknown stop her. Camilla takes a long, deep inhale through her nose and lets it out in a ragged breath through her mouth like Elyse taught her to do when she needs grounding.

Placing her hand on the door handle, she thinks, *It's now or never.* Quickly jerking the door open and swinging her legs out of the SUV, Camilla lands on two solid feet, even though her legs feel tingly and weak.

Camilla steps one foot in front of the other on the cracked sidewalk. The single-hinged gait offers no resistance to her touch, encouraging her to press forward. Now Camilla has momentum and easily bounds the uneven concrete steps up to Golden's front door. She uses the same momentum to eagerly knock on the door, knowing if she hesitates she may turn around. After knocking, she steps away from the small window in the front door and off to the side of the door. She's seen one too many instances where some uninvited visitor received blasts through an unopened door. Camilla hears a commotion coming from the other side of the door and her heart begins to race. She narrows her eyes, listening intently to the sounds on the other side of the door.

"Who the fuck is it?" A woman's voice shouts from the other side.

Camilla hadn't expected the gruff response, but she knew she had to answer the question.

"It's Camilla. I'm here to see Golden."

Fuck! Camilla hates how Golden's name sounds on her tongue. It feels unfamiliar in her mouth, and she knows it probably sounds even worse to the person on the other side of the door. She hears the woman pause behind the door, then the front door flies open, and Camilla is greeted by one of the most beautiful women she's ever seen. The older woman glares at her through the closed screen door, not saying anything. She lets her hazel eyes penetrate Camilla's. The pair stand in silence for a moment before Camilla breaks it.

"Hey, I'm looking for Golden. Is she home?" Camilla asks, lifting her right brow in anticipation.

"Who the fuck are you? I gotta ask you again?" Althea asks with a snarl.

Camilla can see this woman isn't going to budge on letting her know about Golden's whereabouts, nor is she going to unlock the screen door to allow Camilla access. So, Camilla decides to tell the truth under Althea's weighted gaze.

"Listen, let me cut the shit," Camilla says. "I think I may be Golden's sister, well half-sister, and I wanted to..." Camilla hesitates and it's Althea's turn to lift a brow in anticipation of Camilla's request.

"To what?" Althea cuts Camilla off and scoffs. "I don't know what the fuck it is you *think* you know. What's your name again?"

Camilla tries to keep her patience. As the daughter of a queen pin, she isn't used to people readily disrespecting her. "Camilla Rose."

All the color drains from Althea's face. But before she can answer, Camilla's eyes shift behind Althea as Golden appears in her five-ten figure and bronze-cocoa skin. Her emerald eyes now fixate on Camilla.

"What the fuck is going on out here?" Golden demands.

Camilla's mouth is wagging. She scrambles for a response while taking in Golden's beauty. She thought that Althea was beautiful when she first saw her, but Golden is absolutely stunning! The video she saw of Golden on her brother's cell didn't do the woman walking toward her justice. Golden repeats her question, standing beside Althea, burning a hole in her head waiting for an answer. Camilla hadn't realized how loud her exchange with Althea had been until Golden came to the front door, clearly agitated.

"Hi, I'm—" Camilla begins, but Althea slams the door in her face before she can introduce herself.

Camilla had dealt with a lot in her past, but she'd never experienced this much rudeness or disrespect from a stranger. She tunes in and intently listens to the commotion behind the door. She hears shouting, then the door flies open, causing the mini blinds to swing from side to side, almost hitting Golden in the face. Althea is grabbing Golden's arm, trying to hold her back from opening the door. Finally, Althea throws up her hands with a resounding shout, "Fine! Go ahead then!"

"Now, who are you?" Golden asks, slightly out of breath from struggling to get possession of the door from her mother.

"I'm Camilla Rose."

The two stare at one another, hazel and emerald eyes connecting as the women process Camilla's words.

"Excuse me," Golden says. "What did you say your name is?"

"I'm Camilla Rose. I think you may be my half-sister, Golden." Camilla lets a nervous, crooked smile play on her lips, because she half-believes her own words at this moment. Golden's eyes grow wide with shock as she processes the stranger's words.

"Fuck you, bitch!" Althea yells from behind Golden while walking away from the open door, then sits on the worn, brown couch. She reaches for her pack of cigarettes and taps the top, making a single shoot halfway out of the pack. She lights her cigarette while taking a deep pull.

"Somebody sent yo' ass on a bogus journey, bitch! If you think you're Golden's sister, somebody been lying to yo' ass." Althea takes a long puff of her cigarette and laser-focuses her hazel eyes toward Camilla.

"Look here, bitch. Ain't nobody talking to yo' dumb ass." Camilla's patience has worn out.

"Hold the fuck on, bitch. Who the fuck you think you talkin' to?" Golden asks Camilla with a roll of her neck. She didn't agree with her mother's behavior most days, but she'll be damned if she let anyone else disrespect her.

Golden starts to unlock and open the screen door, forcing Camilla to take a step back. This was not how Camilla had envisioned her first meeting with Golden.

Camilla places both of her hands up in defense and takes two steps back, landing on the first porch step.

"My bad," she says. "Let me apologize, I meant no disrespect. I lost my cool for a minute. I'm not used to dealing with disrespect," Camilla matter-of-factly states and continues. "Look, I came here to find you and see if we can put together some pieces of our pasts because I think I've been fed a whole lot of lies," Camilla raises her voice and directs it toward Althea who moves behind Golden.

"And I wanna get to the bottom of it all."

Golden narrows her eyes at Camilla then whips her twenty-four-inch ponytail around to look at her mother.

"Why, you say she ain't my sister? You knew about her and didn't say nothing?" Golden turns her full body with her arms folded in front of her chest waiting for Althea to answer.

"I heard some shit way back." Althea steps past Golden and onto the porch to face Camilla. Then she takes another pull of her cigarette so deep that Camilla sees the tobacco turn bright red while the white of the cigarette disintegrates. Althea locks eyes with Camilla as she takes a long pull of her cigarette. She takes her index finger and dramatically ashes her cigarette with her arm fully extended in front of her while maintaining eye contact with Camilla.

"I also seen yo' picture when you was born and I told Diamond…"

A lump catches in Althea's throat as she says her late lover's name. She swallows hard and chokes down her tears, but Golden and Camilla can see the tears pooling in the corner of Althea's eyes. She takes another pull from her cigarette to steady herself, throws it down on the porch, and twists the toe of her tattered pink slippers to put it out.

She continues, "I told Diamond that was not his baby."

"Momma!" Golden screeches. "Why would you say that?" Golden spins around to look at Camilla. "Look, I'm sorry. She don't have the best manners, but one thing my momma ain't is a liar."

Golden detects sadness in Camilla's eyes, but little does she know, it's really rage settling in.

Who the fuck does this old bitch think she talking to? Camilla thinks. *I should slap the shit outta her right now!* Camilla tries to reign in her emotions and concentrate on Althea's words instead. She came for a purpose; she wants answers to her past. She decides to fight through the spite in Althea's words and search for the truth between.

"Yeah, why *would* you say that?" Camilla asks aloud.

She came here for answers and that's what she is gonna get. She decides right then that she isn't leaving without hearing what this woman has to say, no matter how bad it hurts. Camilla is well aware that there are three sides to every story. She desires the truth. Since she couldn't get it from her own mother, she thinks perhaps she can get it from Golden's mother.

"You drink dark?" Althea asks Camilla.

Camilla nods. "Yeah."

Camilla walks hesitantly into the house with Althea, passing by a confused Golden through the front door, ready for answers.

CHAPTER ELEVEN

DIAMOND (AUGUST 1990)

Diamond sat in the driver's seat of his royal blue box Chevy. He was parked in the driveway of the small house he bought for cash from a foreclosure listing when he moved to his new city about three hours south of Chicago. The house wasn't much, but it was all his. He immediately started looking to hire contractors to modernize the home to his liking. He decided to keep the outside as-is, with a few cosmetic changes to the siding and the yard in order not to make the house stand out from the rest of the neighborhood. However, he planned for the inside of the home to have all of the latest finishes and a customized look. He wanted his plush, red carpet and black sinks with gold finishes like the movie *Scarface*.

The contractors were installing the sinks and would be out of his hair soon. He was happy that his vision was coming to fruition. His circular bed was being delivered the next day, so he wanted to make sure all the sinks, tubs, and plumbing were completed as the contractor promised. He started to feel that things were all falling into place;

even his grandmother decided to follow him to his new city. She said there was nothing left for her in Chicago, and she could always find a new church home. Diamond was excited that Grandmother agreed to move to central Illinois with him.

Diamond's grandmother was his entire world. She was the only family he knew since he never met his father, and his mother had always been strung out on drugs. His grandmother Mary—or Grandmother as he liked to call her—raised Diamond from when he was three years old, and she was more like a mother to him than a grandmother. So, making the decision to move was easy for Grandmother. She didn't want to be left alone in Chicago, and she didn't want Diamond alone in a new city even though he was almost twenty.

He was waiting for a call from his right-hand man after meeting with their new drug connect when Diamond felt his pager buzz. He unclipped it from his belt and saw a message from LeBaron. The code *A1111* let Diamond know that LeBaron received a new shipment of cocaine and it was good quality. Diamond and LeBaron used a set of codes for years during their drug careers. The number one rule in selling drugs is to not get caught—and if you do get caught, to not give police ammunition to lock you away.

Diamond smiled at his beeper. All his plans were coming together since he'd left Chicago only one month before to start his own drug empire. He then felt a pang of guilt thinking of the people he left behind to start his legacy. Rica's face flashed across Diamond's mind, and he shook his head, trying to forget the memory of her standing in her driveway holding their daughter with an angry, tear-stained face the day he left.

Rica must've sensed Diamond thinking about her, because Diamond felt his Nokia phone vibrating in his pocket. He opened it and pressed the green phone button to answer the call.

"Hello." Diamond breathed heavily into the receiver. He was growing tired of Rica calling every few days asking him when he was coming back to Chicago. She acted as if she hadn't created a whole drug empire with him and LeBaron over the past few years and didn't understand the amount of work and dedication it took.

"Damn, well fuck you, too!" Rica replied, picking up on Diamond's annoyance.

"Naw, baby. It ain't even like that. Wassup? I was just about to check on the contractors to see how the house is coming along."

"Aw, yeah?" Rica's tone changed to a purr. "So, you getting our room ready, baby? I can't wait to see you. I miss you so much."

Diamond didn't respond to either Rica's question or admission. He didn't believe in saying anything he didn't mean, no matter whose feelings it hurt. That was one of the things that drew Rica to Diamond: he never cowered for anyone, not even her.

The two sat in silence for a moment until Diamond spoke. "Hey, I gotta go, but I'll call you later from a pay phone. Okay?" Diamond waited for an answer but only received a dial tone as Rica hung up without answering him.

Rica and Diamond's relationship had been strained for about a year prior to the birth of their baby girl Camilla. Diamond couldn't put his finger on when or how their dynamic changed, but he definitely noticed the shift. Rica used to listen to Diamond and his ideas for expansion, but in the year preceding her getting pregnant, he noticed Rica becoming more adversarial in their conversations about business and which direction they should take to expand. Rica believed the best way to expand was to get in good with an established drug family and convince them to give them more weight to move. However, Diamond was tired of being the middleman and wanted to be his own boss. He thought the best way to do that was to find a new distributor and carve out their own territory. Rica and LeBaron both agreed they needed to expand if they wanted to make more money and be the drug lords they always aspired to be, but they all disagreed on the means to accomplish their goals. LeBaron was always in the middle and would go with whoever made the most economic sense. Hence, LeBaron followed Diamond to a new city to establish their own drug empire while Rica stayed back working for the same connect they'd had since they were teenagers.

Diamond let out a sigh, shaking his head at Rica's hot temper. She always found a way to throw tantrums when she didn't get her way, and today was no exception. Now that Diamond was away and not interacting with Rica, he began to see how controlling and volatile she was. He also welcomed the physical distance between them so he could figure out when and how things had changed.

Rica and Diamond dated since they were in high school. They felt an instant connection and consequently lost their virginity to one another in their freshman year, at least that is the story that Rica told Diamond. They also bonded over their home lives and being brought up on the streets of Chicago in the late eighties when the drug epidemic was starting to hit the black community the hardest. Chicago saw upstanding men spiral downward into lives of drugs and crime to feed their habit. The nuclear black family was never the same after the eighties drug epidemic. In the nineties, when crack was introduced into the black community, Rica and her crew became rich beyond their young imaginings.

Diamond's phone buzzed again. Frowning, he looked at the caller ID, expecting to see Rica's number after she hung up on him, looking for another argument. But it was Grandmother, and his whole demeanor changed as he answered the phone.

"So, how's my favorite girl doin' today?"

"Hey baby, just calling to tell you thank you for sending those boys over to the house to help me pack."

"You ain't gotta thank me," he said. "Oh, the movers will be there in two days and you should be able to pick up your keys tomorrow after you get off the train."

"Wait, what you mean the movers are coming after I leave? Now you know I don't like nobody all in my stuff, Diamond."

Diamond hated when his grandmother called him by his government name. She didn't do it often, but when she did, he knew that she meant what she said.

"Yes, ma'am, I know. But this ain't just anybody. You know the movers who are coming. It's one of the deacon's sons from your church who has his own moving company. Remember?"

"Oh yeah, that's right. Well, I guess that will be alright." Grandmother conceded.

"Good. Your train ticket will be waiting at the counter for you. I already paid for it, so all you gotta do is show up. I'm having Al pick you up about an hour before the train is supposed to leave. Okay?"

"Boy! You ain't gotta talk to me like I'm some chile," Grandmother scolded Diamond.

Diamond lowered his voice to a whisper. "Now you know I would never do that, Grandmother. I'm just excited about you coming."

"I know, baby, me too," Grandmother said softly. "So, what you gonna do about Rica and the baby?"

Diamond hated talking about Rica to his grandmother. He knew that Grandmother never really liked Rica and was only asking for the sake of his daughter Camilla. Since before Camilla was born, all Diamond and Rica did was argue. He was surprised when she got pregnant from one of their make-up sex sessions. After she told him she was pregnant, Diamond decided he would be the best dad ever, because he didn't want his child growing up without a father like he did. Camilla was the light of his life! He loved her curly hair and toffee-colored skin, and he melted every time her chestnut eyes locked on his. However, he knew that his and Rica's relationship had run its course, and he was no longer in love with her. He even questioned whether he was ever in love with her or had his feelings stemmed from her being the girl he lost his virginity to at fourteen.

"Honestly, Grandmother, I don't know what I'm gonna do. I don't wanna be with Rica anymore, but I wanna be there for my seed. What you think I should do?" Diamond waited for his grandmother's sage advice.

Grandmother took her time in speaking because she knew how much Diamond leaned on her advice. "Baby, you know I love you, right?"

"Yes, ma'am." Diamond had no clue where his grandmother was headed with her statement.

"Good. I wanna make sure you know that. But I ain't neva liked that girl Rica. She just so ghetto and tries to rule over you. I know y'all was young when you started dating, and that's a whole other thing I won't get into right now. But, baby, that woman is no good and is gonna take you down right along with her."

Diamond let his grandmother's words sink in. He knew she would never say anything out of spite, but he didn't understand where all of this was coming from.

"What you mean?" Diamond asked, sounding like his seven-year-old self.

"See, I didn't wanna say anything, and I tend to stay outta your business unless you directly ask me. So now Imma tell you what I think. That girl ain't no good and is gonna bring you down. A woman knows women." Grandmother ended her sentence with a finality that Diamond couldn't argue with.

"Well, what about Milla, that's my heart?"

Grandmother was silent.

"Hello, Grandmother? Are you still there?" Diamond asked after a deafening silence fell over the line.

"Yes, baby, your grandmother is here. Oh shoot, there's somebody at the door. Let me get up from here. I think the boys are finally done packing and I need to inspect their work." Grandmother chuckled.

"Okay, woman, you go on ahead and play supervisor and I'll see you tomorrow. Love you."

"Love you too, baby." Grandmother ended the phone call.

After hanging up, Diamond was curious about the status of his own house and decided to finally get out of his car to check the progress.

***

Diamond was sixteen years old and considered an up-and-coming legend in the city due to his ruthlessness and ability to move weight in Chicago during a time when the police department was its most corrupt and everyone had their hand out for a payoff. The nineties were a different time: age didn't limit your earning potential and Diamond was known as the guy who had connections to every known drug lord moving weight in the city. Most importantly, they all respected him.

Diamond stood at six-four with a slender, athletic build. He always kept a low fade that showcased his 360º waves with a crispy line. During his elementary school years, his classmates made fun of how dark-skinned he was. However, as he moved to middle school and high school, women began to view his onyx skin as desirable. His perfect white smile drew women in, and it was the last thing his enemies saw as he snuffed out their lives. His striated muscles indicated that he was slim but strong from his daily weightlifting practices. Diamond was always a skinny kid growing up, and he used to get picked on because of his small stature, so he started lifting weights to exert his physical dominance over his bullies...and it worked.

By the time Diamond was fifteen years old, everyone at his high school knew that he was not the one to be tested, because he could fight and was strong enough to take out two opponents at one time. Most of his peers thought that Diamond loved to fight, but he hated it and viewed it as a necessary skill for living in the greedy streets of Chicago. In the late eighties and mid-nineties, if you weren't ruthless, then you were easily swallowed up by either drugs, sex, gang violence, or police brutality. Everyone was a type of predator. Each one sought a way to violate and get over on the next person. Women used their sexuality to get over on men. Men used their money and influence to get over on women. Drug dealers used drugs to hook users who would forfeit their very lives for the misfortune of choosing a path of addiction. Gangs used intimidation and a sense of belonging to entice members to join their organizations. Police used coercion to get informants to trade their loyalty for their freedom. Everyone had their place in the game, but the best players knew their positions and how to play them.

Chapter Twelve

LeBaron (October 1985)

LeBaron was the most ruthless man Diamond had ever met. Luckily for Diamond, LeBaron was his right-hand and best friend. The two had been friends since elementary school where they'd met after LeBaron came to Diamond's rescue after three boys attempted to jump Diamond after school. The three boys were runners for one of the low-level local drug dealers. Diamond's mother was a known alcoholic around the neighborhood and had just been introduced to crack. Diamond's mother owed money to the drug dealer, and he thought that by hurting her son, his mother would pay what she owed. Unbeknownst to the drug dealer, Diamond lived with his grandmother and had no contact with his mother ever since she left him for her boyfriend five years prior. The only parental figure Diamond ever really knew was his grandmother Mary. He never knew his father and had no other close relatives, because his mother had alienated him from all other family members with her alcohol and drug abuse.

"Get the fuck off him!" LeBaron yelled through cracks in his voice, mustering the most menacing tone he could. He threw each boy off Diamond, who was curled up in a ball on the ground. LeBaron was two years older than Diamond, but he had been held back twice, so they were in the same grade.

The boys began to scatter, because they didn't want any altercations with LeBaron—his reputation as a brawler preceded him. LeBaron was in foster care shortly after his birth. He had moved from placement to placement but finally found a home with an older couple who showed LeBaron respect but didn't ask too many questions about how he spent his time away from the house or who he ran with. LeBaron's foster parents made an agreement with him on the first day he entered their home that if the police weren't called and he respected their property, they would stay off his back and let him come and go as he pleased. They were only interested in the foster care check and were both collecting disability to sustain their lifestyle, so they didn't want to mess up their income. LeBaron agreed to their conditions. He kept his word to respect their property and never give the police a chance to knock on their door.

This freedom allowed LeBaron to become streetwise and ruthless well before his thirteenth birthday. While other kids were concerned about playing Super Mario Brothers on Nintendo, he was focused on peddling dime bags of weed and loose cigarettes outside the black American Legions and small hole-in-the-wall clubs in Chicago. He found that the "old heads" respected his hustle and wouldn't steal from him. They were his most loyal customers. LeBaron would ride his bike across town to sell his products. He figured the police would never suspect a kid riding a bike to be a drug dealer. So, he used his youth to his advantage.

"Aye man, you alright?" LeBaron asked Diamond while offering him his hand to help him off the ground.

"Yeah, man, thanks," Diamond replied. His eyes were on the verge of tears. He was so angry that his absentee mother was still bringing her destructiveness into his life, despite her physical absence.

"What was all that about?" LeBaron asked. "Why was it a three-on-one fight?"

"Just some shit about my mom," Diamond answered, hanging his head in shame.

LeBaron noticed the shift in Diamond's demeanor. "Look man, you gonna have to learn how to fight and get strong."

Diamond, at eleven years old and a grandma's boy, had no clue why this stranger had taken an interest in him, but he was appreciative of the advice. The two stood in silence on the edge of the field behind the school.

LeBaron dropped into the push-up position. "See, do these to help you get stronger, man." As LeBaron began to push out reps, he saw Diamond taking notes of his form and correctly deduced there wasn't a man in the home to show his new friend how to increase his physical strength.

LeBaron jumped up, brushing the grass from his sweater. "Now you try."

Diamond hesitantly assumed the position and attempted a push-up but could barely perform one. Instead of laughing, LeBaron encouraged Diamond.

"Don't worry, man. The more you do, the stronger you get. Then nobody will fuck with you."

Diamond got up from the push-up position, dusting himself off as well. "Hey, man, my grandma is probably waiting for me. Thanks."

Diamond saw a flicker of anxiety in LeBaron's eyes at the mention of his grandmother. "Hey, you can come over. My grandmother is always cooking something. And if I ain't home soon, the whole neighborhood is gonna be looking for me."

"Okay."

The two headed in the direction of Diamond's home without speaking another word as they walked.

***

"Hey, Grandmother, this my new friend. Can he stay for dinner?" Diamond asked, already knowing what his grandmother would say. But first she had to interrogate her new guest.

"Sure, baby," she said. "So, young man, what's your name?"

"Umm ...LeBaron. But everybody call me LB."

"That's a nice name. You hungry?"

"Umm...yeah."

Grandmother raised one eyebrow, squinting her eyes and staring at LeBaron.

"Umm...yes, ma'am."

Grandmother softened her gaze. "Okay, baby. Go wash your hands and I'll fix y'all plates."

LeBaron let out a breath he hadn't known he'd been holding. He wasn't raised to have manners but knew what they were. He also never had an opportunity to use manners, because most of the adults he dealt with didn't garner any of his respect. He felt something different from Diamond's grandmother, which was mutual respect. So, he felt comfortable giving her his respect.

LeBaron and Diamond washed their hands in the house's single bathroom. It was small but comfortable, just like the rest of Grandmother's house. After they came out of the bathroom, Diamond grabbed plates out of the cabinet.

"The forks are in the drawer." Diamond motioned with his head to one of the drawers next to the refrigerator, but LeBaron stood in the doorway. "Aye, man. Forks over there!"

LeBaron moved from where his feet were planted in the doorway. He'd never sat down to eat with anyone at either his dysfunctional home or any of his foster placements. He preferred to eat in his room so he could store some of his meals, because he was so used to food being scarce. So, the thought of eating in front of people other than at school was a new concept. LeBaron slowly walked over to the drawer under the approving gaze of Diamond's grandmother.

"Go ahead and grab a fork and a spoon for everybody so we can have ice cream for dessert," Grandmother said in the softest, welcoming tone. "Then when you done with that, call yo' folks and let them know you staying for dinner and will be home shortly."

LeBaron quickly turned to face Grandmother with his eyes wide as saucers, because he didn't know how to explain that no one was looking for him or cared about his whereabouts.

"That a problem, young man?" Grandmother asked in a tone just as sweet as her first request.

"No."

Grandmother raised an eyebrow as she made everyone's plate.

"I mean, no, ma'am. It's just that..."

"Gone 'head, chile...spit it out."

"Well, it's just that don't nobody care where I am."

Grandmother turned away from the plates she was making. With a concerned expression, she walked up to LeBaron and faced him.

"What you mean, baby, that don't nobody care 'bout where you are? Where's yo' Mama? She gone?" Grandmother was aware of the drug epidemic sweeping the city, because her own daughter had fallen prey to the disease of addiction.

"I don't really know where she is." LeBaron left a long pause that Grandmother didn't rush him through. "I got a foster family."

"Okay, well, there's a phone in the living room right next to the couch. Gone 'head and call them and let me speak to them please," Grandmother sweetly ordered.

LeBaron usually had issues with authority attempting to tell him what to do, but he felt an instant connection to Diamond's grandmother. She wasn't pushy or overbearing. He could also hear the sincerity in her tone. He was going to fake a call to his foster parents, because he knew they wouldn't care if he never came home again. But as long as the foster check came each month, they were satisfied.

LeBaron walked over to the telephone and dialed the number to his foster parents' house. He listened for an answer while secretly hoping they wouldn't pick up. As the phone rang, his heart began to beat faster in anticipation. *What am I gonna say to them?* LeBaron thought.

"Hello?" His foster mother picked up as the rate of LeBaron's heartbeat raced even faster now.

"Umm...hey, this is Le...LB and umm, I'm at a friend's house for dinner." LeBaron stammered. "His grandma wanna talk to you."

LeBaron set the receiver facedown before his foster mother could respond and walked back toward the kitchen where he saw a heaping plate of fried pork chops, smothered potatoes and onions, and a side of spinach. There was also a tall glass of red Kool-Aide that Diamond had just poured. Grandmother passed him and gave him a sweet smile as she went to pick up the phone. LeBaron drowned out the conversation between Diamond's grandmother and his foster mother, because he already knew that his foster mother was putting on a show like she gave a damn about LeBaron.

Grandmother was back at the small, round dinner table with a warm smile on her face. She motioned for LeBaron to sit down, because he was still standing behind his chair staring at the food with his mouth watering.

"Okay, baby, go on and bless the food, Diamond," Grandma said with a sweet smile, her gold tooth making her smile shine even brighter against her smooth dark skin.

"God, bless this food for our bodies we are about to receive and bless the hands that prepared it. Amen."

"Amen," Grandmother replied while LeBaron said nothing.

He wasn't used to seeing anyone pray over their food out loud that wasn't a preacher or in a church setting.

Grandmother gave LeBaron a nod and held out her hand, motioning for him to eat. He cleaned his plate.

BROTHERS (NOVEMBER 1989)

Diamond and LeBaron became fast friends from the day they met. LeBaron was a permanent fixture at Diamond's house, because it was the only house he ever visited that felt like home.

"C'mon with yo' slow ass!" Diamond teased LeBaron.

"Nigga, you the one that's slow. Remember? I'm the starter while you ride the bench." LeBaron answered while taking off at top speed toward Diamond's grandmother's house.

"Cheatin' ass!" Diamond yelled and gave chase. They had an ongoing bet that whoever made it to Grandmother's house first was excused from doing the dinner dishes. The race was always cut-throat, and neither of the pair was above cheating to win their innocent rivalry.

LeBaron and Diamond burst through the screen door and fell in a heap on top of each other. "Now if y'all tear up my screen door, I'm taking it out on asses! Grandmother scolded the teenage boys as they lay in a breathless tangle of long limbs and strained muscles. "And y'all can both do the dishes after dinner since it was a tie. Now go wash up for dinner and get out them school clothes. Y'all smell like a pack of wild animals." Grandmother turned away from the boys to hide her amusement.

LB and Diamond let out exasperated sighs as they disentangled from one another. "I would've won if yo' ass hadn't cheated." Diamond sulked while walking toward the bedroom he shared with LB.

Grandmother made a deal with LB's foster parents that LB could stay with her as long as they took him to regular doctor and dentist visits. Grandmother never mentioned money, so LeBaron's foster parents didn't mention money in-kind.

"LeBaron, your turn for grace," Grandmother charmingly stated while bowing her head.

LeBaron still wasn't used to saying grace or living in a civilized home with a set dinnertime and rules. However, he was beginning to like the structured lifestyle that Diamond and his grandmother offered unconditionally. He was used to people offering him things with strings and favors attached. When he was given his first pack to sell, it was wrapped in smiles and offered as a way to help him be independent, because the older boy offering the drugs to sell was disguised with a smile. LeBaron got used to the money flowing to his pockets, so he continued to look for work—be it drug runs, drop-offs, delivering messages, or pulling stick-ups. He was down to do almost anything to keep his pockets laced, his stomach full, and his clothes fly. He still hustled, but now he did it between the hours of five p.m. and nine p.m., because Grandmother didn't play games. If he wasn't home when the streetlights came on, then he would be locked out of the house. He found out the hard way one night and never did it again. What surprised him most was when he returned the next day after school with his head hanging in shame, Grandmother reached under his chin, lifted his head, and told him to never bow his head to anyone and never be ashamed of his actions. She told him to do better.

That's what he loved most about Diamond's grandmother: she never admonished or humiliated him for his mistakes. She allowed him to make the mistakes, recognize them, then course correct. For that, he always gave Grandmother respect and contributed to the household what his hustle money could provide. Grandmother never chastised LeBaron for his street activities either; she only cared if he or Diamond were in a gang. She knew that living a street life was the reality of most teens in urban Chicago, no matter what side you were from. However, if they were gonna hustle, Grandmother wanted the pair to hustle smarter, not harder. And she expected them not to get caught, because she "wasn't visiting no jailhouse" as she would often tell the boys.

LeBaron stopped at the cookie tin containing Grandmother's knitting and sewing materials to drop a couple hundred dollars inside. He started putting money there because he wanted to pay Grandmother for her kindness and generosity. Diamond revealed that his mother left him with his grandmother when he was only an infant, and Grandmother used food stamps, Section 8, and a small pension her late husband left for her. Grandmother made the best out of a bad situation and never let herself, nor Diamond, go hungry or without utilities. She kept a small garden on the side of the house that helped supplement their meals. Diamond never really knew how poor they were, because every night he went to bed full and loved. Now that LeBaron was part of their family, he made sure to contribute to bills so that Grandmother could spend the leftover money on Diamond's thrift store clothes and shoes, which he was frequently teased about. In Chicago, clothes and style went far in establishing and commanding your respect in the hood, and Diamond had neither.

After placing the money inside Grandmother's cookie tin, he went into his bedroom to change his school clothes. When he walked in their room, he noticed Diamond holding a dime bag of weed in his left hand and an open Nike box in his right. *Damn*, LeBaron thought. Diamond found his hiding spot. He thought that if he hid his stash in plain sight, neither Diamond nor Grandmother would find it.

"Aye, what's this man. I know you ain't selling..." Diamond's voice trailed off as LeBaron swiftly closed the door behind him and flew over to Diamond with two steps with his six-three frame.

"Hold that shit down! You want her to hear and put me out?" LeBaron grabbed his weed and shoe box from Diamond's hands. He quickly counted the baggies to make sure none were missing—he had to account for every single dime bag with no excuses for Fat Ron.

"What you doin' with that, LB?"

"What the fuck you think I'm doin', Diamond?"

The twosome glared at each other so hard, they saw their reflection in the other's pupils. "Look, man, I been hustling a long time, and I've been giving your grandmother money since I've been living here. Ain't nothing free in life."

Silence ensued while Diamond processed that his best friend was selling weed and he'd been giving his grandmother money. A pang of guilt and embarrassment began to fill Diamond's chest, forcing him to sit on the edge of his twin-sized bed. He'd never considered the financial strain his grandmother must be under, attempting to take care of him without a job. After securing his shoe box, LeBaron sat across from Diamond on his own twin bed. The room was so small that their knees nearly touched.

"You think you can teach me?" Diamond asked, eyes strained, patiently awaiting his friend's answer.

The two jumped as Grandmother knocked on the door and quickly opened it without waiting for an answer on the other side. "What the heck is wrong with y'all?" Grandmother asked without waiting for an answer. "Come eat. Food is getting cold."

Grandmother left as quickly as she came, leaving the two boys' hearts hammering in their chests. They didn't know how long Grandmother had been outside the door before knocking, because they hadn't heard her approaching footsteps.

The dinner table was quiet that night, which was a far cry from the boys' usual joaning each other and talking about basketball. The clinking of forks on plates and the occasional gulp of Kool-Aide was all to be heard. Grandmother lifted a suspicious eyebrow at her boys but attributed their strange behavior to a disagreement.

Grandmother decided to break the silence. "Y'all know y'all ain't blood-related, but you're even closer than blood. You know why?" Grandmother waited for an answer.

Bewildered and shaken out of their thoughts, the boys shook their heads *no*.

"Y'all are closer than blood because y'all are the family that each other chose. Y'all done both seen how somebody related by blood can do you more harm than a stranger on the street. But not you two. Y'all chose each other to be one another's family. Now that's a bond stronger than any blood bond." Grandmother demanded eye contact from LeBaron, then Diamond.

"You understand?"

"Yes, ma'am," they replied in a singsong manner.

"Good. Now wash these dishes while I read my word then get ready to watch JR 'n them."

The two stood and proceeded to clear the table and start the dish water. Grandmother didn't miss her Friday night lineup of *Dallas* and *Falcon Crest*; she didn't care what was going on. Diamond and LeBaron gave one another a knowing smile, because they were thinking this exact thought at that exact moment. After finishing the dishes together, the boys quickly worked on their homework in silence. They would have uninterrupted time to discuss their earlier interaction when Grandmother was engulfed in her Friday night soap operas.

***

"Take me to meet Fat Ron tomorrow," Diamond demanded.

"What, nigga?" LeBaron turned to face Diamond while they lay in the darkness. "I thought you didn't know what the fuck was going on?"

"I've been around drugs since the day I was born."

Grandmother's shows broke up the silence as the two weighed their next words carefully.

"I was born addicted," said Diamond. "A gift from my momma. I will never use that shit and vowed I would never sell it either. But you made me see a way to get us out this hell hole. And if we work together, we can do it faster. Watch each other's backs. Not let anybody get over on us."

LeBaron listened to his fourteen-year-old friend sounding like a grown man. It made sense to combine their efforts and double their profits. Plus, there was no one on Earth LeBaron trusted more than his chosen brother.

"Bet."

Chapter Fourteen

THE HUSTLE (FEBRUARY 1990)

Diamond was born to be a hustler, and he loved the fast life even more than LeBaron. Diamond met with Fat Ron and began slinging dimes and nicks after school. He told his grandmother that he got a job at a corner store in a different neighborhood, because they were the only ones that would hire a teenager to clean up and run the register. Since the corner store was in a different neighborhood, he knew that neither his grandmother nor her church friends would venture into that area because most of them didn't drive. He told Grandmother he took the bus after school to his job. As long as he was home before dinner, there wouldn't be any questions.

"I wanted to see you in action at work today, but you don't work there, huh?" Grandmother peered into Diamond's almond orbs.

Diamond knew that whenever his grandmother asked a question that it was best to come clean, because she already knew the answer.

Diamond put down his fork and finished chewing the cubed steak Grandmother had made for dinner. LeBaron held his head low, lifting his eyebrows, slowly chewing his steak as he awaited Diamond's answer. LeBaron knew that Diamond's answer would determine both of their fates.

Diamond grabbed his paper towel and wiped his mouth in slow motion.

"Grandmother, I lied to you because I didn't want you to worry about me out here in these streets," said Diamond. "I been working for Fat Ron, but I wanna have *my own* business one day. I wanna have my own empire, but enough to create wealth for my family, so we don't ever have to struggle again. I wanna move you out the hood, so you don't have to worry about walking down the block to the church house and getting knocked over the head and robbed. I promise you that I will do all of these things, but I know that I can't do them without your love and consent."

Diamond measured Grandmother's body language. He'd been planning to give her this speech since he first started working for Fat Ron. He hated keeping secrets from his grandmother. She was his best friend, even more so than LeBaron, and she needed to know how he felt.

"And before you say anything," Diamond continued. "I want to let you know that I'm dropping out of high school and getting my GED, but LeBaron will continue. He has a real chance to go to the NBA." Diamond didn't look at his friend. He knew shock would be written all over LB's face.

"I promise I'll never bring drugs or violence into this house. As soon as I'm able, we're gonna move outta this house. I'm gonna buy you a house, still on the east side of town, but just a better street because I can't have my girl away from her church friends." Diamond gave

Grandmother a twinkling smile that made whatever he was saying irresistible. "Those are my terms. Or I can move out. But I'm not gonna stop hustling. It's in my blood and you know it. You've been known it, right?"

Grandmother sat silent for a few moments, processing everything her grandson told her. "I trust you, baby, and it looks like you got your mind made up. So, there ain't much I can do other than pray for your safety. I've taught you everything you need to know to protect yourself in this world. Now it will be up to the streets to teach you how to be your own man. I love you, son."

Grandmother slowly got up from her chair, taking a step toward Diamond and placing a firm kiss on his forehead. "I always knew the streets was gonna come calling, I just didn't know it was gonna be this soon." Grandmother sighed, walking over to the trash and emptying her plate. Her appetite was gone. She started to run the dish water.

"What the fuck you mean, Imma stay in school and play ball? You my daddy now, making decisions for me?" LeBaron asked through clenched teeth.

Diamond inched in closer to LeBaron's face so that his grandmother wouldn't hear their conversation. "No, nigga. I'm just tryna save you from yourself. I look up to you, and you taught me the game. You got talent *and* you gonna get out the hood, regardless. Me on the other hand...all I got is the streets."

The two sneered at one another through gritted teeth. Neither of them were willing to concede or be the first to look away.

"I made some lemon pound cake, y'all's favorite," Grandmother said and slid a piece of cake in front of both boys. As she did, they separated and smiled.

"Thank you," they said in unison.

"You're welcome. Now eat up. I gotta have my boys strong to take over the world." Grandmother smiled, hugging them both to her bosom. She felt LeBaron and Diamond melt into her.

They never had anyone to accept them fully other than Grandmother, and for that, these two boys would do anything to make her happy. They would also do anything to anyone that made her less than happy.

"Diamond, make sure you get your study materials for your GED testing tomorrow from your counselor since you been skipping," Grandmother said. "You almost seventeen, so they shouldn't say anything. Get the information before they put you out. I gotta go up to the school and withdraw you, so I won't go to jail for truancy."

"Yes, ma'am." Diamond said hesitantly.

"What?" said Grandmother. "Ain't that what you wanted to hear?"

"I mean...yes, ma'am, but I just thought that you was gonna put up a fight about me dropping out."

Grandmother sat back down at the table while the boys finished their pound cake and laid her open hands on the table as an invitation. "Listen to me, boys, and I mean listen hard. I know we live in the belly of Chicago that spits out young men left and right. But not my boys." Grandmother squeezed their hands tightly.

"Baby, I knew school wasn't for you. You only tolerated it once you met LB. But I knew once you got a taste of them streets, it was gonna have a hold on ya' just like yo' momma."

Diamond's head quickly spun in his grandmother's direction. Grandmother squeezed his hand tighter and held it firmly in her hand. "Now, before you get yo' britches all twisted; all I'm saying is that the streets are in yo' blood. They was in yo' grandaddy's blood too. Nothing to be ashamed about. It's better to know what's in your blood and play to your strengths. Just promise me one thing. Both of you." Grandmother's eyes pleaded, looking from one set of dark eyes to the other.

"Anything," Diamond responded with a nod.

"Anything, you got it," LeBaron echoed.

"Promise me you'll never touch that shit! I don't care how curious you get. Not even a drop. And promise me you'll never let anyone come between you. Promise me!" Grandmother shouted and made the boys jolt to attention, because she never raised her voice.

"Okay, we promise," LeBaron spoke for the pair.

Grandmother tenderly held LeBaron's chin. "I know, baby. Now y'all get up and clean this kitchen."

"Yes, ma'am," the two replied in unison.

Chapter Fifteen

RICA (SUMMER 1991)

"Hurry up or we gonna miss all the ballers! I'm gonna leave yo' slow ass! All the fine niggas gonna be taken by the time we make it to the court," Gina yelled upstairs to her best friend.

"I'm coming, hoe, damn!" Rica checked her outfit one more time before leaving to ride through the streets of Chicago looking for trouble. Rica bolted down the steps in her booty shorts, Air Max, and her favorite Cross Colors short-sleeve shirt. She brushed her hair up in her signature high ponytail and looked in the mirror, satisfied there were no fly-aways. She grabbed her favorite cherry flavored gloss off her vanity and applied it, puckering her soft, pink lips and pressing them together to ensure the shine spread evenly. Rica thought about all the ballers that would be at the basketball courts since it was the first day of summer. The thought made her hurry downstairs. She was putting in her favorite pair of doorknocker earrings as she made it to the last step.

"Okay, bitch, I'm ready," Rica said, slightly out of breath.

"Bout time, bitch…let's go. I'm driving," Gina stated and headed toward the front door of Rica's house, pushing the screen door open.

Rica's brothers were outside in the driveway working on the old school box Chevy they shared.

"Where the hell you going in them little ass shorts, Rica?" Her older brother asked.

Rica waved him away and kept walking toward Gina's bright red, two-door, drop-top Corvette convertible. Gina's father was the president of the local Bank of America, which was rare for a black man. He was well-respected and liked, because he made it a point to help black families attain the American dream of home ownership. Although, he moved out of the West Side of Chicago years ago to raise his family in the nearby suburbs to avoid crime. Gina and Rica met at summer camp in the eighth grade and have been best friends ever since. Gina loved hood shit and Rica wanted the finer things in life, so they balanced each other perfectly.

"We going riding, Enzo," Rica said. "Why? You my daddy now?"

"Aye, cut the fucking attitude. You know Daddy put me in charge while he's locked up," Enzo bellowed as he walked toward the girls.

"You know these men out here only want one thing, Rica. You gotta be smarter than them. Stop tryna grow up so damn fast. You know I'm just tryna protect you, right?" Enzo's voice softened while joined by his brother Ricky.

"Yeah, Rica, slow yo' ass down. And if you gonna be out here, make sure you got your strap with you. You know these mu'fuckers see a pretty face and a fat ass and don't hear the word *no*," Ricky added. He never tried to filter his thoughts.

Rica spun around with her ponytail following. "You right, Enzo. I know what these fools are on out here, and I ain't playin'. You know you, Daddy, and Ricky raised me better than that." Rica grabbed the door handle of Gina's car. "And yes, brother, you know I stay strapped." Rica opened up her purse and showed the .22 that her father gave her when she turned twelve and got her first period.

"That's my girl," Ricky said lovingly. "Y'all be safe. You got your pager on you?"

"Yeah, and Gina got a car phone. We'll be fine."

Gina was lowering the top of her Corvette while she bumped "Around the Way Girl" by LL Cool J. The sound was bumping through the Alpine system that Gina's dad had custom installed.

"I'll be home by dinner. Love y'all," Rica yelled over LL Cool J.

Gina screeched her tires while pulling off. She knew that Rica's brothers hated it when she did it, so it was mandatory.

***

"Oh, hell yeah, it's thick as hell out here!" Rica exclaimed over the music. "It's hella mu'fuckas out here today."

As Rica and Gina pulled into the parking lot, they leaned back in their seats, trying to act cool. All the while, they darted their eyes from side to side, assessing which ballers' cars were in the parking lot. The girls had to be strategic about where they parked. They needed to stay incognito, because they were talking to more than one boy, and they didn't want to be caught talking to one while another one was watching. They had to keep their game tight.

They found a parking space at the far end of the parking lot. It was also near the road so they could quickly exit if tempers started running high and someone decided to start poppin' off. Gina turned down

"Summertime" by DJ Jazzy Jeff & the Fresh Prince, so they could still enjoy it but be able to set their game plan.

"Aye, you see your boy out there hoopin'?" Gina teased Rica.

"That ain't my boy, that's yo' boy," Rica said. "You the one that's had a crush on him since last year and ain't said shit."

"Fuck you, bitch, and you the one that said he fine as hell and you would love for him to be your first," Gina replied, knowing that line would frustrate Rica because it was the truth. Rica's only reply was a scowl.

"Damn he *do* look good though," Rica admitted. "Let's get out and sit on the hood. Oh, hold up, there go your boy, Jason."

"With his fine ass!" said Gina. "Them green eyes do it for me every fucking time. And I know he got a big dick! You can see it poking in them damn shorts. Whew! He just ain't got no damn money. What's the point of having a fine ass man that's broke? All them muscles just going to waste." Gina scrunched her nose in disgust.

"Hell naw!" They chimed simultaneously and broke out into a fit of laughter. Gina turned her key all the way back to keep the music pumping and they got out of the car.

"Oh shit, don't look, G, here come Dolla," Rica taunted and giggled.

Dolla was one of the biggest drug dealers on the West Side. He had his hands in a bit of everything, and the hood loved him. Dolla was the type of nigga that showed love everywhere he went. The hood rats loved him because he didn't mind breaking them off a little change. The other drug bosses loved him because he kept to his territory and handled disputes as amicably as possible. He wasn't very smart though and spent most of what he earned on hoes, jewelry, and cars.

"Aye, G!"

The girls acted like they didn't hear Dolla and kept giggling and talking to each other.

"Aye, G...G!" Dolla hollered over the music of his bass bumping out of his speakers.

"Gina, I know you hear me, girl!"

Gina whipped her hair around, making the bangs of her Halle Berry haircut shake. She put her hand over her eyes as a sunshade. "Hey, Dolla!"

She slid off the hood of her car and sauntered over to Dolla's money-green BMW with gold flecks in the paint while her ass swayed in her striped shorts and matching green halter top. "Girl, watch this." Gina whispered to Rica.

They had an ongoing competition to see how much money they could get from any man they considered a baller. Their goal was to see how much money they could get them to trick without giving them any pussy. The key to the game was to never go to their house, someone else's house, or a hotel. Rica and Gina had more game than the hardest pimp because they learned from the best, Rica's brothers.

While Gina was running game on Dolla, Rica turned her attention to the court and the groups of people gathered in the park. She noticed that the game Jason was playing in was ending, but that wasn't who caught her attention. There was a tall, walnut-skinned brotha with his shirt off walking her way. She involuntarily licked her lips, mesmerized by each sure-footed step he took toward her. Her breath hitched in her chest. As he got closer, she noticed his waves centered between a close fade. He took his shirt off and wiped the sweat from the front of his abs, which instantly made Rica twist her hips on the hot hood of Gina's car.

Damn girl, get it to-fucking-gether, she thought and shifted her weight into a power-position by leaning back on her hands and crossing her ankles, tipping her head back, and looking the stranger in his eyes as he approached. With each step, her thundering heartbeat betrayed her outward calm appearance.

"So, I seen you watching me play." LeBaron flashed Rica a brilliant smile, showing his naturally straight teeth.

"And you are?" Rica asked.

"Awe...you don't know me, baby?"

"Hell no! I don't know you, and I ain't yo' baby."

"My bad, girl, damn, you ain't gotta act like that. Don't you go to Marshall?" LeBaron asked, fully knowing he'd seen Rica in the hallway during passing periods. She always seemed preoccupied with the wannabe ballers and the older dudes that hung around the high school and at sporting events.

"What, you stalkin' me or something?" Rica questioned. She was always on alert and bounced off the hood of the car to walk over to the passenger side.

"Hold up, wait," LeBaron said while grabbing Rica's elbow.

Rica's eyes bored into LeBaron's hand and he removed it slowly, holding up both of his hands in defense. "My fault, beautiful. I meant no disrespect. I just seen you at school. I play for the team at Marshall. Number 34."

"Oh wait, you number 34? At Marshall?" Rica softened.

"Yeah, that's me. So, you know me, huh?" LeBaron confidently smiled at Rica. He knew everyone knew him in the city if they followed basketball in the slightest, because he was on track to be drafted into the NBA if all the speculation about his talent and ranking were to be believed.

Rica softened and the dollar signs started to twinkle in her eyes. She thought to herself that this fine, tall specimen of a man standing before her could be her ticket out the hood. She saw her life flash before her eyes: shopping bags busting, her hair whipped by with the latest styles, her wrists, neck, and fingers dripping in diamonds and gold. Rica was so caught up in her reverie that she didn't hear LeBaron's question until he repeated himself.

"So, what's your name, beautiful?"

"Oh, it's Rica. Nice to meet you...what'd you say your name was, Mr. Number 34?"

"Ha, there you go! My name is LeBaron, but everybody calls me LB. Nice to meet you, Rica. Aye, maybe I can call you sometime if you ain't got a boyfriend."

"Naw, I ain't got a boyfriend." Rica turned around and purposefully bent over the passenger side door to retrieve her purse and get a pen and paper. She didn't need to look up to know that LeBaron's eyes were glued to her ass and thighs in her shorts. "Here." She whipped around and caught his eyes trained to her ass—just as she suspected—and let out a chuckle.

Rica wrote her name and number on a scrap of paper. She greedily licked her top lip as she hungrily took in LeBaron. He took the piece of paper from her and saw the little heart she'd drawn at the end of her name made his dick jump.

"So, can I call you tonight, beautiful?"

"Yeah, you can." Rica answered confidently, still holding onto the piece of paper while LeBaron held it. The pair locked eyes as the cheers of the crowd and music from Dolla's and other cars faded into the background.

Rica noticed LeBaron's eyes shift to something behind her.

"Aye, nigga! You done hoopin'?" Diamond called out.

Rica whipped her head around, nearly hitting LeBaron in the face with her ponytail.

"Yeah, bruh, gimme a minute."

In the few seconds that Rica turned her head, she assessed the man LeBaron was talking to was somebody she would be interested in. His deep waves and chocolate skin glistened in the Chicago sunlight, framed in the window of his gray box Chevy.

Rica faced LeBaron. "That your homeboy?"

"Yeah, my brother from another mother."

"Okay...okay, I see. Well, look, hit me up later when you get cleaned up and maybe you and my girl and your homeboy can get up."

"Okay, that's what's up. I'm gonna hit you in a few hours. Write down your pager number cuz I know y'all gonna be in the streets. It's nice as fuck out."

"Okay," Rica said with a smile, tilting her head flirtatiously.

"A'ight, beautiful, see you in a minute." LeBaron smoothed down his waves and walked to Diamond's car, feeling Rica's eyes on him. LeBaron threw up the deuces to Dolla as he walked past his car to the passenger side of Diamond's ride.

Rica resumed her spot leaning on the hood of Gina's car and waited for her to finish her conversation with Dolla.

"Biiiiitch! Both them niggas was fine as fuck!" Gina squealed as she noticed the blunt Gina got from Dolla. "I know that look, bitch. Which one you want, cuz I'll take either one, shit!"

"See, bitch, that's why I fucks witchu." Rica laughed and dapped up Gina while leaning into her. She dug her lighter out of her tight shorts and passed it to Gina. "No, but for real, you know ol' boy I was talking to? I've heard my brothers talking about him. He's about to go to the league."

"Oh, word?" Gina sat back waiting for Rica to pass the lighter.

"Yeah, but the one who drove up, his friend. I can tell he gettin' money right now."

"So, what you gonna do, friend?" said Gina. "See which one got the bigger dick?"

The two looked at each other and fell out in laughter all over Gina's hood.

"I don't know, bitch. I gotta see which one I'm feelin' more. But they supposed to get up with us later. So, it's whatever."

"Well, you already know what I'm on whatever you on, so I'm wit it. Just let me know," Gina said and took a pull of the blunt.

"C'mon, friend, let's go get changed and get something to eat right quick before we meet up," said Rica. "I wanna make sure my coochie's fresh."

Chapter Sixteen

INFATUATION (SUMMER 1991)

"**C**'mon man, just go with me to meet up with these girls. You see how fine ol' girl was that I was talking to at the park? Damn, man, you buggin'!" LeBaron begged Diamond to go with him as his wingman to meet Rica and Gina at the Red Roof Inn.

"Man, you know I got runs to make and ain't gonna miss out on money for some bitches just so you can get yo' dick wet," Diamond complained while counting his money and bundling it in thousand-dollar wads.

"Man, damn, you know I ain't tryna keep you from your bread, but I need somebody for ol' girl's friend. C'mon, man! And her friend got a fat ass. You seen her at the park talking to Dolla, right? I know you did, nigga. You don't miss shit," LeBaron egged on.

"Yeah, I seen her ass talking to Dolla. Damn gold digger," Diamond said. "I hope she know I ain't no damn trick. Never have been and never will be."

"I know, nigga, damn. So, I can hit 'em back and tell 'em to meet us at the Roof?" LeBaron asked with a smirk and started to page Rica.

Diamond shook his head thinking about his brother's thristiness while still bundling his money.

Rica called LeBaron's cell a few minutes later. "Yeah, meet us at the Roof."

"Hell, naw, girl, ain't nobody tryna fuck!" LeBaron told Rica over the phone. "And ain't nobody tryna get caught up at no park or at our people's house either. Unless you want us to pull up to yo' crib?"

LeBaron waited for Rica's response. He knew she didn't want him to pull up to her house. Her brothers were crazy and wouldn't appreciate a black guy coming to call on their sister. They let it be known that she was only to talk to other Puerto Ricans, even though the Puerto Rican community was small on the West Side of Chicago.

"Cool...bet," said LeBaron. "See you in about an hour. Yeah, I'm bringing my homeboy, Diamond, for your girl. A'ight...in a minute." LeBaron ended the phone call and was met by Diamond's disapproving look.

"Thirsty-ass nigga."

"Aye, fuck you. I'm just focused on other shit than money my nigga, like pussy. You remember pussy, my nigga?" LeBaron teased.

"You need to be focused on ball and getting the fuck up outta here." Diamond nodded his head around their shared room.

The pair still shared a bedroom in Grandmother's house even though they both stood well over six feet.

"Aye, but seriously though, don't get caught up with these hoes, man," Diamond said. "They see you and see dolla signs. And I heard about that girl and her friend."

"Now what the fuck you done heard, nigga? You don't even go nowhere?" LeBaron teased.

"Listen, the streets talk, and I listen. Everybody ain't lying, G. Just be careful. If you gonna fuck, make sure you strapped."

Silence fell in the small room as Diamond continued to count his money and LeBaron looked in their closet for an outfit to wear. "I hear you, bruh. I wanna get out the hood just as much as the next nigga. Maybe even more," LeBaron said more to himself than Diamond.

"You still got the hook up at the room?" LeBaron asked.

"Yeah, nigga, calm yo' ass down. I keep a room at the Roof. I'm gonna stop by the store and get something for these hoes to drank. I'll pick up some blunts too. I gotchu, nigga. I call dibs on the shower." Diamond laughed and bolted for the bathroom.

LeBaron tried to grab Diamond, but he slipped out of his grasp and ran into the bathroom, slamming the door.

"Y'all stop with all that stomping around!" Grandmother called from the front room where she was watching *Guiding Light*. "I'm trying to watch my stories."

***

LeBaron paged Rica the room number. He and Diamond made it to the room in the late afternoon after stopping at the liquor store for strawberry Boone's Farm, Phillys, and snacks to munch on. LeBaron also brought his boom box and a booklet of CDs. Music would help relax the girls. It was the beginning of a great party.

When he heard a light knock on the door, LeBaron put down the remote and crossed the room in two long strides. Diamond shook his head and thought, *thirsty ass.*

With his head cocked back, attempting to look cool, LeBaron bit his bottom lip and opened the door for the girls. He let out a soft hum of approval as Rica passed in front of him, her CK One perfume following her in a sensuous cloud. She bit her lip, too, in approval of how fine LeBaron looked in his Cross Colors patchwork hoodie, baggy light blue jeans, and white and red Air Jordans. Her eyes quickly scanned to Diamond as he lay on the other double bed, flipping through the pages of *Jet* magazine.

"Y'all smoke?" LeBaron raised his eyebrows as he asked the girls.

"Hell yeah!" Gina replied.

"Depends on what it is," said Rica. "Whether it's dirt or not."

Diamond looked up from his magazine for the first time since the girls had arrived, narrowing his eyes at Rica. Diamond was supplying the free weed to impress LeBaron's crush, even though he didn't see why he was so enamored with her. She was cute but had a bad attitude, and as far as Diamond was concerned, he wanted to keep his distance. He only came to the hotel room with LeBaron because he had begged him to. LeBaron knew Rica wouldn't come to a room by herself, so he had to have someone to keep Gina company while he tried to talk Rica's panties off.

"Roll up then," LeBaron said and tossed Rica a baggie.

Rica examined the weed, rolling the baggie between her fingers before opening it to give a sniff.

"Hmph, I'm straight. Gina, you can roll if you want."

"Okay girl, I gotchu."

Diamond quickly repositioned himself, sitting on the edge of the double bed. "What's wrong with the weed?"

"Awe, nothing," Rica lied and started cracking her gum and blowing nervous bubbles.

Diamond stood, offended Rica didn't think his weed was good enough to smoke.

"Why don't you wanna smoke? That shit ain't laced, and it's the best in the city." Diamond slightly raised his baritone voice and the girls froze. They'd never heard him speak, and by his tone, he was clearly offended.

The girls started laughing in LeBaron and Diamond's face while the boys grew angry because they didn't understand the joke.

"What's so damn funny?" LeBaron asked, confused and looking from the girls back to Diamond.

The girls attempted to come down from their laughing fit and get serious, because the boys weren't laughing with them. Rica quickly realized the weed belonged to Diamond and that's why he got defensive so quickly.

"I meaaaaan...y'all can smoke that, but me and my girl gonna smoke this," Rica said and brought out a fat baggie of weed.

"Damn, girl!" LeBaron said, grabbing for the bag of weed. Rica yanked it out of his reach.

"Naw, you ain't about to waste my shit! I'll roll. Y'all got some blunts?

"Huhn," Diamond said with an attitude and tossed the box of Phillys onto the other bed.

"Well, damn, you need to get yo' boy. Why he actin' all funky?" Rica asked as she reached for the box of Phillys and prepared to roll a blunt.

"He a'ight." LeBaron ticked his head to the side nonchalantly. Then he went over to the boom box and put on Al Green's *Greatest Hits*.

The foursome began to relax as Diamond went back to flipping through the pages of his magazine. Gina stretched her arms behind her and lolled her head backward. She popped her gum with her eyes closed, listening to the mellow tones of "Tired of Being Alone."

"So, that's yo' shit?" Rica asked. She sealed the blunt between her tongue and top lip, then dried it with a lighter.

Her question hung in the air, because neither Diamond nor LeBaron wanted to claim the rejected weed. Rica gave up waiting for an answer with a shrug. She lit the blunt, taking two pulls. Then she passed the blunt to Gina and twisted the cap off her strawberry Faygo. The smell of potent weed wafted through the air.

"Aye, ain't y'all gonna put a towel up against the door?" Gina asked with her top lip raised and brows knitted with concern. The last thing she needed was to get busted smoking weed with two boys in a hotel room. Neither of the boys moved while the girls tensed up.

"Naw, we know the manager. We cool," LeBaron replied and the girls relaxed.

"What the hell y'all listening to anyway? This old-ass music." Gina teased LeBaron and Diamond.

"Our grandmamma loves Al Green." Diamond peered at Gina, then went back to looking at his copy of *Jet*.

"Y'all don't look like brothers," Gina blurted out, the weed taking effect.

Diamond walked over to the dresser and started to open the Boones Farm. "Y'all drank?"

"Hell, yeah!" Gina replied. Diamond nodded and poured cups for Rica, LeBaron, and Gina. He handed Rica her cup first.

LeBaron took a big gulp from his red cup, then took a puff from the blunt and started a coughing fit.

"Damn, nigga. See, I told you. Y'all been smoking on that dirt," Ricca affirmed. "Can't even handle that shit."

She felt eyes on her and looked across the room. Diamond's intense gaze fell on her face and caught her off guard. She quickly recovered, but she couldn't deny the heat growing between her legs. Rica shifted her weight and re-crossed her legs, bouncing her leg while her sandal dangled off her bubble-gum pink toes.

Rica watched Diamond from across the room and wondered if he was breathing, because she didn't notice him blink either. Her heart picked up and she started to hear it beating in her ears thanks to the mixture of the weed and the cheap wine. She had never felt so uncomfortable under a man's gaze before. Rica was used to men being intimidated by her and being the first to look away. But not Diamond; he held her gaze without shame—without fear.

"Yeah, we grew up like brothers," LeBaron replied to Gina's comment about them not looking like brothers. His eyes darted across the room from Diamond to Rica and then back again as he made the connection that they were feeling each other.

Gina was oblivious to the brewing connection and kept talking to LeBaron while her voice faded into the background.

"It's gettin' stuffy in here. Y'all wanna go for a ride? Then we can come back to the room. I just can't sit here listening to the oldies. No offense." Gina apologized, looking from LeBaron to Diamond.

"It's all good. Aye, D. Let me get the keys," LeBaron asked. Diamond didn't hesitate and tossed LeBaron his keys.

"Aye, girl, you coming?"

"I'm gonna chill here for a minute." Rica faced Gina so that she was the only person who could see her face. She made an expression that told Gina to go and that she was cool.

"A'ight, we gonna hit a couple corners and be back in a minute," Gina said.

Neither Rica nor Diamond said anything, because they were back to staring at one another. LeBaron shook his head at Diamond and left to leave.

"You got the room key?" Gina asked.

"Imma just knock when we get back." LeBaron smiled as he headed out the door and whispered, "We don't wanna disturb anybody."

Laughing and acting like they were tiptoeing, Gina and LeBaron closed the hotel room door and got into Diamond's Chevy.

Rica got up to make herself another drink and didn't speak until she heard Diamond's car pulling away from the hotel parking lot. "So, that's the weed you selling? You get it from Fat Ron, huh?"

Diamond narrowed his eyes and silently stared at Ricca. *How in the fuck she know I sell weed and that it's Fat Ron's weed? What the fuck?*

"My brothers sell weed. Probably the best weed in the city," Rica stated matter-of-factly as Diamond scoffed and rolled his eyes.

"What, you don't believe me? Here, let me see your weed." Rica held out her hand. Once Diamond realized she wasn't taking no for an answer, he retrieved it from his pocket and placed the baggie in her palm.

"You see this, how crumbly it is? That lets me know it's dirt. And look at all these damn seeds and stems. Maybe a crackhead will buy it, but not no true bud-head. They know the difference between good weed and bullshit." She handed him back his baggie.

"How you know so much about weed?" Diamond asked while pouring himself a small drink of Boones Farm.

"My daddy taught me before he got locked up. And my brothers too."

"Hmmm...I see. So, you a queen pin?" Diamond joked.

"No, not yet." Rica simply replied, leaving silence for both of them to process her foreshadowing.

Diamond decided that he believed her. He believed that Rica could probably do anything she wanted to and that turned him on more than he'd ever been turned on before by any of the girls he'd been involved with. He was genuinely intrigued and wanted to get to know this girl.

Diamond quickly grabbed Rica by the waist and brought her body flushed with his, pressing his pelvis into his, so that she could feel how hard he was. Rica gasped in response to Diamond's quick movements while her eyes were ablaze with undeniable desire.

She let out a surprised gasp, because up until now Diamond acted more annoyed with her than aroused. When Rica first met Diamond, she was instantly attracted, but she wanted to play it cool in front of Gina—and definitely in front of LeBaron. Her mind began to swirl in anticipation of Diamond's next move. She parted her lips, taking shallow breaths while her heart hammered in her chest. Rica just knew that Diamond could feel her heart beating into his chest. She tried to swallow her spit to control her heart rate, but her mouth had gone dry due to the few pulls of the blunt she had smoked.

Diamond loved the way he knocked Rica off-kilter and surprised her with his confident move. He used her speechlessness to his advantage. Rica had a smart mouth, and he didn't want to give her a chance to mess up the moment. He looked deep into her eyes, the fire starting to swell and her body stiffening in his arms in a natural fight-or-flight response. He knew he had half a second to respond before she pulled away, cussed him out, or both. So, he pressed his full lips to hers without hesitation.

His kiss was urgent and full of teenage longing. Rica felt the heat and tingle between the two of them that had been building since Diamond locked eyes with her across the room. Diamond felt her slightly tense, then relaxed and leaned into his kiss. That was the green light Diamond was waiting for; he wanted her body to respond to his.

It betrayed her tough-girl exterior, and she wrapped her arms around Diamond's shoulders.

Rica parted Diamond's lips with her tongue to deepen their kiss. She pressed her pelvis into him even further as she massaged her tongue onto his while gripping the back of his head. Then she let her hands trail down his chest as she found the bottom of his shirt. She was now in her animalist mode and sought out the flesh of his abs that hardened under her soft hands.

Diamond leaned in even further, arching Rica's back. He grabbed two handfuls of Rica's ass. As he cupped it, she moaned with pleasure in response to his strong hands possessing her. Diamond grabbed the back of Rica's head as he dove his tongue deeper into Rica's mouth, imagining it was his dick she was tasting instead. Diamond thought of LeBaron and pulled back abruptly, taking one full step back to look at Rica with her lips swollen from his kisses and eyelids low with desire and surprise at the abrupt loss of contact.

"What about my boy, LB? Ain't you come here for him?" Diamond asked, panting.

Rica responded by closing the distance between them and gently placing her hands on either side of Diamond's face. "We just met yesterday. So, there is no me and LeBaron."

Rica waited for her words to penetrate Diamond's psyche. She aided him by nodding in agreement, so he would believe that he wasn't betraying his best friend—his brother.

"You saw how easily he left with my girl, right?" said Rica. He just wanted some pussy and I sho' wasn't gonna give it to him. So, he left with the next best option. Not talking down on my girl, but I know how she gets down."

Diamond took a half-step back, contemplating his next move. He felt he had to create physical distance between himself and Rica so he could think straight. Then he took another look in her deep, brown eyes and fell under their spell. He laid his conscious aside and let his body decide. He wanted Rica and no one was going to keep him from her. He saw his future in her eyes. She was bad, had body, and was street smart. Everything he was looking for in a girl. He had to make her his.

He crashed into her, hooked his thumbs in the belt loops of her shorts, and pressed her into his chest once again. He felt her nipples harden through her thin bra as she moaned and wrapped her arms around his neck.

"I'm gonna make you mine. You belong to me now," Diamond said as he spun Rica around and slowly guided her toward the bed.

"Is that right?" Rica asked between deep, tongue kisses. "And what makes you think I wanna be somebody's?"

"Because that pussy is thumping and letting me know it's mine."

Rica stopped kissing Diamond, slightly embarrassed because she'd never been so caught up in lust before. She got angry at her body for betraying her.

"Don't worry. I'm not gonna just fuck you and leave you. You belong to me, and I'll give you whatever you want." Diamond hovered over Rica, his promises falling on her lips. "I wanna be the best fucking drug dealer in Chicago and beyond. And I want you by my side." Diamond smothered Rica in another deep kiss. "What you got to say about that, Rica?" Diamond moved his hand up her thigh that was hitched around his waist.

Rica moaned in response.

"I need to hear you, baby. I know what I want when I see it and I want you." Diamond pleaded.

He glided his hand to the inside of her thigh as Rica spread her legs to let him have access to her pussy. Diamond read her mind and moved his fingers further up Rica's thigh and under the hem of her shorts. His fingers sought out the heat of her wet pussy. Diamond moved Rica's panties to the side and his fingers found her wet folds as she hummed with pleasure into his mouth.

"Please, baby, say yes, that you'll be mine. I can't fuck you if you don't belong to me," Diamond softly demanded. Rica opened her eyes in response to the yearning in his voice.

Rica never met a man who begged to be with her before trying to enter her. Most boys her age did everything *but* make a commitment. Diamond was different from any man she had dealt with up until this point. Her brothers and father had given her the game and taught her how to finesse men out of their money by giving them the illusion of her affection. However, she never put herself in situations where her virginity could be compromised. She usually only gave hand jobs to get what she wanted from the men she dated. She wanted her first time to be special and now she was contemplating giving it up on a rented mattress with a man she'd just met.

Rica's head reared back in pleasure as Diamond continued to massage her pearl into ecstasy. Her head was swimming with the voices of her father and brother telling her to wait for marriage—but she knew that if given the chance, they would sell her virginity to the highest bidder if it strengthened their drug empire alliances. Rica planned to give her body when and where she pleased and not for anyone's pleasure but her own.

She grabbed Diamond's wrist to stop his onslaught on her engorged pearl so she could think clearly.

"You really mean it?" she asked. "You want me to be your girl?"

"Yes. I knew you would be mine when I first saw you at the courts yesterday. I was gonna let you go because my brother was interested first, but you said it's nothing. So, yeah. I want you to be mine."

Rica nodded her head *yes*.

Diamond stared into Rica's eyes, edging her on. "I need to hear you say it, baby."

"Yes."

Diamond unleashed all his passion onto Rica's lips, pressing his hard dick against her side. Rica reached for the button on her shorts and undid them. Diamond quickly pulled her shorts off, exposing Rica's white, cotton panties.

"Let me taste you, baby," Diamond asked with urgency while pulling her panties off.

Diamond dove his face into Rica's soft fold while sucking and massaging her clit with the precision of an experienced lover, racking Rica's body with pleasure. Rica opened her legs wider to give Diamond more access to her pearl. She'd had head before, but never like this. She could feel the passion of Diamond's kiss on her pearl just as deep as if he were kissing her pouty lips.

Rica's head tipped back in pleasure as an orgasm ripped through her body. Wave after wave of pleasure rocked her body as Diamond thrust his middle finger into Rica's warm abyss. Rica gasped as Diamond added two fingers and pumped in and out while Rica rode the wave of her continuous orgasm.

Diamond came up to kiss Rica on the lips as her body subsided through its last wave of pleasure.

"Damn, you so wet for me, baby. Is this my pussy?

Rica smiled, her brow now beaded with a fine sheen of sweat.

"Tell me it's mine, baby," Diamond asked as he fished for a condom in his pocket. "Can I have my pussy, baby?"

"Yes," Rica answered breathlessly. She'd never been this turned on before and couldn't believe she was about to have sex for the first time. She watched as Diamond took off his shirt, unbuckled his pants, and dropped his jeans to the floor. Rica's eyes grew large in anticipation of seeing what had been pressing on her pelvis, waiting to enter her. Diamond slid off his black and white striped boxers to reveal his long, thick dick as it bounced to life upon being freed.

Rica gave a smile of approval and scooted back onto the center of the bed as Diamond followed her, opening the condom with his teeth. Rica waited while Diamond slipped on the rubber and started to rub his dick against her wet folds.

"Mmm...I feel that pussy getting hot waiting for me. You ready for me, baby?" Diamond asked in a low, hoarse tone full of desire. Not waiting for Rica to answer, he pressed himself into her in one full thrust to the hilt.

Rica gulped in air, adjusting to the pain and fullness of Diamond inside of her. Rica quickly reached up to push Diamond's chest to stop him.

"What is it, baby?" Diamond groaned into Rica's ear, lightly grazing her earlobe between his teeth.

"Just hold up, gimme a minute." Rica panted as her heart made her blood woosh in her ears.

Diamond, still inside Rica, pulled out slightly—enough to look deep into her eyes. "Is this your first time?"

Rica slowly nodded.

"Damn, baby, why didn't you tell me? It should've been more special than this. Uh uhn...we need to stop." Diamond began to pull out from between Rica's thighs, but she quickly wrapped both legs around his waist, not letting him move further.

"I want you." Rica and Diamond's desire reflected in each other's eyes, expressing more than their words could say.

"Fuck!" Diamond groaned in frustration and pushed deeply back into Rica. "You feel so fucking good."

Diamond gripped one of Rica's breasts that neatly fit in his large palm and teased her nipped until it pebbled. With a groan of pleasure, Diamond opened his mouth wide to devour Rica's breast as he sucked and fucked her into another orgasm, starting at the base of her spine and spreading throughout her body. Diamond found his release as he penetrated deeper inside Rica's softening folds.

Diamond held the base of the condom and withdrew from Rica, falling to the side of her in a heap of sweat-kissed flesh.

"Damn, baby, that was good. You know it only gets better from here." Diamond encouraged Rica with a sweet kiss on her forehead. "Lemme get this shower started. C'mon. Oh, and you need to get on birth control, so I can be in that pussy raw." Diamond gave Rica a small pat on the side of her thigh, then helped her to a sitting position.

Rica raised her eyebrows. She'd never had a man be so upfront about his feelings. Nor had she ever taken a shower with anyone before, let alone a man. Diamond sensed her apprehension.

"I'm gonna start the water for you, so you can take a quick shower before your girl and LB get back. Then I'll hop in. Cool?"

Rica stood, giving Diamond a quick smile, then tensing at the soreness she felt between her legs. She grabbed her clothes off the floor and covered her body as she tip-toed toward the bathroom. Diamond grabbed her wrist as she walked past him and pulled her naked body to his as he looked into her eyes. "You're mine now. I'm gonna do everything in my power to make you happy."

Rica smiled and bowed her head, feeling her face becoming heated with joy. She believed Diamond's promises. Rica didn't usually believe anything that came out of a man's mouth, unless they were from her father or brothers. Her experience with men led her to believe that they lied to get what they wanted from women and after they got their desires met, they would discard whoever fulfilled said desire. She vowed she would never be one of those discarded women. So, she used men for material things in exchange for the illusion of having their desires met. She and Gina would sit and laugh about all the schemes they ran on the men they encountered, which made them the best of friends.

Rica smiled while she showered and gently bathed her newfound womanhood. She noticed a slight tinge of pink at the bottom of the white, porcelain tub. She wasn't shocked at the sight of blood, because Gina had already told her that she may bleed her first time—Gina was well experienced in sex. She quickly dried off and dressed so Diamond could get in the shower before Gina and LeBaron got back. She wondered how long they'd been alone, trying to gauge how much time they had left together.

Diamond gave her a quick kiss as he entered the shower and a smile played on his lips. Rica went over to the dresser where the Boone's Farm was and made another drink. Then she took the blunt that she and Gina had put out earlier and lit it. She hoped the smell of the weed would cover the smell of sex in the air. She heard the soft hum of a car engine outside of the hotel room and Diamond simultaneously exiting the bathroom.

"Hello, beautiful," he said while bending down and placing another kiss on her lips as she exhaled smoke. "Don't tell me you a weed-head?"

"I'm not. I was just trying to cover up the smell." Rica hesitated. "The smell of us," she continued. "I'm gonna introduce you to my people and get you set up with a real plug in a few days. Just let me talk to my brothers. And make sho' yo' money is right cuz they don't play."

"Fa sho'. One thing about me you gonna learn is my bread and business stay tight." Diamond gave her another kiss and gripped her chin while he stood back admiring Rica's beauty.

"Can't believe you all mine," Diamond stated with a finality just as a small knock came at the hotel room door. Rica and Diamond looked at each other and smiled bashfully.

Rica got up from the bed, crossed the room, and opened the door.

"Oooh, girl, I gotta pee!" Gina declared as soon as Rica opened the door. She made a quick dash to the bathroom.

Rica laughed, moving out of the way. She sat on the bed, sipping her drink while not daring to look in LeBaron's direction for fear of him knowing his friend had her spread-eagle moments before he and Gina walked into the hotel room. So, she decided to take the focus off herself.

"What y'all get into?" Rica asked while looking over the top of her cup. LeBaron hovered around the door while nervously shifting his eyes from the floor to Rica's face.

"Nothing. Chillin'. Went riding and ended up by the school." LeBaron let a sly smile slip past his lips.

Rica knew what that smile was about. She already knew her friend Gina; that girl loved sucking dick. And judging by the combination of relaxed and nervous demeanor of LeBaron, she could tell he was the happy recipient of Gina's desires.

"All right, girl, you ready to break out?" Gina asked before she had cleared the bathroom door.

"Yeah, I'm ready," Rica said. She stood and crossed the small room. Diamond was leaning against the dresser with his hands behind him and feet crossed at the ankles. Rica placed her hand on his chest and slipped her number into his pocket. "Call me." She whispered into his ear and gave him a quick peck on the cheek.

Diamond nodded and watched Rica turn on her heels, heading toward the hotel door. "Okay, girl." Gina let out a squeal and followed Rica out the door without saying goodbye to LeBaron.

"Damn, D. Bro, you ain't waste no time, did you?" LeBaron asked as soon as he heard the girls' car doors close.

"C'mon, man, let's clean up and get outta here. I still got some runs to make. You coming with me or you going to the crib?" Diamond continued without answering LeBaron's inquiry.

"Damn, nigga, it's like that? She must got that fire, huh?"

"Aye, nigga, mind yo' business and don't talk about my girl."

"Yo' girl? Since when, my nigga? You just met her ass, and she came here for me?" LeBaron became irritated.

"I asked her and she said she just met you yesterday. So, I thought you didn't have a claim to her since you left with ol' girl. You fucked right?" Diamond questioned LeBaron.

They'd never let a woman come between them before. They had an agreement to never date or have sex with a girl the other one had. So, this was new territory for them.

"Aye, man, you got it." LeBaron approached Diamond with his hand raised for a dap and embraced his brother.

Chapter Seventeen

BRICK BY BRICK (SPRING 1992)

Rica came through as promised. She introduced Diamond to her brothers who got the okay from their father to involve him in their family business. Her brothers started Diamond off with a couple of pounds of weed to see how fast he could move it before entrusting and upgrading him to "white." Working with Rica's family was a drug dealer's dream, because now Diamond was connected to one of the largest Puerto Rican crime families in the Americas.

In a few short months, Diamond was able to move LeBaron, Grandmother, and himself out of their two-bedroom house into a newer four-bedroom in a black, middle-class neighborhood. Grandmother didn't want to move too far away from her church. She compromised a short fifteen-minute drive to church to move to a safer part of the city. Plus, they couldn't move too far from LeBaron's high school since he'd become the starting power forward on the basketball team.

LeBaron was heading into his senior year and was in the running to be a first-round NBA draft pick. With LeBaron on the team, Marshall High School had a winning squad and were dominating the season. They were projected to win the state championship. Grandmother and Diamond were so proud of LeBaron, because even though he envied the money Diamond was bringing in through his fledgling empire, he had avoided getting involved with the drug game.

Although Diamond made sure that LaBaron had everything he could possibly want or need, LeBaron felt like he should be taking care of himself and not accepting help from his brother. He never accepted handouts before. Now the roles were reversed; LeBaron was no longer the only one involved in street life. When Diamond and his grandmother came into his life, they changed it for the better. LeBaron felt slightly guilty for not being able to fully return the favor. However, he had plans to repay Diamond and his grandmother for their generosity when he made it to the NBA. He never wanted a college degree. All he wanted was the lifestyle, accolades, and women that came along with NBA money.

"Aye, man, you coming to the game tonight, right? Six o'clock man, don't be late," LeBaron reminded Diamond.

"Chill, nigga, I'm gonna be there. I gotta keep track of your stats. You know them scouts are gonna be there tonight, too, so make sure you ball on them fools," Diamond encouraged.

"You already know," LeBaron said while dapping up Diamond.

"We gotta be at the gym by four though. Can you drop me off?" LeBaron asked Diamond. "You know I hate to drive on gameday."

"You know I got you. You almost ready?"

"Yeah, just let me get my uniform and bag and I'll meet you in the car," LeBaron replied.

Diamond gave Grandmother a kiss and reminded her that the two of them would be out late because it was game night. The whole West Side came out for the high school basketball games. All the dope dealers came to flash their cars, jewelry, and money, while alumni who didn't make it to the league or college came to the games to relive their glory days. There were also plenty of women in the stands, from young to old, on the hunt for a baller. The city streets would be packed and full of excitement tonight.

Diamond made sure his corner boys were ready to serve his customers. When there were sporting events, he always experienced a spike in business, because everyone wanted to party. People found any excuse to party and get high; it just depended on how hard they wanted to party. Diamond made sure he had a variety of work his customers would enjoy.

While he waited for LeBaron to get in the car, Diamond made a few calls on the car phone using special slang that only he and his corner boys understood. "Yo, keep them caps on the pens because night school is in session," Diamond said. This statement let his squad know to be ready for tonight because they were going to make a lot of money on game night.

After he was satisfied that business was running smoothly, he turned some music on. Diamond kept his head on a swivel. He checked his side and rearview mirrors to make sure no one caught him slipping in the driveway. He didn't keep any of his drugs at Grandmother's house, but the thieves didn't know that. To his dismay, he'd become a well-known drug dealer in some parts of the city. Diamond thought that he could anonymously amass a drug empire, but that was only reserved for the bigger bosses. The more money he made, the further he would get from the day-to-day operations and the more anonymity he would gain. This was his one and only goal: to get as far away from Chicago street life as soon as possible. Eventually, he wanted to start a family and move them out of the city.

When LeBaron came out of the house, Diamond moved his pistol from his lap to under the seat—just in case.

"Damn, nigga, took you long enough," Diamond said as LeBaron climbed into the passenger seat of his box Chevy. Diamond checked his mirrors again as he backed out of the driveway.

"Yeah, I almost forgot my lucky boxers. I had to grab them. You know I gotta have them for gameday. They ain't failed me yet," LeBaron said, smiling in Diamond's direction.

Diamond smiled in response, because he knew LeBaron was right. Every time his brother wore his lucky boxers, not only did his team win, but his game stats were off the charts: scoring, offensive and defensive rebounds, and three-pointers. LeBaron heard through the grapevine that a Duke scout may be at the game that night. The scout had already visited two of Marshall's rival high schools.

"Aye, man, I know you got a lot riding on tonight's game because the Duke scout is gonna be there. But make sure you're playing for you and not for them," Diamond said over the bass of the music.

LeBaron looked at his brother and nodded in agreement. The two shared a knowing smile. They were both well on their way to achieving their dreams. Riding through the crisp spring air of Chicago, the pair felt invincible. All of their hard work and years of turmoil were coming to an end.

Diamond's thirst for a mother figure was quenched with the love of his grandmother and the love he got from the streets. He also had Rica in his life, who had added a woman's touch. She was just as much a visionary as he was. She also had dreams of becoming a queen pin. Together, they felt invincible.

LeBaron's hoop dreams were also coming true. All the years of abandonment and foster homes became a distant memory thanks to the love and acceptance of Diamond and Grandmother. The two relaxed into the tufted, velvet seats, savoring this moment.

Diamond suddenly saw red and blue lights flashing in the rearview. He was so lost in thought, he hadn't noticed the Chicago Police pull behind him.

"Aye, keep cool, nigga. I'm gonna pull over. I wasn't speeding. They just pulling me because I'm a nigga driving a clean Chevy."

LeBaron narrowed his eyes and nodded. He already knew the drill. The CPD was notorious for harassing young black men, because they assumed they were all drug dealers and riding dirty. However, in this case the CPD would be correct.

Diamond put on his blinker, rolled down his windows, and came to a stop. He looked at the officers in his rearview mirror. Of course, one of them was the neighborhood bully Hendricks. He loved to jump out on his boys working the corner. Hendricks was a dirty cop and often took bribes. Diamond knew he could play this traffic stop one of two ways: He could bribe Hendricks, or he could play the entitled role, knowing he hadn't broken any traffic laws. Diamond also knew he had his burner under his seat. But he would never consent to a search and seizure. The officers didn't have probable cause to search his vehicle, because he hadn't broken any traffic laws.

The two officers sat in the car for a long moment and then a second CPD car pulled up behind Hendricks's car with his lights on. Diamond and LeBaron looked at each other, because a second car in a routine traffic stop was never good.

"Turn off your ignition, throw the keys on the pavement, and place your hands on the outside of the car," Hendricks's voice blared through a megaphone.

Diamond complied with the request. He knew he was past the point of negotiations. Asking the officer what the problem was and why he was being pulled over was not an option. He knew this traffic stop was about life or death and he intended to live. He would let his lawyer fight afterward.

"Aye, be cool, nigga," he mumbled under his breath to LeBaron.

They were both aware their lives now hung in the balance and there was a fifty-fifty chance they would make it out alive, depending on their next moves.

"Driver, open your car door from the outside and step out. Place your hands behind your head and interlace your fingers," Hendricks demanded over the megaphone. "Now, turn your back to us and walk backward away from the car."

Diamond complied and an officer from the second CPD car rushed up with his gun drawn and pressed the weapon to the back of Diamond's head. "Yeah, boy, thought you was the shit, huh? We got your ass now, buddy." The officer's breath lingered with the faint smell of beer, while it singed Diamond's nose. The officer placed cuffs on him. "You got anything in your pockets like drugs, guns, or needles? Huh, boy? Answer me," the officer demanded as he searched Diamond's pockets and pulled out his wallet, two condoms, and six hundred dollars in hundred-and twenty-dollar bills.

Unsatisfied that Diamond didn't have drugs or a gun on him, the officer led Diamond to the curb and slammed him down. Diamond hit the ground hard, because he didn't have his hands free to break his fall. He thought to ask the officer why he was being detained. However, he knew that the combination of ego and alcohol would only turn into a confrontation—police brutality or his own death. So, he remained quiet and sat on the curb silently.

"Passenger, open the door from the outside and step out," Hendricks commanded LeBaron over the megaphone. "Place your hands behind your head and interlace your fingers."

The other officer who had cuffed Diamond came over to place cuffs on LeBaron. Then he searched him and slammed him on the curb next to Diamond. The two brothers stared at each other with fire blazing behind their brown eyes. The pair stared at each other, their chests rising and falling in tandem while the night air pierced their nostrils. LeBaron's eyes were tearing up. Diamond knew his brother was about to lose his shit. He gave a millimeter shake of his head, unnoticeable by any onlookers, but LeBaron saw it and followed Diamond's instruction to keep quiet.

"Well, well, well, what we got here boys?" Hendricks's voice snatched the attention of LeBaron and Diamond. LeBaron's eyes widened at the sight of Diamond's Glock in an evidence bag that Officer Hendricks was holding up for them to see.

"Oh, and a Marshall uniform too, boss. I guess they were gonna go shoot someone at the game tonight." The intoxicated officer smiled with glassy eyes. "We gotta call this in, boss."

"Yeah, we do. Wait, what number is on that jersey?" Hendricks asked while crossing the back of the Chevy over to the passenger side where the other officer held LeBaron's jersey. "Number 34?"

LeBaron looked straight ahead. He could hear in the officer's tone that he recognized LeBaron's number. The whole West side was proud of Marshall and the possibility of them sweeping the high school championship.

"Aye, which one of you is LeBaron Tate?"

The pair sat silent on the pavement, not moving and not looking in the direction of the officers.

"Oh okay, got a bunch of martyrs I see. Well, I know one thing. One of your asses is going down for this gun. So, whose gun is this?" Hendricks asked while walking over to stand in front of LeBaron and Diamond. "We got you boys on intent to fire a weapon at a high school basketball game. So, whose is it?"

"It's mine," LeBaron said.

Diamond whipped his head to look at LeBaron in disbelief. They'd always agreed that if they were ever pulled over, they wouldn't answer any questions because it could be used against them.

"Wait, Tate, this is your gun?" Hendricks asked quizzically. He recognized LeBaron from the newspaper and knew that he was a star athlete slated for the first-round NBA draft or a Big-10 college. Hendricks walked over to where LeBaron sat on the curb. "Son, do you know what you're doing? If you say this is your gun, then we gotta book you," Hendricks stated. His whole demeanor had changed toward the two young men sitting on the curb. Before he pulled them over, they were just two juvenile delinquents. Now he realized one of the young man's life with promise was about to be forfeited.

"I said it's mine," LeBaron replied with fire in his eyes and tears welling. He refused to let fall.

"Okay, son." Hendricks let out a breath, hung his head and paused. "Stand up. I'm gonna read you your rights." Hendricks helped LeBaron up from the curb, read him his rights, and placed him in the back of the police car.

Hendricks walked back over to where Diamond was sitting and stared at him for a long time. Diamond didn't meet Hendricks's eyes. He didn't want the officer to see the fear and guilt on his face. His facade was cracking because his brother was taking the fall for him. Hendricks pulled Diamond to his feet and uncuffed him.

"Which precinct are you taking him to?" Diamond wanted to know so he could have his lawyer meet him at the jail. Diamond didn't want LeBaron to spend any undue time in jail. He also knew that his fingerprints were the only ones on the gun. Diamond waited for Hendricks to answer while the two stood toe-to-toe, neither one willing to break eye contact.

"The Eleventh Precinct, but we're takin' him to county based on the gun charge," Hendricks replied and turned away toward his vehicle.

Diamond took one look at his brother in the back of the police car and yelled out to Officer Hendricks, "I'm gonna follow y'all."

Hendricks nodded in agreement and continued walking. He got into the car, turned off his lights, and pulled off toward the police station.

Diamond pressed *one* on his mobile phone that was pre-programmed for his lawyer. He'd taken the advice of Rica's brothers and retained a lawyer who specializes in defending their niche clientele in the drug game. By the time he reached the county jail, he had already spoken to his attorney and told him about the illegal search and seizure. He also gave his attorney the badge number of the officer who had alcohol on his breath. His attorney thanked him for the information and headed to jail. Since LeBaron was eighteen, the police didn't need to contact a parent or guardian.

As Diamond pulled into a parking spot in front of the county jail, he called LeBaron's coach to explain his absence. "Aye coach, this is LB's cousin. We were on our way to the gym and were illegally stopped by the police. LB was detained."

"What do you mean? LB was detained by the police?" The coach questioned.

"I got my lawyer working on it and LB will be out tonight but will miss tonight's game," Diamond informed the coach.

After a long pause, the coach replied, "He knew that scouts were gonna be here tonight." He took a long pause, "I guess there's nothing else we can do for now. Look, thanks for the heads up. I gotta redo our game plan for tonight." The coach hung up without saying goodbye.

Satisfied that he covered all his bases, Diamond headed into the county jail to post bond for LeBaron. Luckily, he kept extra cash in a hidden compartment of the back seat of his car for occasions like these. He never wanted to use a bail bondsman, because their fees were too high, and he didn't need or want anyone else in his financials if it wasn't necessary.

He went inside the jail and waited for LeBaron's lawyer. It took about five hours for the police to process, charge, and post LeBaron's bond before he was released. Diamond waited for his brother outside because he couldn't stand to inhale the stale air of the county jail. He remembered the smell from having to accompany his grandmother one too many times when picking up his mother after numerous prostitution and disorderly conduct charges.

LeBaron walked out of the county jail with his head hung and his uniform slung over his right shoulder. He felt Diamond's eyes on him and lifted his eyes from the sidewalk. He didn't want his brother to see the worry in his eyes. So, he raised his head, rolled his shoulders back, and lengthened his stride toward Diamond.

"Let's get the fuck outta here, bro," LeBaron said as he walked up and dapped Diamond.

"Say less," Diamond replied.

CHAPTER EIGHTEEN

180°

LeBaron woke to the smell of bacon frying. He smiled, knowing that Grandmother was in the kitchen preparing his favorite post-game breakfast: bacon, over-easy eggs, pancakes, and fried potatoes with onions. He got out of bed and headed to the bathroom to brush his teeth and wash his face before breakfast. Grandmother didn't play about coming to the kitchen table with last night still on you.

"LeBaron!" Grandmother shouted. "Get yo' ass in here."

LeBaron tore out of the bathroom with his toothbrush still in his mouth. He'd only heard Grandmother curse a handful of times, so he knew she meant business. Diamond heard the commotion and came running out of his bedroom wearing only his sleeper shorts.

"What the hell is this?" Grandmother asked while facing LeBaron, then motioning to the TV.

The morning news was on and it was showing a picture of LeBaron's mugshot from the night before.

"Turn it up," Diamond demanded, so he could hear the news anchor.

"The Chicago Police Department is cracking down on gun violence as we move from spring into summer when gun deaths soar. Last night this man, eighteen-year-old LeBaron Tate, was arrested on possession of a firearm during a routine traffic stop. Mr. Tate is also the power forward for Marshall Metropolitan High School. Mr. Tate was unavailable for questioning and is out on bond pending his charges. Mr. Tate is also slated to go in the first-round of the NBA draft this season, but he was not present at last night's game against their rival school. We will keep you posted as this story develops," the news anchor concluded.

"Such a shame," the co-anchor lamented and moved on to the next news topic.

Grandmother grabbed the remote, turned to face LeBaron, and sat in her favorite recliner. LeBaron and Diamond followed suit and sat on the couch. LeBaron put his head in his hands, shaking his head, and began to sniffle. Diamond didn't dare look his grandmother in the eye; she would know it was his fault that LeBaron was on the news.

"No wonder I had seven voicemails on the machine when I woke up this morning," said Grandmother. "I didn't pay it any mind because I knew both you boys were home and safe. Whoever is on those voicemails must've seen the story on the six o'clock news." Grandmother was putting the story together, bit by bit.

She silently waited for LeBaron to give her an explanation. With his head still in his hands, LeBaron explained what happened.

"Me and D got pulled over last night for nothin'. We wasn't speeding or nothin'. Then the police told us to get out the car with our hands up and they searched the car and found D's gun," LeBaron's voice cracked.

Grandmother's head quickly turned to Diamond. "You make this right. That's all I'm gonna say. I'm glad y'all safe cuz you already know how it could've gone wrong. All I care about is you both coming home safe. That's all. You hear me, LB?" Grandmother waited for LeBaron to meet her eyes, full of worry and concern.

"Yes, ma'am," LeBaron weakly replied.

"You hear me, Diamond?" Grandmother demanded.

"Yes, ma'am," Diamond replied. "I'll make it right, I promise."

However, Diamond wasn't so sure he would be able to make things completely right, especially since LeBaron's mugshot was already on the news and the whole city would know about his arrest by noon. He was also confident that by tomorrow the story would be uncontrollable and morph into a life of its own, no matter what the truth was. The current narrative was that the starting high school basketball player was arrested on a gun charge and missed one of the most important games leading up to the state championships.

"I already got my lawyer on the case," Diamond confirmed while looking at LeBaron, who still held his head in his hands while frustratingly rubbing his waves. LeBaron snapped out of his contemplation and looked at Diamond with pleading eyes reddened from his night of crying.

Grandmother looked from one set of brown eyes to the other while her shoulders sagged in disappointment. Chicago swallowed young men up and she thought herself foolish to think her boys would be exempt from the harsh streets. She had been hopeful up until this moment when her greatest fears came to fruition with the airing of the news segment. She had faith that Diamond would make things right for LeBaron, but she knew deep in her heart that LeBaron's basketball days were behind him. The news would sensationalize the story whether LeBaron was found guilty or not, and that made her worried for her boys and their future.

"Y'all get cleaned up for breakfast. LB, you gonna need your strength for the days ahead, baby. You hear me, LB?" Grandmother asked. Her pitch increased with her second question as she noticed LeBaron lost in deep thought. She could see him understanding in real time that his basketball career was over too.

LeBaron slowly rose from where he was planted on the couch. His limbs felt heavy with regret. He was disappointed that they were targeted that night and pulled over for *driving while black*. He was enraged, because he knew that all his hard work had now been in vain.

As LeBaron walked to the bathroom, the house phone's shrill cry rang out. The three looked at one another, wondering who could be calling this early on a Saturday morning. LeBaron rolled his shoulders back, balled his fist, and crossed the room in three strides to reach the phone that sat beside Grandmother's brown, leather recliner.

"Hello." LeBaron's voice came out in a scratchy, hollow tone as he anticipated the caller. He was silent, listening to the voice on the other end. Diamond noted LeBaron's jaw clenching and his eyes blinking rapidly as he attempted to hold back his tears.

Diamond and his grandmother crossed the room to LeBaron's side, trying to hear what the caller was saying.

"Okay, I understand, coach," LeBaron croaked. His voice cracked on his last word. He hung up the receiver, avoiding Diamond's and Grandmother's eyes. There was nothing to say, because everyone in the room knew that LeBaron was let go from the team.

"I'll be back," LeBaron said while still avoiding the gazes of the two people he loved most in the world. He stormed toward the door and snagged Diamond's keys from the nail that held them. LeBaron left the house without uttering another word. Diamond and Grandmother looked after him with worry on their faces.

LeBaron fired up the engine and peeled out. He needed space to think and process his next steps. All his dreams of going to the NBA had been shattered overnight. LeBaron aimlessly drove around the city. His body instinctively knew where it wanted to go as he turned the steering wheel hand-over-hand into the gravel parking lot of his favorite park with a basketball court. LeBaron parked the car and sat staring at the court with hot tears streaming down his face. He used his shirt sleeve to wipe away the tears. He felt the need to put his body in motion, so he turned off the car and grabbed his basketball that was still in his duffel bag from the night before.

LeBaron walked toward the court, ignoring the early morning chill that bit his cheeks. It was still early March, and spring hadn't relieved Chicago of her bitter cold yet. Plus, LeBaron was still in his PJ pants and long-sleeved shirt he wore to bed. The wind urged him to get his blood pumping to quiet his chattering teeth. LeBaron started off with a few three-pointers with thoughts of his coach's words echoing through his memory.

LB, we have to let you go, buddy, until all this blows over. This is coming from the school district, not me. But I wanted to be the one who told you. We're gonna fight this all the way, LB. We need you on the team. And don't worry about the recruiters. You haven't been found guilty of any crimes, but I'm gonna be honest. It may scare away some. But don't worry about that now. Get a good lawyer and stay up on your game. I'll call you when I have any updates.

LeBaron ran full speed at the rim with Coach Chambers's words reverberating. He dunked his ball and the swish of the net whizzed in his ears as both feet came down on the court. LeBaron dribbled, posted up, and pretended he was playing against his greatest opponent. He was so engrossed in his own thoughts that he was oblivious to the car that pulled up next to Diamond's Chevy. Rica got out of the car and headed toward the courts where LeBaron was still unaware of her presence. Rica stopped halfway to the courts and cupped her hands around her mouth in a makeshift megaphone. She called LeBaron's name, but the combination of his thoughts and the bouncing basketball filled the empty space of silence across the court, making it impossible for LeBaron to hear her.

Irritated, Rica moved closer. As she got closer, she noted he still had on his PJs that he'd sweated through completely. It was clear that he was not in a good headspace. Rica didn't want to startle him, so she walked to the edge of the court and called his name again.

"LeBaron...LB."

LeBaron paused mid-pump, turned toward Rica and froze. His mouth was open and his eyebrows were knitted together. He wondered why she was there. LeBaron slowly lowered his basketball from above his head and held it underneath his left arm.

"What you doin' here, Rica?" LeBaron panted. His heart was hammering out of his chest from the exertion his body was demanding of it.

"Just got off the phone with Diamond and he was worried," Rica replied with a shy shrug.

She hadn't had much contact with LeBaron after she and Diamond made it official after the night that was supposed to be *their* first date. It had been a few months since she saw him, and his face seemed like it had aged ten years.

LeBaron shifted his weight and scowled. "I said, what you doin' here?" He didn't give a damn if Diamond sent her. *And why would he send her, of all people,* he wondered.

As if she read his thoughts, Rica stammered, "Di-Diamond didn't send me. He just told me what happened and said you took off in his car. I decided to come here and look for you because he was worried about you.”

“Is that right?” LeBaron replied condescendingly.

Rica squinted and focused on LeBaron’s deep brown eyes that reflected fire, disappointment, and regret all at once.

“Yeah, that’s right. Why don’t you come on and get in the car and warm up. You out here in your jammies.” Rica pointed at LeBaron’s damp clothes.

LeBaron looked down at his shirt as if seeing it for the first time. He shifted his weight, now more conscious of himself and surroundings.

“You didn’t answer my question, Rica. Why the fuck you here?” LeBaron demanded.

His eyes pierced through Rica’s soul, making her breath hitch in her throat. She dryly swallowed the words that were on the tip of her tongue. She wanted to tell LeBaron that his brother was worried about him and she was too. She wanted to assure him that everything would be all right and that Diamond was working on his lawyer. She wanted to hug him and comfort him. *No, that’s not right,* Rica thought as she shook her head. She didn’t want to hug him, because he was Diamond’s brother. The man who she loved and was planning on building a drug empire with. The only man’s dick that ever graced her tongue. *Diamond,* she reminded herself. That’s why she was there—for him.

LeBaron slowly advanced toward Rica, rolling his basketball from one palm to the other, closing the distance between them. Rica shook her head, breaking her internal dialogue. She could see the fine mist of steam rising from LeBaron’s body in the crisp Chicago air. He looked like an angel walking in clouds with his brown orbs darkening while targeting hers. LeBaron dipped his head as his eyes grew low and he entered Rica’s space.

Rica stiffened upon LeBaron's approach as her mouth unwillingly held itself open, attempting to formulate the words that would halt his advances, but she felt an all-too-familiar throb in her pussy taking control. As LeBaron got close, Rica lifted her eyes to meet his gaze as he towered over her five-foot-five frame.

"I—" Rica tried to form words as LeBaron's mouth came crashing down over hers. Rica's breath was taken away as she felt the unexpected warmth of LeBaron's lips. His tongue found its way to part her lips. Her head was dizzy with confusion as she tried to reconcile the warmth radiating from her moist center. LeBaron grabbed the back of Rica's loose, low ponytail, deepening their kiss.

"You were supposed to be mine first," LeBaron growled into Rica's mouth.

LeBaron grabbed the small of Rica's back, holding her close to his body. She felt his dick hardening against her hip and down her thigh. She returned LeBaron's kiss while her heart hammered in her chest. She felt LeBaron smile into her lips and her feet left the ground as he walked forward. Rica was completely lost in their kiss until she felt her body moving, broke their kiss, and opened her eyes.

Rica searched LeBaron's face for some semblance of Diamond's brother, but all she saw was a man on fire with passion and eyes for only her. LeBaron noted Rica's body tensing up and looked deeply into her eyes, searching for the *yes* he craved. His body, mind, and soul needed a release and Rica was the woman to give him the relief he sought.

Rica stared into his eyes and gave a small nod as she felt her nipples pebble and strain against her bra. LeBaron nodded in return and quickly moved toward the park pavilion. He pressed Rica up against the enormous gray stone of the pavilion pillar. Rica sucked in air as the cold of the stone penetrated through her jean jacket. LeBaron raised Rica's shirt and freed one of her breasts from her bra. He devoured it, sucking and teasing her nipple with precision. LeBaron moaned in satisfaction as he freed her other breast. Rica hissed at the cold touch of his hand, but the coldness was short-lived as LeBaron engulfed her other breast in his hot mouth.

Rica lost all sense of time and space. She greedily shoved her right hand into LeBaron's pajama pants. A smile crossed her lips as she discovered LeBaron's massive girth and length. Rica stroked and gripped LeBaron's dick as they massaged their tongues deep into each other's mouths. Rica felt LeBaron's dick harden even more, and pre-cum oozed from his dick. Rica used the natural lubrication to glide up and down his shaft.

"Suck it, baby," LeBaron requested with yearning.

Rica pushed LeBaron back a few inches and pressed her back off the pillar. She squatted as her knees hit the cold, dormant earth. She greedily eyed LeBaron's dick. She wanted to remember every curve of his dick to make her betrayal worthwhile. She opened her mouth and took LeBaron inside her hot mouth as her breath rose in puffs of vapor in the early morning hours. Rica worked her head back and forth, enjoying the taste of LeBaron on her tongue.

LeBaron let out a guttural groan as he tipped his head back and enjoyed the attention.

"Let me feel you, baby. Stand up," LeBaron cooed. He gently placed his hands on Rica's shoulders and unexpectedly spun her around. LeBaron pulled down Rica's Nike windbreaker pants to her thighs and rubbed his thick girth on her ass. His other hand burrowed under her shirt and found her breast, teasing her nipple between his thumb and pointer finger. Rica let out a moan of pleasure while she bit her lip in anticipation of LeBaron entering her. She didn't have to wait long.

LeBaron placed his other hand on Rica's back to bend her over. He angled himself at her center and glided himself against her soft folds.

Rica bent over further, closed her eyes, and waited for the suspense of penetration, but LeBaron took his time as if they were not outside in a park.

"Damn, baby, you wet for me, huh?" LeBaron asked in a sexy growl.

Rica nodded, going crazy waiting to feel LeBaron inside her walls. *Please hurry up*, she begged in her head.

As soon as the thought passed through her mind, LeBaron thrust himself into Rica in one motion. The sudden fullness took her breath away and LeBaron felt her tense.

"I got you, baby. I got you," LeBaron's deep tenor croaked into Rica's ear as she felt his warm stomach lean onto her ass cheeks and back. She nodded and felt her walls loosen. So did LeBaron. He pumped in and out of Rica as they both panted and rocked into each other's rhythm. LeBaron reached around to find Rica's pearl, stroking it and pounding into her with the same reckless ferocity.

Rica's legs began to shake, her orgasm rising at her core. "Oh my god," she panted. She had never had an orgasm that fast in her life.

"Yeah, baby, come all over this dick," LeBaron encouraged her as he felt his sac begin to tighten in anticipation of his own release.

Rica let go and felt her release as she increased her rhythm, sliding back and forth onto LeBaron. Rica's pants were now around her ankles as she tried to find some stability with the stone pillars to hold her upright on her weakening legs. As she found her release, so did LeBaron, with a loud grunt that echoed throughout the concrete pavilion. LeBaron felt his sac tighten and the shudder of his release fill Rica as he grabbed her closer.

"Mmm, take all this nut, baby. Keep it open for me," LeBaron demanded as the last quivers of his release left his body.

He slowly removed himself from Rica as the pair came back down to earth, letting their heartbeats return to normal. Rica, on wobbly legs, slowly reached down to pull up her pants and panties as she felt her softened center release some of LeBaron that was slowly leaking out of her. LeBaron pulled up his pants and staggered to a nearby picnic table underneath the pavilion while Rica turned around and pressed her head to the cold stones. As her body became less sensitive, she opened her eyes and looked at her surroundings. She couldn't believe herself; she just fucked her boyfriend's brother. And to make matters worse—if they could get any worse—she fucked him outside in the park where anyone could've rolled up and caught them.

"Come here," LeBaron's voice broke through Rica's thoughts.

Rica inhaled a deep breath, bouncing herself free from the stone wall. Her feet felt ladened with guilt as she walked over to where LeBaron sat on the bench. He reached out and grasped both of her hands and looked up into her eyes.

"I will never forget this moment for the rest of my life. It was special, and you gave me what I needed. I didn't know what I was about to do. Hell, I still don't. My life as I know it is over. Basketball is over for me."

Rica tensed and prepared herself to refute LeBaron's words, but he tightened his grip on her hands.

"Look, it's okay. I've been up all night thinking about it. I've made peace with it," LeBaron looked earnest in his admission. "I think it's time for me to put all my energy into something else."

LeBaron paused, looking into Rica's eyes with tears forming at the edges. She waited for him to finish his thought.

"I wanna be the biggest fucking drug dealer in Chicago, then the world." LeBaron's dark eyes narrowed and focused on Rica, letting her know he was serious.

Rica took a step back and snatched her hands free from his, leaving LeBaron in shock.

"Well, you can't be the biggest fucking drug dealer in the city because that's gonna be me," Rica countered.

The two let each other's words penetrate the crisp, early morning air.

LeBaron leaned back on the picnic table. "I see. Does my brother know this?"

Rica shrugged one shoulder. "I may have mentioned it."

Again, silence.

"Well, why don't we do that shit together? We can have each other's backs. With your connects, D's hustle, and my grind, nobody will be able to touch us," LeBaron said. Silence stretched between the two.

"Whatchu think?" LeBaron impatiently awaited Rica's answer.

Rica shifted her weight, thinking about LeBaron's proposal and how it could work. She thought of the future and how each of their strengths would build their empire. She started to see a plan forming. LeBaron smiled, because he could see the sparkle in her eyes as well. He listened to Diamond talk about how smart Rica was whenever the couple wasn't conjoined.

"Maybe it could work. But on one condition." Rica raised her pointer finger and closed the distance between her and LeBaron.

"Damn, why you walking up on me? What?" LeBaron asked.

"You never tell Diamond about this." She motioned between the two of them. "I don't give a fuck if you have a change of heart or start to feel guilty and want to clear your conscious. We take this shit to the fucking grave, my G."

Rica and LeBaron stared at each other, knowing that if Diamond ever found out about the two of them, they would both be dead.

"I can agree to that. But talk to yourself about feeling guilty and shit. You'll break before I do."

"Not a fucking chance, nigga. I love D and wanna be his wife one day," Rica admitted.

LeBaron replied with a snort of disbelief. "Yeah, okay, miss wifey. You still got my dick on your breath and my seed in your pussy, talking about marrying my brother."

Rica cocked her head to the side in disbelief. *This nigga!* she thought. She couldn't believe that LeBaron had the nerve to disrespect her to her face after sharing an intimate moment together. Things quickly turned left in the hood, and she was always ready to go toe-to-toe with whoever was foolish enough to disrespect her.

Rica turned the spaghetti strap of her small, crossbody purse she had twisted around her body and popped open the metallic clasp. She quickly pulled out her .22 and pointed it in LeBaron's direction.

LeBaron narrowed his eyes. "You pull that shit, you better kill me."

"Think I won't? Nigga, try me! Don't you ever in your fucking life disrespect me," Rica spat while holding the .22 with a two-hand grip like her father taught her.

LeBaron knew that Rica would shoot and ask questions later. After a moment passed between the two, LeBaron yielded.

"You got it," he said, holding both his hands up in surrender.

"Like I was saying, you keep your mouth shut about what happened here today. And it's never gonna happen again, okay? And I will marry D," Rica demanded as she lowered her weapon and secured it in her bag.

"Whatever you say, Rica. Let's just focus on business. I'll bring it up to D about me joining the business."

"Okay, cool," Rica replied, adjusting her purse's shoulder strap. Then Rica nervously looked over her shoulder toward their cars.

"Let me leave first, then you can leave after me. I'm gonna go to the store and pick up some shit to get fresh, then to the crib. You go home and wash me off you, ASAP. Don't want that nigga to smell me on you. He swears he knows what I smell like."

"What you mean, some shit to get fresh?" LeBaron was curious.

"Getting some shit to take a bath in. Vinegar and some other shit. I gotta get you off me. I'm not tryna get caught slippin'."

LeBaron raised his eyebrow in curiosity, because he had no idea what bathing in vinegar had to do with washing off the scent of another man's dick. He was all for it as long as they didn't get caught.

LeBaron nodded and a smile splayed across his face as he watched Rica walk to her car thinking that it was gonna take more than a bath to wash him off her. He could even tell her walk had changed. He looked after her in awe. Of all the girls in the world he would fuck in a park, Rica was the last girl to cross his mind. He walked back over to the side of the court where he dropped his basketball and went back to shooting a few more hoops until he left. A smile tickled the corner of his lips the whole way home.

CHAPTER NINETEEN

GOOD BUSINESS (FALL 1992)

Diamond agreed to let LeBaron join his business enterprise, with himself as the leader and Rica second in command. Rica was true to her word and set up another meeting with her brothers' supplier to request more product. Their business was growing so fast, the trio had to hire people they had grown up with whom they trusted.

LeBaron's lawyer was able to get his case thrown out due to harassment. Their lawyer also took the issue a step further and filed a civil suit against the city of Chicago for harassment and racial profiling. They were awarded six million in damages, which was unheard of at that time. The Chicago Police Department was put on notice that if they ever harassed Diamond or LeBaron again, their lawyer would bankrupt the CPD.

Without the real threat of being arrested, Diamond was able to run his drug business with impunity. However, the threat of a federal investigation was all too real. Neither Diamond nor LeBaron were stupid enough to play Russian roulette with the Feds. So, they kept their drug sales and spending under the radar. They never had extravagant cars, jewelry, or clothes.

LeBaron's lawyer secured an interview on WGN-TV that would air on all the time slots to clear his client's name in the court of public opinion. Although the local community believed in LeBaron's innocence, the college scout visits dried up, just as he'd expected. But now the trio had the seed money from LeBaron's settlement to completely cut out Fat Ron as their connect and get their drugs directly from the connect that Rica's brothers used.

Little did Rica know, her father was securing the family's drug connections while in prison. He was validating them with the top crime families in Puerto Rico. His drug and prison connects secured them a small piece of a large family crime syndicate in Puerto Rico that had to be solidified by marriage and money.

Rica's father betrothed the daughters of the highest-level members of the drug syndicate in Puerto Rico to her brothers. Rica's oldest brother moved back to Puerto Rico to learn the business while she and her middle brother continued operations in Chicago.

"Meet me at the spot tonight to go over some business," Diamond whispered into LeBaron's ear as he dapped him up.

LeBaron nodded in agreement, wondering what Diamond wanted to talk about that had to wait until they got to their warehouse. Later that night, LeBaron pulled up to the warehouse to meet Diamond. Despite knowing they had spotters on the roofs of the surrounding buildings pulling surveillance, LeBaron stepped out apprehensively, keeping his head on a swivel. His eyes quickly darted left and right to make sure he wasn't being watched or ambushed. He tentatively opened the door, finding Diamond and Rica waiting for him.

LeBaron walked up to Diamond, dapped him up, and gave Rica a thin-lipped nod. She barely noticed his presence with her nose in the air. LeBaron ignored her antics, because he didn't want to draw any undue attention to the two of them or raise any suspicions with Diamond. His brother loved Rica, and he didn't want to take that away from him when all he and Rica shared was a primal desire for one another's flesh. They'd had sex several times after the park incident. They tried to stay away from one another, but the sexual pull was too strong for either of them to resist.

They would mostly hook up when Diamond went on trips outside of Chicago to build relationships and do business reconnaissance. The last time they met up, LeBaron said he felt bad about cheating with his brother's girl and wanted to cut the relationship off. But Rica threatened to somehow let it slip that they were fucking and that they'd both die. She wasn't ready to let LeBaron go. He was always nervous when Diamond called an impromptu meeting. He never knew if it was because his brother had found out about him and his girl and was ready to end his life or if he just wanted to talk about business. So, he had to play it cool.

"What's up, D?" LeBaron questioned. "Why you call me all the way down here that couldn't wait until tomorrow?"

"I been thinking it's time to expand our operation outside of Chicago and I want to discuss it with you. Rica don't think it's a good idea, but I wanna hear what you got to say." Diamond walked over to a semi-circle of chairs arranged on the side of the warehouse.

LeBaron followed suit and sat down while Rica followed and angrily crossed her legs. She knew she would be outvoted by the two of them, but she wanted to hear Diamond's explanation as to why he thought that an expansion outside of Chicago would help build their empire.

"Let me hear your plan, bruh," LeBaron said.

Diamond laid out his well thought-out plan. He'd already done some reconnaissance in Springfield—the state's capital city, although everybody thinks it's Chicago. Springfield had the potential to be a money maker if they marketed sections of their business to different demographics. He knew there was a market for cocaine for the white boys who worked in government and crack for the corner boys to sell. Diamond also told LB and Rica about his plans to start a real estate company where they could buy trailer parks, fix them up, and flip them with little to no risk and high profit margins. He wanted some parts of their business to be legitimate to cover for the illegal activities. Collecting rent was a great way to wash their illegal money if the books were done right.

Since LB had an interest in finance and had graduated from high school with honors, Diamond had him take a few classes at Chicago State. Because they had income from their business, LeBaron didn't need scholarships to afford his education. Through his classes, LeBaron made some business contacts who taught him business law too. He also kept his classmates supplied with uppers to handle their rigorous coursework at the university. Diamond knew that LeBaron's education would help their business in the long run by finding new ways to launder their money.

During their warehouse meeting, Diamond talked about how disjointed the major players were in Springfield. There was room for growth for the trio to come in and take over because of their superior product and competitive prices. He'd spoken to a few people during his trips to Springfield, and he was confident they were ready to make a move and become the major supplier in the area.

The drug dealers he talked to and gained rapport with were tired of scrimping by and making small change. They had plans to get their families out of the hood and attain the American dream by any means necessary.

LeBaron listened to his brother's plan closely and asked questions when he needed clarification. He was mostly on board with the move but still had a few questions. Most importantly, he wanted to know where Rica stood, because her own selfish desires to be a queen pin could deter their plans. He was afraid Diamond would put too much stock in her feelings and yield to whatever she thought rather than thinking rationally about their collective goals.

"Rica, what you think?" LeBaron asked after Diamond finished his pitch.

"I think we got a good thing here in Chicago. We're gaining more turf every month and making a good profit, too—more than we thought possible. We also have the bosses in Puerto Rico to answer to," Rica replied.

"Yeah, but, babe, didn't we say we want an empire? We can't do that shit by being focused only on Chicago. I think you being short-sighted, boo," Diamond said gently.

"Have you talked to Grandmother?" LeBaron asked tentatively. He knew that if their grandmother didn't approve of the move, talking about expanding their territory further south would be futile.

"Not yet," Diamond said, wiping his face in frustration. "We should meet up with her tomorrow and talk it out with her."

LeBaron nodded in agreement.

"So, if y'all granny don't approve of an expansion then y'all ain't gonna do it?" Rica questioned, getting louder with each word. "I mean, next you gonna ask her if it's okay what draws to wear? I mean fuck!"

"Aye, watch yo' fucking mouth!" Diamond popped off before LeBaron had the chance to check Rica's reckless mouth.

There were two things neither Diamond nor LeBaron played about, and those two things were God and their grandmother, in that order. If their grandmother didn't approve, then it wouldn't happen, period.

LeBaron had a snarl on his face. "We'll all ask Grandmother tomorrow. We'll tell her our plan and see what she says. Either she gives us her blessing or not. Either way is a win, whatever *we* decide," LeBaron said with finality and stood.

Getting ready to leave, he dapped up Diamond. He didn't like being in Rica's presence any more than he had to. Plus, she was looking especially delectable tonight in her waist-length fox fur jacket that was way too hot for the late spring weather. Her face naturally glowed with a hint of cherry lip gloss that was intoxicating from where his chair was placed in their small semi-circle. Before little LB stood at attention, picturing Rica's glossy lips wrapped around him, he made his exit.

Chapter Twenty

DONE IN THE DARK (SUMMER 1995)

"Hey, Grandmother, can you come in here for a moment, please?" Diamond yelled into the kitchen.

He thought this would be the perfect time to tell Grandmother that he was moving to Springfield for six months, now that they had the capital and product to expand their business into a new city. After LeBaron almost caught a case and they won a lawsuit against the CPD, Diamond and LeBaron decided it would be best to come clean with Grandmother about Diamond's occupation as a drug dealer. They didn't want to hold anything back from her, because they could potentially put her in danger if she wasn't aware of their ambitions.

Grandmother was characteristically understanding when they explained their level of involvement in Chicago's drug game. She knew the streets of Chicago were rough and that if you stayed long enough you were bound to get mixed up in some shit. She just didn't want her boys involved with gangs. She told them once that the only people who benefited from joining a gang were the people in charge. She also felt that if they were going to get money, the illegal route, the least they could do was be their own bosses. So, LeBaron and Diamond took her advice to heart and set out to become the biggest, most cunning drug dealers Chicago had ever seen.

It had been two years since LeBaron, Diamond, and Rica discussed broadening their business to include cities in central Illinois. They'd all been working diligently to chisel out new territory that had already been claimed by other gangs and crews. But those types of moves were usually a catalyst for bloodshed, and Diamond wanted to avoid violence until it was necessary.

So, after two years of hustling and grinding, the trio agreed that Diamond would travel back and forth to Springfield, and they would decide—as a crew and with Grandmother's blessing—if a more permanent move would be needed in the future. As for now, Diamond traveled about three hours south of Chicago to the new city to keep an eye on their fledgling investment while LeBaron and Rica kept an eye on business back home.

"Gimme a minute. I'm tryna' finish the gravy for these poke chops," Grandmother yelled.

Diamond and LeBaron made themselves comfortable on the dark green leather couch but left a space in the middle for Rica. A knock came lightly on the screen door.

"Now who is that?" Grandmother hollered from the kitchen.

"It's Rica, Grandmother," Diamond shouted.

Diamond heard a grunt from the kitchen and decided to ignore it. He hoped his grandmother was going to be on her best behavior today since Rica was arriving. Grandmother kissed her teeth and shook her head in disapproval while the sound of her house shoes could be heard shuffling throughout the kitchen. She made her disdain of Rica very clear, but she never gave a specific reason why she didn't care for her.

The trio sat nervously on the couch, the squeak of Rica's bare thighs on the leather betraying her every move. They patiently waited for Grandmother to come to a stopping point while making dinner.

"Now what's this all about?" Grandmother asked while untying her apron. She looped it over her head to remove it, eyeing the pensive faces of Diamond, LeBaron, and Rica as they awaited her entrance into the living room. Diamond began talking before his grandmother settled in.

"Grandmother, we all been thinking about expanding the business further south, as you know. Cuz we wanna have a slice of our own pie and the market is ripe for the taking. We got the product, *and* we got the people to move it." Diamond paused, letting his words sink in.

Grandmother sat, unloading her 215-pound frame into her matching recliner. She continued to listen to Diamond's plan all the way through without interrupting him with questions. She believed in letting a person get their thoughts out before interrupting them, and she also expected the same. The only way the trio knew she was listening was by her eyes darting to each of their faces, studying their reactions while Diamond revealed his plan. She noted Rica's body language was fidgety when Diamond mentioned moving away six months at a time to oversee business operations. She also read LeBaron's body language and surmised that he would support his brother no matter what. But then Grandmother noticed that when LeBaron shifted, Rica slightly shifted as well. The leather couch amplified their movements. Her keen intuition noted that Rica's knees were slightly turned toward LeBaron instead of Diamond. She sat back in observance, because if she knew anything in all her fifty-six years of living, it was that the body never lied.

Diamond grew more nervous as he took in Grandmother's energy shift. He assumed it was because she didn't support his plans. So, Diamond hurried through the rest of his plan and nervously asked if she had any questions.

"So, who would stay in Springfield to keep an eye on the business?" Grandmother asked.

"As you know, I've been the one going back and forth and getting everything set up. I was thinking that Rica could move with me and LB can stay here and run the business in Chicago," Diamond stated.

"I see," Grandmother replied, nodding while raising her right eyebrow.

Diamond began to stutter nervously, "I-i-i-it would only be for six months at that, that I would be gone. Then, I would come back and check on the business here because we don't wanna talk too much on the phone, ya' know?"

Grandmother cut in, "LB needs to go with you and Rica needs to stay here near *her own* family."

Grandmother's statement carried finality and authority, which only confused Diamond—particularly her use of the phrase *own family*.

He felt that the plan he presented was well thought-out and sensical. He wanted to be with Rica, so leaving her behind in Chicago was not an option. Diamond was confused about why his grandmother never liked Rica. For the first time, he started feeling angry with Grandmother for her unsubstantiated distaste for Rica. His grandmother was never warm toward his girl, which was odd because his grandmother was one of the nicest and most giving individuals he'd ever met. He asked her about her dislike for Rica one day, but his grandmother just dismissed his accusations as his imagination. But he knew better. He knew Grandmother didn't like Rica; he just didn't know why.

Rica, who was quiet up until that point, was offended. She wondered why their grandmother singled her out to stay back. And to stay near *her family* of all things. She instantly got angry.

Who the fuck does this old lady think she is? She don't run shit! Most of all me, she thought.

Grandmother saw the disgust on Rica's face. The young woman hadn't learned how to hide her emotions yet, and Grandmother let out a chuckle that took the trio by surprise.

"Baby, you need to stay home cuz you having a baby of your own." Grandmother's words hung in the air.

"What you talkin' about, a baby?" Diamond asked, puzzled.

"Ask your girl. Y'all been using protection?"

"Dang, Grandmother, you all in the business," Diamond retorted, now embarrassed that his sex life was on display.

Grandmother didn't miss LeBaron avoiding her knowing gaze. She also saw Rica's shoulders sag with realization. Rica had heard that old people could tell if you were pregnant just by looking at you, but of course, she had never experienced the phenomenon herself. She thought that maybe she could be pregnant but wasn't for sure. She hadn't taken a pregnancy test, because she was uncertain about whether she was going to keep the baby or not if she was pregnant.

"She on the pill." Diamond interrupted everyone's thoughts.

Rica hung her head.

"Right, baby?"

"I wasn't sure, babe. I haven't taken a test yet," Rica looked in Diamond's direction with huge tears pooling at the bottom of her honey-colored eyes.

Diamond got up from the couch, kneeled in front of Rica and gave her a tight bear hug and pressed her to the back of the couch, overjoyed. He always wanted a family of his own and he knew that he wanted to marry Rica one day. Rica allowed her tears to fall as she shut her eyes and felt love wash over her in a wave of heat and desire.

Diamond released Rica, wildly searching her face, trying to see the tell-tale signs that his grandmother had seen to predict her pregnancy but couldn't. He wiped away her tears as he lovingly kissed her cheeks.

LeBaron reached down to dap Diamond while raising him into an embrace. However, the slightly nervous quiver to LB's congratulations was not lost on Grandmother. She knew her boys all too well.

"Well, baby, it's time you get a test and figure out what you gonna do." Grandmother gave Rica a straight-faced nod with her eyes darting from Diamond to LeBaron.

What the fuck? Rica thought for a moment. *Does Grandmother know something is going on between me and LB or was she just talking about me having to make a choice about whether to keep the baby or not?*

"Well, this has been heavy and you two have a lot to talk about. But baby or not, I think Rica should stay here and handle the business while you and LB go down to Springfield. You know you got some cousins down there that are hungry and ready." Grandmother nodded in Diamond's direction.

Diamond was doing a poor job of managing his emotions. He had thought Rica was on birth control all this time. That's why he didn't hesitate to spread his seed freely. "Yeah, we got a lot to talk about," Diamond muttered under his breath while his adrenaline began to subside.

"Boys, go for a ride. I wanna talk to Rica by myself," Grandmother said sweetly, and the boys obliged her wishes.

"We gonna sit down and eat. Go to the store and get me some white bread for these poke chops. LB, you know you can't eat 'em without white bread," she said with a knowing smile.

Grandmother walked to the kitchen, expecting Rica to follow as the boys went out the front door.

Grandmother shuffled to the stove, her worn grey house shoes on the linoleum floor, the only sound in the kitchen, and fixed them both plates. The gravy had started to burn, so Grandmother ditched the idea of smothered pork chops.

"So, why you tryna trap my grandson?" Grandmother asked while sliding a plate of pork chops, green beans, and mashed potatoes topped with bacon bits.

"Huh?" Rica replied.

"You huh, you heard," Grandmother replied smartly and waited for Rica's answer.

"I don't know what you're talking about." Rica shook her head emphatically.

"Cut the shit, little girl," Grandmother demanded and leaned in, pointing her finger in Rica's face. "You never got on birth control, thinking you was gonna trap my grandson cuz he a good nigga and will take care of his seed. But that ain't his seed, is it, gal?" Grandmother's sepia eyes burned into Rica's honey-colored ones.

Deafening silence pierced the air while Grandmother awaited Rica's lies.

"No, I hadn't started my pills yet. But I was gonna go get them, but I got busy. And it is his baby!" Rica lied.

"So, you got time to run around the city fucking, but not enough time to take yo' ass to Planned Parenthood to get on birth control. And I know my grandson, he woulda wrapped it up if he knew you wasn't on birth control. So, that's how I know yo' little ass lied about being on it." Grandmother leaned in. Her words pierced Rica's ears like an arrow hitting its bullseye. "And you want me to believe that's my grandson's baby?' Grandmother questioned and let out a boisterous laugh.

"I ain't been with nobody else," Rica yelled unconvincingly.

"Now, you and I both know that ain't true. And if Diamond ever finds out..." Grandmother trailed off. "You better hope it is and he doesn't."

Just as she finished her last sentence, the front door cracked open. LeBaron and Diamond entered and walked into the kitchen. Both young men stopped their haughty chatter when they noted the serious looks on Grandmother's and Rica's faces.

"Damn, what's all the long faces for?" Diamond questioned as he got closer, searching Rica's face.

"Oh, nothing, just having a little girl chat is all, said Grandmother. "Ain't that right, Rica?"

"Yeah," Rica replied flatly.

"Y'all wash up while I fix y'all plates and we can all eat." Grandmother nodded sweetly in LeBaron's direction as he shifted his gaze from hers.

***

Rica decided to keep her baby. She didn't want to lose Diamond or her fairytale of them being the "first family" in their drug empire that they could pass on to their children. When she finally made it to the doctor, she was further along than she thought. She found out that she had an incompetent cervix, so her doctor suggested a procedure to close her cervix with stitches to prevent preterm birth, and she was put on bedrest.

Rica delivered the baby only one month prematurely, and Diamond was able to be present for the emergency C-section, which made Rica feel like they were lucky to be starting their family. She willfully put a fortress around her mind to block all the memories she shared with LeBaron, and she resigned herself to having Diamond's baby. She also bartered with God that if her baby girl was delivered safely, then she would never indulge her fleshly desires for LeBaron again.

"Let me see my grandbaby," Grandmother demanded, reaching for eight hour-old Camilla.

"She been kind of fussy. The nurse said I should try and breast feed her again to try and get her settled," Rica said weakly.

She wanted to enjoy her new family—just the three of them—for as long as possible. Her brothers and aunts had just left the hospital, bringing congratulations in the form of balloons, teddy bears, clothes, and diapers, because Rica hadn't had a chance to have a baby shower. She kept refusing her aunt's insistent demands to have one. Rica wasn't sure if she was going to carry her baby to term, and she didn't want to deal with the aftermath of having baby stuff with no baby.

She was exhausted by their visit and wanted to tell Diamond's grandmother to come back tomorrow. But Rica knew Diamond would snap if she forced him to turn her away. So, she decided to grin and bear it.

Although she and Grandmother had a tiff early on in her pregnancy, they learned to get along for the health of her unborn baby. Neither of them wanted their negative energy to cause a miscarriage, so Grandmother put her intuition aside and welcomed Rica with open arms. She resigned to wait and see the baby in person before passing final judgment upon Rica. Grandmother also decided that even if

Rica's baby resembled Diamond, she would push him to get a blood test. She was from the old school that believed "if you feed them long enough, they start to look like you." She was adamant her grandson would not be stuck to a child or a woman who didn't truly belong to him.

"Oh, look at those sweet little rosy cheeks." Grandmother fawned over the baby as she sat on the small couch that Diamond had slept on while Rica was in the hospital recovering from her C-section.

"She's so sweet, grandson. Just precious. What's her name? Cuz y'all never told nobody," Grandmother reminded Diamond. She barely looked in Rica's direction.

"Camilla Rose," Rica's voice croaked from nervousness.

Grandmother raised her eyebrow, "Camilla Rose, huh? But y'all not married though," Grandmother stated the obvious.

"Don't start," said Diamond. "Not today."

"I'm just stating a fact, not trying to upset y'all. Camilla Rose," Grandmother repeated, trying the new name out on her tongue. "Oh, I see a little brown trying to show through on the tops of her ears. Maybe she'll get a little color like you, grandson."

"Or maybe she'll just take after her momma." Diamond replied.

Diamond was growing weary of his grandmother's innuendos about Camilla not being his. She'd been adamant from day one that Diamond get a blood test. He was irritated with his grandmother's meddling. She kept insinuating that Rica cheated on him and that Camilla could possibly belong to someone else. But he couldn't deny that he didn't feel the connection he thought he would feel after seeing his daughter for the first time. He was unsure if his grandmother's thoughts had tainted his feelings or if his own intuition was kicking in. Either way, he resigned to get a blood test when he was ready.

Camilla's soft cries interrupted his reverie.

"Here, baby," Grandmother said as she stood and passed Camilla back to Rica. "I think she may be hungry. I'll see y'all later. I'm gonna head out and let you get some rest."

As Grandmother was leaving, she passed LeBaron in the hallway.

"You coming to see your brother's baby?"

"Yes, ma'am, I brought the baby some stuff my girl bought," LeBaron replied.

"Hmph, and you think Rica gonna accept some gifts for her baby from the next bitch? You got a lot more balls than I thought, boy, or you just dumb as hell. But anyway, I'm fixin' to go. Don't go in there and start no mess. Rica is fragile right now and don't need the stress so she can feed that baby. You hear me?" Grandmother firmly grabbed LeBaron's chin, forcing him to look her in the eyes. "Y'all both my baby boys. You know I love you both equally and it breaks my heart to see y'all going through this mess." Grandmother hissed the last syllable.

"Grandmother, I don't know what you talking about," LeBaron lied.

"I've tried to lay low and drop hints to your brother to get a blood test for that baby. I know it's gonna break his heart when he finds out that baby ain't his."

LeBaron started to protest, but Grandmother quickly pulled him to her chest in a tight hug.

"He can never know, LB. I can't lose my sons, you hear me? I can't lose neither one," Grandmother's voice cracked and tears started to pool. "Listen to me. You be the best uncle ever until he finds out...when he's ready. But don't you give yourself up as the other option. You hear me?"

"Yes, ma'am," was all LeBaron could muster. He feared if he said anything else he wouldn't be able to recover from the guilt that plagued his every thought.

"Go in the washroom, clean your face, then go and see your *niece*." Grandmother motioned toward the bathroom on the opposite side of the hallway.

LeBaron nodded in agreement. Grandmother reached both of her hands up to LeBaron's head and held it, then bent his head down to her lips to steady them both. Grandmother abruptly broke their embrace and walked down the hallway, leaving LeBaron with his thoughts. He decided to take Grandmother's advice to take a moment to himself in the bathroom before going into Rica's hospital room.

The automatic fluorescent lights flickered on and illuminated LeBaron's face. He'd aged several years in the past few months. He leaned in closely to look into his own eyes in the mirror and looked away in shame and regret. *I ain't shit!* he thought.

He splashed cold water on his face several times in a vain attempt to wash away his guilt. He roughly grabbed the brown paper towels to wipe his face and let out a silent scream into the wad. He found himself doing this often when feelings of guilt overwhelmed him. He gathered himself and checked inside the gift bag that his girlfriend packed. He smiled at the small onesies with matching hats and gloves. He was ready to see his daughter.

"Congrats, bruh," LeBaron whispered as he stuck his head inside Rica's hospital room door.

Diamond rose up from his bedside chair to embrace his brother. He couldn't wait to show his princess to her uncle.

"Come check out my baby girl Camilla Rose." Diamond smiled and led LeBaron over to Rica's bed where she swaddled her newborn.

Rica looked up from her baby's face into LeBaron's eyes. Tears started to form in the corners of her eyes.

"My girl was a rock through it all," Diamond beamed. "You wanna hold her?"

LeBaron froze and looked deep into Rica's eyes, searching for the answer he was seeking that he somehow already knew but had to see the truth in her eyes first.

"It's okay, bruh. You ain't gonna hurt her. Here, sit down." Diamond motioned to the bedside chair.

Diamond's touch broke LeBaron out of his reverie as he nodded and slowly walked to the faux leather hospital chair. Diamond gently took Camilla from Rica's arms while panic spread across Rica's face.

Diamond noticed her trepidation. "It's okay, baby. He ain't gonna drop her."

Rica realized her nervous energy was palpable, but her motherly instincts to protect her child were raging inside of her body, riding the wave of her postpartum hormones.

"I know," she replied nervously.

Diamond placed Camilla in his brother's arms as LeBaron lightly bounced the bundle. Diamond gently removed the blanket from Camilla's face to reveal the most beautiful child he'd ever seen with the pinkest cheeks set against her light, sandy complexion. LeBaron's heartbeat stuck in his throat as the newborn struggled to open her eyes and fix onto his as time stopped moving and only she and he existed.

"Aw, babe, she got him. She locked in on him just like she did me, huh?" Diamond joked.

"Yeah," Rica replied timidly.

"Grandmother just left," said Diamond. "She said that her color should come in, in about a month. She said you can tell what a baby's color is gonna be by looking at the edges of their ears or their nail beds.

So, my baby's gonna have a little color? Ain't that right, baby girl?" Diamond cooed over LeBaron's shoulder.

LeBaron tried not to flinch at Diamond's confession, but he knew that if Diamond ever thought that Camilla wasn't his, then they would be having a totally different conversation. LeBaron had seen Diamond become ruthless over the past year while building their empire, and he didn't want to be on the other side of his brother's wrath.

"Cuz if she don't get no color, then I know she ain't mine," Diamond said in a singsong manner. He leaned over LeBaron's shoulder while he held Camilla, nuzzled her neck, and grabbed her tiny fingers.

Rica stirred in her bed, wincing in pain.

"What is it baby?" Diamond asked, concerned.

"I think it's just my uterus contracting. I remember the nurse saying that would happen." Rica's face twisted with agony.

"She's beautiful, man. She really is. Congratulations to both of you. You made a beautiful little girl. I'm gonna head out so y'all can get some rest." LeBaron pulled Camilla away from his chest as a sign for Diamond to take her.

"You leaving already, bruh? You just got here," Diamond pointed out.

"Yeah, man, I got some business to handle but wanted to stop by real quick and see y'all's little angel. Congrats again, bruh." LeBaron leaned in to dap Diamond.

"Okay, man. Let me know if you need anything. They gonna send them home in a few days but I know you gonna hold shit down."

"You already know," LeBaron replied and exited the hospital room with his heart pounding in his chest.

Camilla looked just like LeBaron's mother. Even her rosy cheeks mimicked hers. He thought there was a slight chance that Camilla could be his baby, but he doubted it. But that was before seeing her. He hadn't gotten anyone pregnant in the past, and he had unprotected sex more times than he liked to admit. This was one of the first times he was grateful that his mother had abandoned him, because if Diamond ever saw her face, he would immediately see his daughter reflected. *No one can ever find out*, he thought. *Especially not Diamond.*

It would kill him. Then, he would kill both LeBaron and Rica.

CHAPTER TWENTY-ONE

THE MOVE & SHAKE

Camilla Rose was now almost two years old and was the smartest toddler that Diamond had ever known. He doted on her as if the sun and moon were held in the sky by the gravity of his love for his daughter. Rica protested when Diamond wanted Grandmother to take care of Camilla during the day. Instead, she suggested that Camilla go to her aunt's daycare center a few blocks from Rica's childhood home. Although Diamond didn't like the idea, he agreed so that Camilla would have other kids to socialize with, and he thought that would make Rica happy.

Business was booming, and it was time for Diamond to make his part-time move to Springfield. He was hesitant to leave due to the frigid relationship between his grandmother and Rica. Grandmother continued to question Diamond's parentage.

"I'm gonna miss you when you leave. Promise me you'll call me and Milla every day," Rica demanded as she and Diamond lay in bed the night before he was set to leave for three weeks.

"You know I will, baby. You know I gotta check on my girls and the business. You gonna be able to handle things here while I'm gone?"

"I was born and bred for this shit, even with a baby on my hip." Rica kissed Diamond but noticed he cut their kiss short.

"What's the matter? You been acting funny lately. I mean, damn, you here but not here, even though you still inside me." Rica pushed Diamond out of her and rolled him off to the side.

The room was silent as Rica sat up on the edge of the bed, holding her sheet around her naked form. She wasn't sure if Diamond found her desirable anymore. She now had stretch marks and her once perky breasts were deflated from months of breastfeeding Camilla. Rica asked Diamond if he was still attracted to her and he reassured her that he was, but she knew better. She also knew her man better than he knew himself, but she couldn't quite figure out the source of the wedge between them. She had talked about it with her aunt, who told her sometimes couples went through growing pains after having a baby and adjusting to their new normal and to be patient with Diamond. Rica heeded her aunt's advice and chalked Diamond's distance up to him, adjusting to being a new father and handling the pressure of expanding their business.

"C'mere, girl. You know I love you, don't you? Come back to bed. It's our last few hours together. I don't wanna fight," Diamond pleaded.

Rica thought about all the women who would be drooling over her fine ass chocolate man, a fresh face in their city, and decided to make love to Diamond so good that Rica would etch her pussy in his memory forever. She wasn't going to give up her man without a fight. She wasn't going to throw all her hard work out the window and willingly hand her man to the next bitch. She kept these thoughts in her head while she bucked her hips and met Diamond's rhythm as they both climaxed into a heap of molten flesh.

"Let me get up and get dressed, babe. And thank you for sending me off right." Diamond gave Rica a passionate kiss and headed toward the shower.

Rica sat in post-coital bliss thinking they may have a chance of surviving and going the long-haul in their relationship. Rica let her thoughts drift to a future she always envisioned: her and Diamond old and grey, holding and kissing each other, surrounded by family and friends enjoying the fruits of their labor.

Her blissful daydream was interrupted by Camilla's cries coming through the baby monitor. *Great, she's up*, Rica thought. She put on her robe and shuffled to the nursery to start her and Camilla's day.

"Hey, babe, I'm gonna stop by my grandmother's, then get on the road," Diamond said.

"Wait, you want me to make you some breakfast?" Rica asked, whipping her head around with Camilla on her hip, heading to the kitchen to make pancakes.

"No time, baby. Plus, Grandmother already made a full breakfast for me and LB. You know it's tradition for me to sit with her before I go out of town so we can talk and pray."

Rica huffed, annoyed at the mention of Diamond's grandmother. The two had never really made amends; Rica only tolerated her because Diamond loved her. She was well aware of their ritual of breakfast and prayer every time he went on the road to make a run or take care of business.

"Okay, just call me so I know you made it there safely," Rica said. She trudged over to Diamond and gave him a kiss goodbye, then offered Camilla for him to give her a kiss as well.

"I will, baby," Diamond promised and rushed out the garage door.

***

"Hey, baby, let me get you and LB's plate ready," Grandmother called to Diamond as he headed to the bathroom to wash his hands. As he was finishing up, he heard the door open and close, signaling LB's arrival.

The trio sat at the small, round kitchen table as they had so many other times in the past. So much had changed since that first meal LeBaron shared with Diamond and Grandmother. LeBaron was no longer a lost, angry foster kid looking for love and recognition in the streets. Now he was a grown man with fully realized dreams of his own—now that those plans no longer involved professional basketball. He didn't want to think about the road he would've gone down if he didn't have Grandmother and Diamond in his corner. Diamond had also grown over the years as a businessman and new father. He had employees now and a whole team to answer to that required focus, discipline, and a monstrous amount of violence to keep the empire he'd built since he was slangin' dimes and nicks.

The trio ate and joked around with each other just as they always did. Diamond looked into the eyes of LeBaron and Grandmother while sitting back in his chair, full and satisfied.

"Uh oh, I know that look. What, man? Gone ahead and say it," LeBaron teased.

"Naw, man, you know I was just thinking how much I love y'all. Y'all my family, for real. Grandmother, you took me in when my momma couldn't. You the only momma I know and I just wanna say thank you. You never judged me or LB for the shit we've done or gonna have to do, being wrapped up in the game," Diamond reminisced.

LeBaron hated when Diamond got sentimental, because it only made him open up his healed scars of betrayal with each and every compliment and kind word. LeBaron blew his breath out and adjusted himself in his seat, uncomfortable with Diamond's display of affection.

"I know, I know, man. You probably ain't never gonna get used to me telling y'all how much you mean to me. But I done lost too many people not to tell y'all I love y'all," Diamond said. He reached to give Grandmother a hug and kiss, then gave LeBaron a bear hug.

"All right, enough of that soft shit. You ready, nigga? You got everything you need?" LeBaron asked.

"Yeah, I'm good to go. But there's one thing I wanted to talk about with both of y'all before I get on the road," Diamond said.

"What's up, bruh?" LeBaron asked as Grandmother got up and started clearing the table to wash the breakfast dishes.

"I wanna talk to you about the exit plan. Rica don't ever wanna hear the shit, but I need to talk to you. She lives in this fantasy world like I'm Scarface and shit. She be having her head in the fucking clouds. But I'm thinking about real shit. Hell, Scarface died at the end of that movie, gunned down like a dog in the street. I ain't going out like that, LB. I wanna have an exit plan. I wanna have legit businesses. I had one of my homegirls write all the shit down and print it out on her computer." Diamond got up and walked over to his duffel bag that was sitting by the door and retrieved a large manilla envelope.

"What's that?" LeBaron questioned.

"It's my get out plan," Diamond replied. "It details all the places where I keep my money, passwords, power of attorney, deeds to buildings, all that shit. Everything."

The two of them silently exchanged their love and trust for one another. LeBaron pulled Diamond close to him by the scruff of his neck and connected his forehead with his.

"I got you, bro," LeBaron confirmed.

"I even included a get out plan for you too, bro. We can't do this shit forever. I been putting aside money for you to get your law degree when we done with this shit. I see how much you liked those few business and finance classes you took. And you remember all those laws and are a beast with contracts. Maybe you can put that to use. We gotta have an exit plan, bro. I wanna live to see my babies grow up."

"Wait, what you mean babies, negro?" LeBaron said. Rica pregnant again?"

"Hell, naw, man. To be honest I ain't really been fucking with her like that since Milla was born. But you never know, things may change. But I do know I want another one. You know, some little D's running around the crib." Diamond flashed his million-dollar smile that always set beautifully against the contrast of his coffee-colored skin.

"Anyway, bruh, look it over and we can chop it up when I get back," Diamond said and put the documents back into the folder and handed it to LeBaron.

"Enough said. I got you, bruh. Drive safe. I'll be there in a few days after I check on the traps," LeBaron stated. He dapped up Diamond and headed for the front door. "Love you, Grandmother. I'll be back tomorrow." LeBaron headed out the front door, closing it behind him.

"A'ight old woman, I'm about to head out too. Come give me a hug," Diamond demanded with a playful smile.

"Look, I wanna holla at you about something before you go," Grandmother said while opening a kitchen drawer and retrieving some papers.

"Dang, woman, you serving me?" Diamond joked.

"Naw, nothing like that. I just wanted to give you these papers so you can get the process started to get a blood test for Milla," Grandmother said in a hushed tone.

"C'mon, not that again. Look, I know you don't like Rica, but damn," Diamond said, exasperated.

"First of all, watch your mouth in my house. Second of all, I don't particularly care for the girl, but that ain't the reason I'm giving you these papers. I'm giving them to you because that little girl is two years old, and the older she gets, the more she *don't* look like you or any of our people, and you know it, D." Grandmother paused to soften her tone. "I'm not tryna' hurt you, baby. I'm trying to help you," Grandmother enunciated each word in staccato.

"I know, I just don't wanna talk about that sh—mess right now is all." Diamond rubbed his face in frustration.

"Look, baby, I know. Just think about it. Maybe the trip will give you some time to distance yourself and think about the situation. Maybe give you some perspective. Just promise me you'll consider getting a test. Because if she ain't yours, it's not fair to her or whoever her real daddy may be. Okay, okay, that's all I'm gonna say." Grandmother raised her hands in defense.

"Oh, and I wanted to talk to you about something later on, but since we dropping bombs today...I want you to move to Springfield with me while I'm there. I can't handle business there knowing you're here alone."

"Boy, please. I been grown way before yo' little ass was even thought about," Grandmother joked.

"I know, I know. But it would make me feel better if you came with me in a few weeks. I was thinking about living there permanently. Haven't told Rica or LB yet, but I been thinking about it."

"I tell you what." Grandmother walked over to Diamond and placed her hands on either shoulder. "I'll make you a deal."

"I'm listening," Diamond uneasily replied. He didn't know what Grandmother was going to say.

"If I come and live there, will you get the DNA test for Camilla?"

The question hung in the air like an unwanted scar.

***

Diamond had been in Springfield for a few weeks more than he originally expected. Business was booming and he was hiring more corner boys his cousins referred who'd already put in work and were battle-tested. He was also trying to distance himself from the drug side of his business empire. The more people between him and the drugs, the further he would be from the day-to-day drug operations. Diamond truly saw himself as a businessman. He started rehabbing houses to flip and establish his construction company.

Rica had been calling him all day. He needed a break from her nagging about when he was coming back to Chicago. He had no interest in rushing back since his grandmother had moved to the small town a few weeks ago. He was avoiding Rica, because he knew the next time he saw her, he would have to ask for a blood test for Camilla.

Grandmother was right as usual; the more time he spent away from Rica, the more Diamond started to realize there was a real possibility that Camilla was not his daughter, and it broke his heart. He was angry at the thought of her betrayal, and then he was saddened for Camilla and her future. The one thought he didn't focus on was who Camilla's real father could be. When he tried to think about Rica fucking and sucking on another man, his thoughts turned murderous. So, he didn't like to think about it and let work dominate his thoughts.

Diamond needed to blow off some steam. So, he got fresh in a jean outfit. Although he was a millionaire a few times over, he was still underage and couldn't get into a club, so he decided to head to the skating rink. He heard that it was jumping on the weekend. He thought he would give it a try and see what the skating scene was talking about in the small city compared to Chicago.

As Diamond pulled into the parking lot, he noticed different groups of fine girls heading inside. A group of men were gathered in the corner of the parking lot. He could see their heads all bobbing together at the same time as someone in the center battle-rapped. Then he noticed a girl walking up to the door by herself. She had confidence and was gorgeous. Diamond turned down his music so he wouldn't be distracted—he needed to take in all her beauty: the way her ponytail swung with each step and the way her jeans hugged her ass just right.

Diamond quickly secured his car, observed his surroundings, and headed inside the skating rink, drawn to the front door like a magnet. He paid his entrance fee and scanned the skating rink for his copper-skinned beauty. As he scanned the rink, he saw the object of his attention talking to the DJ. He observed their interaction and how they seemed to know each other. Diamond decided the DJ would be his source of information. All he needed was her name, and he could handle the rest.

"Aye...aye," Diamond yelled over the music and motioned for the DJ.

"Hey, what's up? I ain't doin' requests yet," the DJ replied.

Diamond smiled. "Naw, man, I don't wanna request a song."

The DJ looked at Diamond, puzzled, and removed his headphones from one ear to hear him better.

"I seen you talking to ol' girl." Diamond motioned to Althea as she skated past the DJ booth.

"Yeah, what about her? She ain't for you, dog?"

"Aye, I don't want no problems. I got five hundred dollars. I just want her name is all." Diamond pulled out a wad of cash and counted out five hundred-dollar bills.

The DJ snatched the money and looked around to make sure no one was watching their interaction.

"Her name is Althea, but you ain't hear it from me," the DJ replied. He put three bills in his sock and two in his pocket.

"You real, G, thanks," Diamond replied and walked away.

***

"Can I have a bite?" A deep voice cut through the booming music so close Althea could feel warm breath on her neck and ear. Althea jumped at the closeness and depth of the stranger's voice.

"Oh, I'm sorry if I scared you," the smooth voice said before Althea could turn around and see who dared to invade her private space like that. She was ready to cuss whoever this was up, down, and around the skating rink, but once she saw the face that the voice came from, she sat mid-nacho, stuck in silence.

The man slid into the picnic table bench across from Althea with the biggest, whitest smile she'd ever seen in her life. He unashamedly looked deep into Althea's eyes, still smiling. She was still at a loss for words, because this was a man who clearly was not from her small city. He was wearing a distressed jean jacket with the word *dope* airbrushed across the front, with a fresh white T-shirt underneath.

His skin was deep chocolate and smooth, not a blemish in sight. He was clean-shaven with a low fade. That smile and those lips—Althea squirmed in her seat while the stranger continued his silent appreciation of what he saw before him. He had three-sixty waves on his thick, dark hair that was lined to perfection. Althea took a sip of her soda, because she still didn't know what to say. The usual nasty attitude she had with guys who tried to approach her eluded her.

As she took a sip, Althea looked for the smaller details that Mother Rose taught her to pay attention to. She looked at the stranger's fingernails. *Hmmm...clean and manicured,* she thought. *So, he can't do any hard labor. His hands look soft.*

Then she noticed the earrings in both ears: not too big, not too small. The way the earrings glittered in this light, Althea bet her life the diamonds were real. The pinky ring on his left finger had a diamond encrusted *D* on it. Althea took a moment to soak in all of the stranger's handsome glory, but she pretended to be annoyed. She finished her soda and bobbed her head to the music. The stranger wasn't fazed by Althea ignoring him and continued to grin, his eyes locked on her.

Althea huffed, "So what does the *D* stand for, dickhead?" She motioned toward his pinky ring while still pretending she was drinking her soda.

The stranger completely ignored Althea's smart comment. "So, what's your name?" he asked and sat patiently, waiting for her reply and adjusting his pinky ring with a big smile on his face.

"T.T.," Althea lied. She never gave her real name to strangers.

"For real?" the stranger said matter-of-factly and reached in and grabbed one of Althea's cheesy nachos.

"Ummm, excuse you, greedy! Nobody said you could have any of my nachos!" Althea was pissed. *Who did this guy think he was?* Just coming over and inviting himself to her table and now her nachos?

The stranger just continued to smile at her. When he finished chewing, he said, "That's not what I heard."

"Not what you heard?" Althea had a major attitude now.

"I heard your name was Althea." The stranger sat back and let the fact that he knew her name but she didn't have a clue who he might be sink in.

Althea sighed and rolled her neck and eyes at the same time. Now she was annoyed at the stranger. At first glance, she was really attracted to him, but now that he acted like a know-it-all, she was completely turned off. She started eating her nachos again and watching the skaters. She hoped he would get the hint that she was no longer interested in having a conversation with him and leaving the table out of sheer embarrassment, but no such luck. The stranger just sat there and continued with a huge smile.

"I asked about you," the stranger finally confessed. "Yeah, I saw you talking to the DJ and asked him who you were."

Now Althea was livid. This was so out of character for Jack; he knew better than to talk to guys about her. She was curious about what was so special about this stranger that Jack felt comfortable giving her real name to him. She whipped her long ponytail around, "Who, Jack?"

"Yeah, I asked him what your name was and he told me. That's all I needed to know. I wanted to find out the rest for myself."

Althea sucked her teeth and looked directly at the stranger. "Well, you came and saw." She cocked her head, swung her ponytail again, and rolled her hazel eyes. She was not going to make it easy for him.

Her nacho cheese had grown cold and now she was irritated and ready to leave the rink, but not before she checked Jack. She started to get up to leave and the stranger stood up, too, and quickly moved to her side.

"Lemme throw that away for you." The stranger grabbed her tray.

Althea couldn't help but notice how tall the stranger was. He loomed over her—even with her skates on—with the biggest grin on his face that almost disarmed her again. He had to be at least six-four, she assumed.

"Thanks," Althea begrudgingly offered. Before the stranger could utter another word, Althea was off on her skates, hitting the roller rink floor. Her head was spinning with thoughts. *Who in the heck is this dude and who does he think he is?*

Althea was always leery of over-friendly men. Her mother taught her that men only wanted two things from a woman: sex and to get over. Althea didn't have plans of letting either happen.

She skated around the roller rink three times to clear her head before remembering that she had to check Jack. On her third time around, she rolled into the DJ's booth. Althea cocked her head and stared at Jack. He was expecting this unwelcome interaction all night.

"Heyyy, cuz," Jack stammered.

"Ain't no *hey cuz*! Why you give that dude my name? I don't know him and he sure don't know me. Wait 'til I tell Mother Rose that you been giving out my name to strangers," Althea threatened.

"Now, wait, cuz. Ain't no need to go and tell Mother Rose. The man gave me two-hundred bucks just to tell him your name. He said he ain't want nothing else." Jack pulled out the two crisp hundred-dollar bills. Althea snatched one.

"This is for making sure I don't tell Mother Rose, because you know she don't play." Althea glared at Jack and stood silent, waiting for him to protest, but he knew she was right. He didn't have any reason to give out Althea's real name to a stranger.

Althea's face softened a little. "Look, I won't tell Mother Rose about this, but you gotta be more careful. You know Mother Rose has competition and enemies out here in these streets and we don't know all of them. Could be somebody wanting to hurt me to get to her. You gotta think, cuz." Althea gave Jack a quick hug to let him know she wasn't going to stay mad. "But Imma still keep this bill though." Althea laughed and skated away.

The night was winding down, so Althea thought it would be a great time to make her exit, just in case the stranger or anyone with him was waiting for her to leave. Althea got her shoes out of her locker and went behind the counter of the shoe rental. There was a side exit that only employees used. She always parked her car by this exit, just in case a fight broke out or someone decided to shoot up the place, which was rather frequent. Althea paused and poked her head out the door to make sure there was no one by her car and that she wasn't being watched or followed. She made a quick dash to her car when she heard the stranger's voice.

"So, you just gonna leave without saying goodbye?" He was leaning on the hood of his all-back Lexus, rims shining, bass bumping.

CHAPTER TWENTY-TWO

REVELATIONS (FEBRUARY 2025)

Looking around the house, Camilla sees pictures of Golden with her grandmother, who she recognizes from her obituary and Facebook posts. Camilla's nose burns from the smell of Althea's cigarettes as she takes a seat on the small, brown couch. Althea walks into the kitchen and returns with three mismatched glasses pinched together in one hand and a fifth of Jim Beam in the other. She was balancing her cigarette between her lips.

"Momma, I don't want nothing to drink. It's too damn early," Golden whimpers.

"You gone need this shit after I get done, baby girl," Althea says, then looks at Camilla. "Matter fact, both y'all gone need this shit after I get done."

Camilla and Golden's eyes meet, then back to Althea. She pours them all double shots of Jim Beam and sits in Grandmother's old recliner. She takes her double shot to the head. As she swallows, she nods to Camilla and Golden for them to take theirs. They follow suit, the liquor burning all the way down.

"I met yo' daddy Diamond when he first came here from Chicago. I remember I thought he was the finest, most chocolate man I'd ever seen. But you know I had to play hard to get because I was the shit, too, back then. All the niggas wanted me," Althea muses while Golden pours herself and Camilla another shot.

Golden looks up at Althea and decides to pour her another shot, too. She's never heard her mother talk about how she met her father, and she doesn't want the story to stop. So, she adds liquid courage to her glass to keep the memories flowing.

"Anyways, we were inseparable. I remember meeting Grandmother for the first time. That's Diamond's grandmother—she raised him since he was a baby and moved here with him from Chicago," she explains to Camilla.

"Grandmother didn't like me at first. And I can't blame her. I was some young bitch coming around who thought she knew everything, but ain't know shit." Althea lights another cigarette.

"I got pregnant with you pretty quick and moved in with Diamond and Grandmother, into this very same house cuz Mother Rose, my momma, was locked up. I remember one day after coming home from church, D got a call and he was pissed. He was cussing and shit. And he never lost his cool. So, I snuck up on him to hear who he was talking to and I heard him say he wasn't coming back to Chicago and that he met somebody. Then he said—" Althea pauses, choking back tears while reliving the moment.

"I'll never forget he said, 'Do what you gotta do, but I ain't raising nobody's else's kid. You know and I know she ain't mine.'

"I couldn't believe what I was hearing. I thought I was trippin' so I came around the corner and started snappin' and asking who the fuck was it on the phone. He had to hold my ass down, cuz I was ready to cut his ass—shoot him, or whatever I could get my hands on. He finally calmed me down and said he would explain but wouldn't until I calmed down."

Althea gets up from the recliner to retrieve the bottle, stopping to pour the girls another shot. Then she sits down with the whole bottle. She fills her cup almost to the brim, placing the half-empty bottle on the floor next to the recliner.

"He told me that he was with a girl before he left Chicago and that they were together. They grew up together and were business partners. He said that she got pregnant when she lied and told him she was on birth control, but he was happy, because he always wanted to be a father. But he said when the baby was born, he didn't feel a connection like he thought that he should've. Then he said that as the baby grew a little older, he had doubts that she was his. He even said Grandmother didn't think the baby was his and pressed him to get a blood test, but he never did. And that's all I know. I know he had doubts, and I wish he was here to clear all this shit up." Althea's voice breaks with grief.

"He was my first and only love."

Althea's words permeate the smoke-filled room with a heavy sense of regret and longing that is palpable to Camilla and Golden. The two of them had never experienced a soul-shattering love like Althea was describing. They both secretly wonder what it would feel like to love someone so deeply that your world felt tilted in their absence. Golden wonders if this is how Marquez feels in the way that he loves her. She doesn't doubt it, and it pains her to think about his love unrequited. Camilla simultaneously thinks of Elyse, wondering if her world would crumble if they ever separated. The thought alone makes her chest tighten with anxiety.

Camilla is silent. Golden dares to look at her face, scared to see the pain in her eyes after hearing Althea's revelations. She closes her eyes, gathers courage to speak, and turns to Camilla.

"We can take a blood test," Golden blurts out.

"Huh?" Althea questions, snatching herself out of her grief.

"Yeah, I mean if we blood, then a blood test should show we half-sisters, right?"

Camilla doesn't answer. She is still too stunned by Althea's walk through the past, revealing that Diamond questioned her paternity. She doesn't know whether to believe Althea or not. However, she can't think of a reason why a stranger would lie to her about a dead man not being her father.

"Okay," she hears herself reply weakly before her brain registers the words coming out of her mouth.

Golden shakes her head in disbelief at Camilla agreeing to her proposal so quickly.

"Yeah, I mean, at this point. What I got to lose?"

"All right, that settles it then. I got a homegirl that does blood tests at the county building, and I know she can get us set up and our labs processed. She does it for all the girls at the club who have baby daddies in the streets who don't wanna step foot in the courts. They trust her to take the test.

As the three women settle into the idea of possible outcomes of the blood test and their implications, a heavy knock sounds at the front door. Three pairs of eyes quickly dart back and forth to one another. Camilla surveys Althea and Golden's eyes and notes a hint of surprise, because they usually don't have this many visitors in one day.

Althea raises herself from the comfy recliner and wobbles ever so slightly, showing signs that the liquor is doing its job. She steadies herself and walks toward the door, standing a few inches away.

"Who is it?" She yells loud enough for the other person to hear her on the other side of the door.

"It's LB."

Althea snaps her head in Golden's direction. Their eyes exchanging telepathic thoughts only a mother and daughter share. Golden quickly stands and Camilla, a half-second behind her, stands as well. Camilla's fierce gaze meets Golden's and Althea's as she reaches behind her back and pulls the .45 from her holster. She firmly grips it while pointing it at the floor. She doesn't know what this man wants, but she is pretty sure he followed her. Golden turns and faces the front door while squaring her shoulders.

"What the fuck you want, LB?" Althea shouts through the closed door.

"Look, let me in, Thea. Let me explain. Camilla, I know you're in there too. Just give me a chance to explain everything," LeBaron pleads from the other side of the door.

Camilla shakes her head *no* while peering into Althea's hazel eyes. She hasn't trusted LeBaron since the moment she laid eyes on him, and she certainly doesn't want to be in a confined space with him and two unarmed women and only one clip. She doesn't know his intentions, nor does she want to find out. Her plan concerning LeBaron is to slowly surveille him to figure out his motives for returning to Chicago and now following her here. But time isn't always on her side.

More silence passes between the trio. Camilla still holds her weapon with both hands clasped around the handle and her finger resting on the side of the trigger. Her mother's voice rings in her head: *Don't ever pull yo' shit unless you ready to use it.*

Althea takes two steps toward the door, placing her hand on the doorknob, and looking out the side window. Camilla steps from in front of the couch, leaving Golden's side to stand on the opposite side of the room. In case LeBaron has ulterior motives for his visit, he won't be able to pinpoint their locations all at once from the front door.

Althea opens the front door to a disheveled LeBaron. His beard had slightly grown over his usually smooth face. He wears a suit that didn't travel well, because it's wrinkled and clings to his muscular frame haphazardly.

"What the fuck you want, LB?" Althea yells through the open door but keeps the screen door locked.

"I—I just wanna come in and explain everything. I fucked everything up, Thea. I'm tired" His onyx eyes bore into Althea's with intensity. She can see the weariness gathering at the corners of his eyes, showing his true age.

"Well, well, well. How the mighty has fallen," Althea taunts.

LeBaron's upper lip lightly ticks, letting Althea know she's hit a nerve.

"So, what the fuck you wanna explain, LB? That you fucked your best friend's—no, your *brother's* girl? That's what y'all called each other, right? Brothers?" Althea asks while fishing her cigarettes out of the front pocket of her robe.

When LeBaron doesn't answer, Althea continues. She's on a roll and has been holding back what she wants to say for over twenty years. She doesn't care who her words hurt in the process; she needs this release.

"Then yo' ass not only fucks his girl, but then you knock her ass up and agree with the bitch to pass off *your* fucking daughter as his! That's some cold as shit." Althea pauses to light her cigarette and take a deep inhale.

"Then after he dies, you send Grandmother money for Golden. Oh what, you think I didn't know? Grandmother told me since the first day you sent the money. But what I couldn't understand was why you didn't come around. Why didn't you even come to the funeral? Was it so hard for you? Well, it was hard for me too!" Althea yells.

"To see my man like that. The love of my life shot up like that. And y'all was supposed to be brothers. I never heard about no retaliation. The streets was quiet after he died. You didn't do shit to avenge yo' brother. Did you?"

Althea waits for LeBaron to answer as he hangs his head in shame.

"Did you?" she shouts.

"Thea, please let me just come in and explain," LeBaron pleads with his hands held out.

"Naw, motherfucker. You've had two decades to explain why you didn't show up to your *brother's* funeral. Your fucking brother!"

Althea yells again as her voice echoes through the house and vibrates against the glass of the screen door.

"You've had over twenty years to explain to that girl in there that *you* was her daddy. You've had twenty years to make things right and you didn't. You sorry motherfucker. But for the life of me I can't figure out why you went ghost after Diamond was killed."

"I told you, Thea. Diamond had an exit plan for us to get out the game if anything ever happened," LeBaron pleads.

"That's bullshit and you know it," Althea spits. "Why didn't you come to his funeral, LB? Fuck you being a piece of shit daddy. Why didn't you come to your brother's funeral? It ain't like you killed him."

LeBaron lowers his head, raising his eyes to look at Althea, "It was an accident," he whispers.

Silence.

"What the fuck he say?" Golden chimes, running toward the screen door and pushing Althea out of the way.

"No, wait. Let me explain!" LeBaron backs away as Golden barrels forward and unlocks the screen door so fast that neither Camilla, Althea, nor LeBaron anticipate her reaction.

"You fucking killed him?" Golden screams at the top of her lungs, forcing LeBaron down to the bottom porch step.

"You fucking burrow yourself into my life and you killed my father?" Golden doesn't wait for an answer. She turns on her heels, heading in Camilla's direction.

"Gimme the pistol!" Golden demands.

"I can't do that, shawty," Camilla says calmly. "Hear him out first." Camilla leans forward to whisper in Golden's ear. "No matter what, we gone make that nigga pay for what he did."

She leans back and stares into Golden's emerald eyes, absorbing all the hate and confusion, urging her to trust her. Golden nods in agreement.

"But I'm gonna beat his ass first," Golden affirms. She quickly walks back to the front door toward LeBaron. She grabs the bat that Althea keeps near the door for her unruly dates.

Golden swings the screen door open to face LeBaron just in time to see Althea rushing forward and down the stairs to punch him as she curses him out.

"You took him from me. You fuckin' bastard!"

Golden quickly descends the few steps to reach her mother and LeBaron in the front yard. She takes a swing at LeBaron but misses.

"Wait, let me explain. We were arguing about Camilla. He knew, Thea! He knew she wasn't his. He came to me about it, but things got heated and the gun went off," LeBaron pleads unsuccessfully.

"Then why the fuck was he shot more than once? You fucking liar!' Althea screams at the top of her lungs.

"Aye, what the fuck is going on?" Marquez's voice booms from across the street after hearing Althea's screaming.

"Aye, no offense, but this ain't got nothing to do with you, young blood," LeBaron says, turning in the direction of Marquez.

"The fuck it don't," Marquez says, standing his ground.

"So, you my fucking daddy?" Camilla asks, joining the group outside as they all look up toward the porch.

"Yeah," LeBaron replies with a deep sigh. "I came to Chicago at first, because Rica was trying to hurt Golden by sending her pics from the club to her school."

"What the fuck?" Althea and Marquez say.

"So, that's why you came home?" Althea asks Golden. "You said you was on a break. Not no bullshit about having your pics sent out," Althea says with tears pooling in her eyes and the effects of the liquor wearing off.

"Oh, so you can save her but fuck me, huh?" Camilla asks in a cold tone that sends chills down LeBaron's spine.

He knows where that cold, murderous tone comes from, because he sounds the same way when he's already decided that another man's life is not worth living.

"Listen, I came here thinking I could get to the bottom of the stuff with Golden and maybe try to create a genuine connection with you, too, Camilla," LeBaron says, unconvincingly.

"Naw, nigga, you felt guilty that my momma opened up that wound again and reminded you that you a dirty son-of-a-bitch," Camilla says coldly while still holding her .45 with her hands folded over one another, resting against her stomach.

"Aye, nigga, I don't really know you, but I know you done pissed off a whole house full of women. You need to go, bruh," Marquez demands in his deep baritone, dripping with authority.

A stare down ensues between Camilla, LeBaron, Althea, Golden, and Marquez. Each of them is unwilling to concede. LeBaron takes a step backward but keeps his front facing the group.

"I'm gonna head out and go back to Chicago. Camilla, if you wanna talk, I'll be here for two days, then I'm out. If you want answers about the past, then me and yo' momma can give that to you. If you want," LeBaron says. He slowly walks backward out of the squeaky gate and toward his SUV.

"Naw, nigga I'm good. Ain't had no daddy and don't see a need for one now," Camilla says in the same cold tone as before.

"Awe, hell naw, nigga! You ain't gettin' away again!" Althea charges LeBaron, but Marquez is quicker and holds her back.

"Let me the fuck go, Quez!" Althea thrashes about, trying to free herself from Marquez's strong grip.

"Naw, Ma, let his bitch ass go. That nigga gonna get his" Golden spits onto the ground.

Camilla silently agrees with Golden. She's already formulating a plan for revenge that won't right all the wrongs that have been done over the years but will hopefully offer some sense of solace for the trio.

Chapter Twenty-Three

BEST SERVED COLD

Marquez helps Althea into the house as she breaks down, sobbing. Her reaction to the news that LeBaron killed her lover, and the father of her child has her numb—she is taking the revelation harder than anyone. Althea's life would be completely different if Diamond were still alive; she wouldn't be running around degrading herself with men she never would've given a second glance. He was truly her soulmate. Now Golden fully understands the breadth of her mother's love for her father and the depth of her grief.

"Why the fuck did y'all let him go? He killed Diamond. He killed Diamond," Althea repeats over and over.

Marquez walks her over to the couch while supporting most of her body weight because Althea is too weakened from her confrontation with LeBaron. Althea collapses into Marquez's chest, sobbing uncontrollably as Camilla and Golden reluctantly enter the house. Neither of them wants to be engulfed by Althea's pain, but it's their pain as well. Confusion hangs in the air before Camilla breaks the silence.

"So, my momma knew this nigga was my daddy and ain't said shit for over twenty-five years?" Camilla paces the room and places her .45 into her back holster.

No one responds to her rhetorical question, because everyone else is trying to process the events of the last fifteen minutes.

"Wait, so what happened?" Marquez asks. "Somebody tell me what's going on. Golden?" Marquez gives Althea another squeeze, rocking her while focusing his gaze on Golden and awaiting an answer.

"So, she shows up this morning." Golden motions toward Camilla. "Saying she's my sister."

Marquez's eyes dart in Camilla's direction. But Camilla purposely avoids eye contact. So, Marquez looks back to Golden for an explanation.

"Then Momma said that no, she's not and went into this long explanation about how my dad never thought she was his daughter." Golden paused, feeling the words in her mouth.

She can only imagine how Camilla is feeling right now. Learning that the father she thought was her father isn't and that the man she just met is in fact her father.

"So, then her real daddy shows up, who's LeBaron," Golden says. "But what I can't figure out, Quez, is why the fuck did he come into my life, pretending at first not to know who I am? Anyways, Momma figures out that LeBaron is Camilla's father, but also that he was the one who killed my dad." Golden's voice breaks as she covers her mouth and begins sobbing once the realization fills the air like nerve gas, paralyzing everyone in the room.

"Wait, what?" says Marquez. "So, LeBaron, the dude that got you a job and paid for your school, killed your dad? What the fuck?" Marquez squeezes Althea again as her sobs subside.

"This is some Jerry Springer type shit," Golden says while bending over, holding herself.

"Yeah, some real fucked up shit," Camilla speaks for the first time since LeBaron left and all eyes are on her.

"I'm sorry you had to find shit out like this. I really am," Althea offers in a hushed tone.

"Naw, it's not y'all fault. I came here for answers, and I got them. I just didn't know that the man I was investigating was my father and that my mother knew it but kept it from me too. Both of they asses deserve each other, as far as I'm concerned," Camilla ends flatly.

"Whatchu gonna do?" Golden asks Camilla.

Camilla lets out a laugh. "I don't think you wanna know that, lil' momma. Just know I'm gonna handle that shit. And both they asses is gonna fucking pay. Look, I'm gonna head out. I wish I could say it was nice meeting y'all, but maybe under different circumstances." Camilla ends with a chortle, turns toward the door, and exits Golden and Althea's lives just as quickly as she arrived.

***

Camilla drives back to Chicago in silence, letting the sound of her tires on pavement be the soundtrack to her plans of revenge. She thinks about how Golden said that LeBaron gave her a job and paid for her school, but he couldn't be bothered to make himself known to her. He didn't lift a finger in raising her, nor did he make any attempts to get to know her.

Hot tears stream down Camilla's face, which makes her grow angrier, because she hates crying. She only sheds tears when murder is on her mind, and the only two faces in her mind's eye are those of her parents.

Camilla grips the steering wheel as she toggles between feelings of murder and a longing for a father she's always missed in her life. She had been okay with growing up without a father, but to know that he has been alive all these years and *chose* to stay away is a different type of pain that Camilla won't let go unpunished.

She also thinks about why LeBaron resurfaced all these years later. *Was it for Golden?* she thought. However, she can't figure out why after all this time. Why now? Why did he come out of hiding for Golden and not for her?

Jealousy courses through her veins as the speedometer reaches 100 mph. Her phone rings through the car speakers, breaking her reverie. Camilla notices her speed and decreases it as she sees Elyse's name on her SUV's screen.

"Hey," Camilla greets.

"What happened? What's wrong?" Elyse can hear the tension in Camilla's voice.

"Some fucked up shit went down."

Camilla hears Elyse's breath quicken as she imagines her closing her glass office door and blinds for privacy.

"Tell me everything and don't leave anything out," Elyse demands.

"Okay, so boom, I get there and the girl's momma don't wanna open the door but finally does when I say I think I'm her sister. Then she basically tells me I'm not. Then she says that the dude who I think is my daddy never thought I was his." Camilla pauses for questions from Elyse, but her girlfriend is silent and patiently waits for her to continue.

"Then, that motherfucker LeBaron pops up."

"Wait, what?" says Elyse. "What the fuck?"

"Yeah, that's what I thought too. How the fuck does the person I'm trying to get information about suddenly just show up? Coincidence? I think the fuck not. Anyways, the momma and LeBaron start to get into it. She starts asking him why he never came to his best friend's funeral. And she keeps pressing this nigga and kind of comes up with it on her own that he was the one who really killed his homeboy."

"What the fuck?" Elyse tries to follow Camilla's story.

"Yeah, so basically, LeBaron killed his business partner and best friend. And I think he may have did it because Diamond found out that I was really his daughter."

"Hold up, wait. I'm confused." Elyse pauses Camilla's story.

"Yeah, you following the story right. LeBaron is my daddy, and my momma knew the whole time and kept it from me. Fucking bitch! But what I can't figure out is, why keep this secret for over twenty-five fucking years? Why not tell me who the fuck my daddy really is?"

Silence fills the line while Elyse processes all the information Camilla has given her. "Damn, Cam. She couldn't tell you who your real daddy was, because she already told your stepfather that he was dead. That was probably the only way he married her and allowed her into the family. He would never allow a bastard into his home who would have the potential to take over his empire with her other drug-dealing daddy. So, she had to keep him a secret."

"Damn, baby, you might be right. This bitch did all this lying and scheming for money and power," Camilla says. "You right though. My stepdad didn't play that shit about the family bloodline. He made sure that I wouldn't get shit from his business, only my two brothers. And once my oldest brother died, the business would go to Rico and my momma wouldn't have any power anymore. But if the family knew that my dad was still alive, I would be a threat and so would LeBaron," Camilla deduces.

"Yeah, but that still don't explain why he stayed away. Ain't no excuse for staying away from your child. But wait, then didn't you say that he killed his best friend?" Elyse asks.

"Yeah, ain't that some dirty ass shit?" says Camilla. "That motherfucker is so fucking dirty for that shit. Not only did he fuck on his best friend's girl and got her pregnant, but then he killed his ass too. That nigga gotta pay. They both do," Camilla says with finality.

"I agree with you for once, baby. Them niggas gotta pay. Him and yo' momma." Elyse waits for Camilla's objection that never comes.

"I love you, baby," Camilla says "I'll be home in about two hours."

"I love you, too. Drive safe. I think I got a way we can kill two birds with one stone." Else cracks a half smile.

"And that's why I love yo' ass, because I already knew. See you in a bit, baby," Camilla says, ending the call.

She spends the rest of the car ride thinking of a plan to make her mom and LeBaron pay for their lifetime of deceit.

Death would be too quick, she thinks.

CHAPTER TWENTY-FOUR

DOMINOES

Camilla pulls up to the club, ready to confront her mother about all the truths that were revealed over the last seventy-two hours. Her blood runs hot as she takes three long, calming breaths to slow her heartbeat and lower her anxiety. She sits in the car looking at the text she sent to LeBaron after getting his number from Meechie's source.

> We need to talk.

> Okay sounds good. Let me know when and where.

> The club at noon.

> I'll be there.

Camilla wipes the nervous sweat from her palms and climbs out of her SUV. She quickly heads toward the back door where security greets her with a head nod.

"Aye, that nigga from the other day is coming back through in a few," she says.

"You want me to put his ass down?" the security guard asks.

"Naw, let his ass through. I'm gonna handle his ass myself," Camilla affirms.

"Got it, boss. I ain't like that fancy-ass nigga from when I first met his ass. Let me know if you need anything else," the security guard says. They share a special handshake, and he opens the heavy metal door for her to enter.

"Me either," she replies and walks through the door.

Camilla gets to the main floor of the club and sees her mother sitting at her usual booth smoking on a clove cigarette. She stops momentarily, drinking in the picture of her mother. Her long, beautiful black hair cascades in loose curls around her face, while her long red nails make soft clicking sounds on her cellphone's screen. *She's so beautiful*, Camilla thinks. A sense of longing for her mother's love builds and tightens her chest; she knows her mother will never be able to fill that void. For once, Camilla is finally okay with the idea that her mother's love is unobtainable. Her chest tightness subsides as her feet slowly edge her toward her mother's booth.

As Camilla nears her mother, she wonders how a woman who's done as much dirt as she has can comfortably sit in a booth smoking a cigarette without a care in the world. She thinks her mother is probably able to act so nonchalant for the same reasons she is able to do the dirt she's done over the years. Camilla convinces herself that the dirt her mother did was necessary for her survival or for the betterment of the family business. She chortles to herself, thinking how silly she was in the past—willing to risk it all for a false sense of family that she never belonged to. The only family she has is the one she's created with Elyse and the Circle Boyz.

"What the fuck got you smiling so early?" Rica's voice breaks Camilla out of her thoughts.

"Nothin', Ma. I was just thinking about how pretty you look today and how I must get my good looks from you." Camilla says.

"Hmph. Well, you definitely got good genes," Rica replies, focusing her attention back on her cell.

"My dad was kinda handsome too, huh? I guess I get it from him too, right?" Camilla leads Rica into the conversation she wants.

"Yup, he was handsome. Very handsome," Rica says, meeting Camilla's eyes. She notices something else playing on her daughter's face.

"What's all this about, Milla? Yo' ass getting sentimental again. Yo' ass always get soft around your birthday, asking questions about yo' daddy. That was a long time ago. I was young and I don't wanna talk about it," Rica ends with finality.

Usually, this is where Camilla tends to end the conversation about Diamond, knowing how sad it makes her mother. But now Camilla knows what she mistook for sadness was guilt. Rica never wanted Camilla asking questions but she isn't going to let it go today. On her way back from meeting Golden and Althea, she made the decision that she wants her mother to confess to her lies about who her real father is.

"Yeah, I've seen pictures of him. He was very handsome. All dark chocolate. You would think I would be darker, but I guess I took after your side, huh?" Camilla asks as she takes a seat across from Rica.

Rica pauses mid-scroll. "Yeah, he was dark-skinned. I guess you took after me. I guess I got strong genes."

"Yeah, I guess. But I guess your genes lost out when it came to my brothers cuz they look like Ramon Sr. more than you," Camilla says.

"Where the fuck is all this coming from Milla? I ain't got time for your bullshit and sensitive ass this morning." Rica asks, irritated.

"Nothing, Ma, I'm just talking, damn. Why you so sensitive?" Camilla asks.

Rica doesn't answer and goes back to scrolling.

"So, you said my dad doesn't have any people left, right?" Camilla presses Rica.

"We been through this, Milla. The only family yo' daddy has was his great grandma and she died when he was young. I was his family. His momma was a damn crackhead, and he never knew his daddy. So, I guess it's possible his momma could still be alive, but she ain't want nothing to do with him so I'm pretty sure she ain't gonna be grandmother of the fucking year. You getting on my nerves with all this shit. I'm about done with this conversation, little girl," Rica says.

Camilla knows she's one sentence away from Rica getting up and walking out on their conversation. She knows that whenever Rica is confronted with a topic she doesn't want to discuss, she physically removes herself. She needs her mother to stay seated for their surprise guest.

"My bad. You know how I get around my birthday," Camilla concedes.

The front door opens and light floods the entryway to the club as a tall silhouette walks through the front door. It's Rica's personal security guard.

"We have a visitor. He says he has an appointment, ma'am," the security guard informs Rica in an authoritative voice.

"I don't have any appointments," Rica says with a wave of her hand. "Take care of it."

"It's my twelve o'clock. Let them in," Camilla commands the security guard. He uses his earpiece to signal for the visitor to come inside the club.

"I didn't know we had any meetings scheduled for today. I didn't see anything on my schedule," Rica replies to Camilla.

"Yeah, it was a last-minute thing. My apologies, Mother, I know you hate surprises, but I thought you might like this one."

"Hey, thank you for seeing me, Camilla," LeBaron's baritone voice booms and echoes throughout the empty club.

"What the fuck is this?" Rica says, jumping up.

Her security pulls his weapon from his holster, noticing Rica's startled reaction.

"This is a family thing," Camilla replies to security. "Put your weapon away and step outside."

Rica narrows her eyes into slits, darting from Camilla to LeBaron. She waves her hand at security to clear the room and waits for him to reluctantly leave.

"I'll be right outside if you need me," he replies. He holsters his weapon and closes the front door, returning to his post.

"What the fuck is this about, LeBaron?"

"Camilla invited me here. It's time we all talked," LeBaron replies. His voice drips with regret and a new harshness that Rica hasn't heard before.

"About what?" Rica yells.

"About us, Rica, damn! I'm so fucking tired. I'm tired of all the lies, all of the secrets," LeBaron reveals.

"Secrets? What fucking secrets, LB?" Rica demands, walking closer to LeBaron. She stands in front of him defiantly with her hands on her hips.

"Rica, she knows."

"Knows what, exactly?" Rica asks.

"She knows I'm her dad, Rica."

Rica turns on her heels, walking away from LeBaron to quell her anger and prevent herself from slapping his face. She can't believe his betrayal. They agreed all those years ago that they wouldn't tell anyone, not even Camilla, who her real father was, because it could put their daughter's life in danger, as well as hers for lying to Ramon Sr.

"And how the fuck would she know that, LB?" Rica demands.

"Because I told her, Rica. Look, she went to Golden's house looking for answers. I followed her there and told her, but only because Golden's mom had already told her," LeBaron pleads, moving closer to Rica with his hand outstretched.

"Wait, so you went to see *Golden*?" Rica turns her anger toward Camilla.

"Yeah. I wanted answers, and I knew you weren't going to give them to me. So, I followed the trail you left when you had Rico take video of some girl dancing at a club. You never do anything without a reason. So, I followed the breadcrumbs that led to Golden," Camilla adds, but she doesn't elaborate further.

"So, you went behind my back on some Inspector Gadget shit!" Rica yells.

"No, Ma, I went on a hunt for the truth, because you don't tell me *shit*! I'm not a fucking little girl who just takes your word for shit anymore. Maybe if you had told me the truth, I wouldn't have to go looking for it." Camilla realizes that she's now yelling.

"Look, Rica, I had to tell her she was my daughter, because she already found out and deserves the truth," LeBaron says.

"Oh, ain't you leaving out an important part of the story, father?" Camilla asks LeBaron sarcastically.

LeBaron looks at Camilla with his brows furrowing, pleading with her light brown eyes not to reveal the last bit of truth that he knows will throw Rica into a murderous fit.

"Either you tell her or I will. Your choice, you piece of shit nigga." Camilla spits on the concrete floor.

"Tell me!" Rica shouts. "What the fuck did you do, LB?" Rica asks, closing the distance between her and LeBaron to meet his eyes.

"I...I can't," LeBaron stutters.

"You fucking coward. You motherfuckin' coward. Ma', you never really asked yourself who really killed Diamond? The supposed love of your life. Did it ever occur to you that it could've been your jealous lover?" Camilla states with satisfaction.

"What? What the fuck is she talking about, LB? You betta say something before I call security in here and get to shooting shit up."

"You can't be that dense, Mother Dear. He killed Diamond. He even admitted to it and barely got away from Golden's house alive, because her momma almost killed his ass with her bare hands. Ain't that right, *LB*?" Camilla asks in a mocking tone.

"You dirty motherfucker!" Rica yells as she lunges for LeBaron's throat.

He hadn't expected her quick attack, although he is all too familiar with Rica's temper. Just as Rica wraps her hands around LeBaron's throat, a boom comes from the front of the club and multiple voices yell, "Freeze! FBI!"

A tactical team of ten FBI agents swarm the club from the front and back entrances with their guns raised and pointed at Rica, LeBaron, and Camilla. Rica ignores the flood of agents and continues to try and strangle LeBaron. It takes two agents to loosen her grip and pull her off him.

"Rica Martinez, you're under arrest for conspiracy to sell and distribute narcotics. You have the right to remain silent." One of the FBI agents begins to read Rica her *Miranda* rights.

"Wait, what the fuck is going on?" Rica screams, thrashing about, trying to free herself as her hands are forced behind her back into handcuffs.

The FBI agent begins to Mirandize Rica again as she purses her lips. "Call my fucking lawyer," Rica barks the command to Camilla.

"No," Camilla replies.

"You little fucking bitch," Rica yells with spit flying, trying in vain to free herself from the cuffs and the grip of two agents on either arm.

Two more agents lift LeBaron from the ground, "LeBaron Tate, you are being charged with conspiracy to sell and distribute narcotics, murder in the first degree, and human trafficking."

Now it's LeBaron's turn to buck against the inevitable. He's a lot stronger than Rica, and it takes four FBI agents to wrestle him to the ground and eventually cuff him. For the first time in his life, regret makes tears pool in his eyes. LeBaron couldn't fathom that he would ever be caught for his crimes. He knows that once the FBI gets involved that his life would be over.

LeBaron notices that Camilla isn't placed in cuffs. The realization hits him that all of this is her doing and she set a trap for him and Rica. He doesn't know whether to be proud or disappointed in Camilla's betrayal.

The agents escort LeBaron and Rica out of the front of the club where a crowd of press awaits their arrival. They both wince at the flashes of cameras and barrage of press questions flying at them.

"So, they call you the Queen Pin of Chicago. What do you have to say for yourself, Rica?" one of the reporters shouts from the crowd.

Rica looks in the young woman's direction and notices Camilla standing in the crowd next to the young reporter. Camilla gives Rica a nod, then walks away. She smiles, having given her mother her parting gift. Rica had told Camilla that she always wanted to be known as the *Queen Pin of Chicago*. So, she decided to give her mother just that.

Camilla walks down the street to her SUV, climbs in, and starts the engine. She looks at the back of Rica's head inside the tinted, non-identifiable FBI Suburban. Feelings of guilt overwhelm her as she thinks of her mother being arrested and taken from her life of luxury. But then she stops and thinks about how her mother made her feel her entire life. Camilla always felt like the black sheep—unwanted and unloved. She felt like a burden, a dark spot on her mother's past. Now she knows exactly why. The reflection of her mother's choices came out in her actions toward her.

Camilla's phone buzzes inside her pocket.

"Is it done?" Elyse's voice softly reaches Camilla's ears.

"It's done."

"How do you feel?"

"I don't know yet. Still trying to figure it out. Everything happened so fast," Camilla replies solemnly.

"Come home, baby."

"I'm on my way, love."

CHAPTER TWENTY-FIVE

EPILOGUE (1 YEAR LATER)

Golden sits in her dorm room as she prepares for her final exams. She was allowed back into design school after her lawyers received anonymous information that the video that was sent out to the student body and faculty was revenge porn. Her study session is interrupted by a Facetime call coming through her new laptop.

"Hey, you. How's the studying going?" Marquez asks with a smile.

"It's going better now that I'm talking to you." Golden replies, while biting on her bottom lip. She's taking in the curve of Marquez's traps as he sits on his bed with his shirt off.

"What's that smile for?" Marquez asks.

"Just looking at my man, looking all good over Facetime is all," Golden flirts.

"I love the way that sounds. *Your* man." Marquez replies back and bites his bottom lip in return. "I can't wait to see you next week at graduation. I'm so proud of you. You know that?"

"Thank you, baby, I couldn't have made it without you," Golden replies.

"So, have you narrowed down your job choices yet? Marquez asks.

Golden received two offers from luxury fashion houses and one from an up-and-coming designer for an assistant stylist. Golden's dream is to have her own fashion line one day, but she knows that she needs experience first. She remembers that she needs to learn how to be a good follower before becoming a good leader, like her grandmother counseled her.

"I'm thinking of taking the job with Marcus because he's an up-and-coming designer and a lot of his stuff is on the cutting edge. I think I can really learn a lot from him and get some one-on-one training to build my own portfolio. I think it will be a great steppingstone to having my own brand one day," Golden smiles.

"That's my girl. Always thinking about the future. That's why I love you." Marquez smiles into the camera. Golden can feel his love radiating from miles away.

"I love you too," Golden replies. She never thought that her and Marquez would ever be in the committed relationship they were now in. However, after seeing her mother's grief up close and personal, she realized that she couldn't let true love slip through her fingers just because she was afraid of getting hurt. That was the best decision she ever made.

***

Camilla looks out of her panoramic view of downtown Chicago, taking in the magnificent cityscape. *Damn, I love this view*, she thinks. Her corner office is just as she imagined when she earned her real estate and broker's licenses. However, she never imagined that real estate would become her primary income and that the drug game would no longer be a part of her life. She still has connections with the Circle Boyz, because they're more like family than members of her crew. She'd even convinced a few of them to go legit with her and invest in real estate. Her company Camilla Rose Estates is becoming sought after for commercial and luxury real estate throughout Chicago.

As she looks out across the city, plotting her next move, a knock sounds on her office door. Camilla swivels around her desk chair to face the door.

"Knock...knock," Elyse's soft voice croons from the doorway.

"How's my beautiful wife doing this morning?" Camilla asks, rising from her chair to greet Elyse.

"Mmm, better now that I'm seeing you, bae. Sorry I had to leave so early this morning. You looked so beautiful that I didn't wanna wake you. But I had to head down to the Emerson project because we've been having problems with the supplier. And you know I had to go down there and get they ass together." Elyse smirks as Camilla presses herself into her pelvis for a tight hug.

"And I know you got they ass right together too, huh?" Camilla knowingly asks.

"You already know. So, what's on your agenda for today?" Elyse asks.

"Bae, just ask what you wanna ask. I hate when you beat around the bush," Camilla admits. She takes a few steps back and sits on the edge of her desk while pulling Elyse into her.

"Well, are you gonna go see her? You know she's been asking for you and they supposed to sentence her today."

"Yeah, I know. But I just don't know how I feel about seeing her again. That's my momma and I love her, but I just don't fuck wit her ass. She lied to me my whole life about who I was and where I come from. I just can't let that shit go," Camilla confesses and rests her chin on Elyse's shoulder.

"I know, bae. But you know what they say…forgiveness isn't for the other person, it's for you. Just give her a chance to explain herself. If you don't like what she has to say, then fuck it, you don't ever have to see her ass again. Or you can just say fuck it now and not see her. But either way, you gonna have to forgive her. If not, that shit is gonna eat you alive," Elyse coaches.

"Yeah, you right. But I already know how she is, babe. She's not gonna accept accountability. She's gonna justify why she never told me and then give me a list of excuses. I just don't wanna piss myself off anymore. Plus, she's probably gonna go to prison for the rest of her life and I'm the one to blame. You think she gonna greet me with open arms?" Camilla asks.

Elyse is silent while pondering Camilla's questions. She knows Rica is proud and a borderline narcissist. She also knows that Rica will use her whole visit to blame Camilla for her being in prison rather than accepting responsibility. But she wants peace for her wife.

"Look, bae, I know what you're thinking. I don't want this shit with my mom to bleed into our relationship any more than it has. So, I've made up my mind. I'm not gonna go visit her. Maybe in a few years, but not right now. *But* what I will do is go to therapy. I think I need to talk to somebody about all the shit I've been through," Camilla says.

"Really? I'm so proud of you, baby. That's a huge step!" Elyse kisses Camilla deeply.

"Girl, you gonna get shit started up in here if you don't quit. I'll lift yo' pretty ass up on this desk and make you come on my tongue," Camilla jokingly warns Elyse.

"I dare you," Elyse says lovingly while staring into Camilla's eyes.

"Say less, baby girl."

CHAPTER TWENTY-SIX

THANK YOU

I want to first say thank you first and foremost to my creator for blessing with the gift of storytelling. I oftentimes got in trouble in elementary school. My report cards consistently said, "talks too much." Well, this time it paid off and my talking turned into two novels.

I am so appreciative of all my supporters and those of you that bought my first novel *Golden Rose*, and of those of you who purchased *Golden Rose, Part 2* and are experiencing my art for the first time. I don't take your support for granted. Thank you to those who reposted my social media posts about my novels and told a friend about my storytelling. My heart is full.

A special thank you to my sister and daughter who saw the blood, sweat, tears, and meltdowns as I pressed my way to complete these two novels. A special thanks to my own daughter who forced me to look at the image I wanted to present to her as a woman and example for her to learn and grow into. Honorable mention to my son who was the first person to teach me how to be a mother. You grew and stretched me in the most positive way. Thank you.

These two novels delve into mother-daughter relationships in the hope that through entertainment we all can look at these relationships to internally analyze how they've impacted our lives and the way we relate to one another. My goal is to open dialogue to ensure the next generation of women feel supported and nurtured by their mothers, thus changing negative generational stereotypes and negative ideologies.